Club Serenity

Free Me, Master!

Free Me, Master!

ISBN # 978-1-78686-170-2

©Copyright Dani Rose 2017

Cover Art by Posh Gosh ©Copyright 2017

Interior text design by Claire Siemaszkiewicz

Totally Bound Publishing

Club Serenity

FREE ME, MASTER!

DANI ROSE

Chapter One

Rebecca sat in the booth in the back of the diner with her cappuccino. Her laptop was up and running and, while she sipped her coffee, she was looking for jobs online.

I really don't want another office job, or worse, serving in some restaurant, dammit!

Her mind drifted and she looked out of the window, not really seeing anything, lost in thought. She absentmindedly picked up her cup and took another sip. Her gaze zeroed in on a man that walked by the window.

Wow, nice ass!

Rebecca looked him over. Tall, golden blond hair, muscular, suntanned arms, wide shoulders, corded neck. Really well-built. *Damn, he's hot!* She almost started to drool.

Let it slide, Becca. Not for you. Rebecca sighed. She'd given up on dating. For now. First, she needed to get her life sorted again. She stared at nothing in particular and thought about the last couple of months.

She had handed in her resignation a few months earlier to start her own coaching practice. That had been quite the decision to make, considering she'd had a really good job as an office manager. Her income had been enough to make a nice living. But after ten years, she had gotten fed up with it. She'd seen it all, done it all. Her heart was no longer in her work. She wanted to do something else, something completely new. The safety of her job had turned into a confinement and the need to break free had grown and grown, until she couldn't ignore it anymore.

Thank goodness she had saved through the years, so she could tide herself over for at least six months. If she was frugal.

Being as smart as she was, she had started working on her practice while she was still employed. She had set up a website and found a nice place where she could rent space to work from for a very reasonable price. When she had done all the prep work, she had handed in her resignation.

Her practice was picking up all right, but she didn't have enough clients yet to make a living off it. The best thing to do was to find temp office job before she depleted her savings account.

"Mind if I join you?" A deep, low voice asked, clearly addressing her.

Rebecca looked up into the bluest eyes she had ever seen. *Mr. Nice Ass. Oh, my goodness!*

Her cheeks heated.

Get a grip, Becca! You're forty-two, for God's sake!

She opened her mouth to answer him, but no sound came out. She cleared her throat, his piercing eyes on her. She almost cringed. They seemed to bore right through her, and made her feel as if she'd bared her very soul to him.

"Sure, go ahead," Rebecca replied and quickly turned her gaze to her laptop, pretending to read something.

Why the heck does Mr. Gorgeous have to sit here? There were plenty of empty tables — the diner wasn't all that busy. And why did he make her feel so goddamned awkward?

She tried to focus her attention on the job site, but somehow it didn't work.

"So, what is a nice girl like you doing in a place like this?" His deep voice cut through her jumbled thoughts.

"Wow, that's not very original!" Rebecca blurted, and looked up to meet his gaze. His lips curled as he gave her a sexy smile, and she blushed again.

Mr. Gorgeous leaned forward, holding her with his eyes.

"Oh, trust me." He had lowered his voice as if he was telling her a secret. "I can be very original."

She *so* wanted to avert her gaze, to break free from his hypnotizing blue eyes, but found she couldn't. A slow heat

6

crept up from her neck, all the way to her hairline. She had to be a crimson red now.

So much for being a mature woman, coaching people and giving them dating and relationship advice. *Some coach I am!* This guy had swept her off her feet with just one look and a few words. *How the hell did he do that?*

"Can I tell you a secret, Miss…?" he asked.

"Rebecca," she answered automatically.

Dammit. Now he knows my name. How stupid am I, exactly? Manipulated by someone's good looks and strong eyes. He was probably some perv. But she sensed he wasn't. He didn't look like a freak. His clothes, haircut and the cologne she smelled screamed money. Of course, rich bastards could be pervs just the same, but her gut told her he was a good man. And so far, her intuition had rarely let her down. He did, however, intimidate her tremendously, so she had to try to get rid of him. Fast!

"I'm sorry, but I've got to get back to work now. Nice meeting you," she said, fully aware she was being rather rude, and without waiting for him to reply, she dropped her gaze to her laptop again.

His soft laughter irritated her and she looked up at him and glared. Amusement flickered in his eyes and she couldn't help but smile.

"Tell me why you can't take a break from that laptop for five minutes?" he asked softly.

And before she knew it, she was telling him her story, about quitting her job and starting her practice. How the heck he managed to wangle all that information out of her, she did not understand. She knew coaching techniques and how to get people to talk—she used them herself in her work. This man had gotten completely under her radar.

But it was good to talk to him. Really good. She hadn't even realized she had needed someone to talk to, someone who'd listen and understand. And he did both.

While she was talking, he took her in. He had seen her

a couple of times before in the diner, and somehow, she had caught his attention. He wasn't quite sure why, but he never ignored instincts, and his instinct had drawn him to this woman. Being sensitive and intuitive, he was prone to picking up people's vibes wherever he went. As the owner of a posh BDSM club, his intuition often came in handy to assess situations and people. And as a Master himself, he could easily listen to what someone was telling him and pay attention to body language at the same time, without missing what was being said. Which came in handy now.

As he listened to her story, he looked at the chocolate-brown, wavy hair, the thick, long eyelashes and stunning hazel eyes in a heart-shaped face. A beautiful small nose that turned up a tiny bit at the tip and full lips that begged to be kissed. Or put to work elsewhere on a man's body.

Having seen her before, he knew that she had a good waistline, a slight curve to her lower belly, round hips and a seriously nice ass. Gorgeous tits, too. He guesstimated she was around forty years old, but her breasts still looked firm and full. She was a stunner. A nice, soft woman who he was sure he could get to moan under his hard body.

His cock pulsed to life at the thought. He was forty-four and had a preference for women her age. Mature, sexually at their peak, and usually far more confident than their younger counterparts, both in and out of bed.

He reacted to something she said, and asked her, "So, what kind of job are you looking for, Rebecca?"

She nibbled on her full bottom lip and seemed to think about her answer for a second.

"I'm not quite sure. Not the typical boring office job or waiting on tables," she said, frowning. Then her face brightened. "I want something with a challenge."

"I might have just the job for you!"

Rebecca looked up, surprise clear in her eyes. He smiled at her.

"I'm looking for someone with people skills, who can be trusted with confidential information, has administrative skills, and can easily shift from one task to the next when the situation calls for it. Someone with a brain."

He chuckled when interest piqued in her eyes.

"What kind of business do you run?" Rebecca asked.

"A BDSM club."

She was dumbfounded. *BDSM? He's a Master? No wonder this man is so…overpowering!*

One corner of his mouth turned up.

"I take it you're not familiar with it?" His eyes held something she couldn't quite grasp.

"Y-yes, but… N-no, but… I mean…" she stammered. "I'm not going to be your slave!"

He threw back his head and laughed, a deep, sexy laugh that made her insides stir.

"Have I said something funny?" she raised her chin, slightly embarrassed. This was definitely turning into the weirdest conversation she'd ever had. Thoughts of a sleazy club came to mind, and her running around in skimpy clothing, a fat bastard Dom chasing after her with a whip. *No way!* Or this man chasing after her. This strong, fit man would easily take her down and…

An electric current shot through her core at the thought of what would follow.

She looked at him again. If his club was anything like the owner, it would be far from sleazy. The man sure as hell had style, and by the looks of things, plenty of money to go with it.

His gaze was warm and reassuring when their eyes met again.

"I'm not looking for a slave. I need someone who can help out to keep my club running smoothly. So, you'd have to answer phone calls, run new membership applications by me, look after membership payments, that kind of thing. And you'd need to work behind the reception desk during club nights. And with the nature of the club in mind, confidentiality is of the utmost importance," he explained.

"That does mean that if you accept, I will have you checked out before I hire you."

Rebecca was seriously interested now. She wasn't up for a boring job and this sounded great. Variety, meeting people, a bit of office work, and the buzz of a BDSM club. Sexy. Maybe this would be the miracle she'd prayed for.

They discussed some more details and he answered all her questions.

"Think about it for a few days. Call me when you've made a decision. I'd need it before Friday next, though," he said and gave her a smile. Then he stood and handed her his business card. It read *Club Serenity* in gold relief print.

"Okay, thank you." Rebecca smiled back at him. "Oh, wait. I don't even know your name."

"Master Kyle."

Work at a BDSM club, oh, my God! Talk about synchronicity in life.

She had been in a BDSM relationship for a few years, but when it had started to go sour, the BDSM had ended up on the back burner. She had lost trust in her then partner, and without trust one couldn't engage in BDSM games. That just didn't work.

She hadn't been involved in BDSM for five years now. Every now and then she missed it, although she wasn't quite sure if she really needed or even wanted it in her life again.

In retrospect, she knew that her ex, who used to be her Dom, hadn't really known all that much about BDSM. He hadn't been as experienced as he had made out to be. She had instinctively felt this, even though she had been new to it all herself. Her instinct had kept her from completely submitting to him. Something deep down had made her want to keep her wits about her so she could monitor what he was doing to her—meaning she hadn't really trusted him. The times he had wanted to use nipple clamps or ropes around her breasts had made her uncomfortable. She had been scared he'd leave them on for too long, afraid her body would get damaged. A couple of times, he had let her down emotionally after a scene, as well. That had hurt, and ruined the bit of trust she'd still had in him.

In hindsight, she'd probably ended up topping from the bottom a lot. Had that been because of her sassy nature or not trusting her Dom? She wasn't sure.

Regardless of what had happened, she had never completely lost interest in BDSM. Occasionally she checked a BDSM dating site, and sometimes she read love novels on the subject.

Reading about it all, floggings, whipping, butt plugs, Doms and Masters, always turned her on tremendously. Every time, her pussy would dampen and need would smolder in her core. Sometimes she craved being a submissive, having a Dom or Master. She had enjoyed many of the things she had done and received as a sub.

Rebecca had been the bratty kind of sub. Not always — sometimes she had craved to serve her Dom — but the vibe between her and her ex simply hadn't been right. In a way, she felt that she had never gotten to fully explore her submissive nature. And that side still intrigued her. Her inner sub was still alive, even though it lay dormant most of the time.

But she hadn't a clue if she could still submit to a Dom or Master. Even though she had come a long way since her last relationship, she had gotten hurt badly. Both the sub and the woman in her had gotten damaged by her ex. And the bastard had broken her heart. Rebecca really didn't know if she could ever trust another man again, another Dom, with her heart, body and soul.

Now Mr. Nice Ass, Kyle, no, Master Kyle, had come along and offered her a job at his BDSM club. *How peculiar is that?*

Chapter Two

Rebecca was close to having a nervous breakdown.

What have I done to myself?

On that Wednesday, she had phoned Master Kyle to let him know she'd accept the job. He had wanted her to come over the very same day to sort out the necessary paperwork and he'd started a background check on her. He had shown her the office, where he had cleared out a desk for her, and the reception desk. Master Kyle had suggested she'd start Friday afternoon, so she could settle in a bit before the club opened in the evening. In the afternoon, she could do office work when he had time to help her out, and in the evening, she was to work in the reception area.

It had all sounded easy enough. Nothing that she couldn't handle as a former office manager. She'd be fine. And she was fine, until Friday.

On Friday, she suddenly started to get stressed out. What was she supposed to wear? She had nice clothes for the office, but what about the evening? Was she expected to show up in BDSM gear? And if so, what was she to be? Surely, having a submissive at the door, telling Doms and Masters the club rules, would be considered a bit odd? Alternatively, she could easily dress up as a Domme, a female Top. People often mistook her for being one, since she was a strong woman, and apparently, came across as being dominant. Admittedly, some of the typical Domme outfits did appeal to her. But she was no Domme, and it would feel off to dress like one. What if a male submissive threw himself at her feet?

The thought had made her giggle. But, in all honesty, she

wouldn't know what to do with a sub. The thought of one throwing himself at her feet only made her want to run to her Master for safety and security.

Her Master. She didn't have one. In spite of the odd longing in her gut, she really didn't know *if* she wanted one. Ever.

In the end, she had decided to wear a nice bustier, a short black skirt, black mesh pantyhose and high-heeled shoes that didn't scream 'Domme' or 'Mistress'. She'd briefly considered wearing her high-heeled thigh boots. She loved those boots, but they were far too Mistressy. Kyle would likely have a fit if she turned up in those, and after that he'd give her hell. A shiver ran up her spine. Crossing Master Kyle would not be a smart move, even though thinking about it made her insides quiver.

When she showed up in the reception area, Master Kyle looked her over and whistled. Her cheeks flushed. He looked damned hot himself in black leathers and a black shirt with press studs. The top buttons were undone and revealed a sprinkling of crisp golden blond chest hair.

Yummy. How about I run my fingers through that, Master Kyle?

"Thank you!" She looked at him through her eyelashes and gave him a sultry smile. "Looking good, too!"

Master Kyle raised an eyebrow and crooked his finger, motioning her to come to him. She swallowed. He looked so…Master-like all of a sudden. He towered over her and his piercing blue eyes made her want to drop to her knees to beg him for…anything and everything. Whatever he was willing to give. Like a spanking.

I'd love a good spanking. Master Kyle taking complete control, tossing her over his lap, slapping her bottom with a hard hand. She dampened.

His perceptive gaze saw her every reaction. Her sudden arousal and reaction to his command were very interesting. But now was not the right time to explore. Not with the club about to open.

He put his hand under her chin to lift her head. She let out a breath and her pupils dilated.

Yep, he had employed himself a subbie. A very attractive subbie. His cock agreed.

Not now, Kyle. Wrong time. Wrong place.

He almost chuckled. How could a BDSM club be the wrong place to play with a sub? Wrong time, agreed. He couldn't really drag his new employee indoors to flog her ass, play with her breasts, and fuck her hard when they were both ready for it. Not the wrong place, just the wrong time.

He sighed, wishing he was Master of his cock, so he could tell it to go down. The woman was still looking up at him with her puppy eyes. Kyle shook off the kinky thoughts of what he wanted to do with her and focused on the situation at hand. Up to a point, an experienced Master could switch things on and off. Except for his dick.

"Rebecca, you cannot address Masters and Doms that way. You will address them with respect and the appropriate title. When you're not sure, you call them Sir. Understood?" He gave her his Master-look. Her knees wobbled. "So how do you address me, Rebecca?"

Her hazel eyes were huge when she whispered, "Master Kyle, Sir."

"Good girl." Master Kyle smiled at her, his eyes warm again, and he rubbed his knuckles over her cheek. "Now go to the reception desk. I will send over another sub to help you out until you know the ropes."

A sub who knows the ropes?

She giggled. "Nice play on words, Sir."

Laughter glinted in his eyes and he gave her a devastating smile.

"You will get the feel of the ropes, as well. Soon. Sub." With those words, he left her standing there, flabbergasted.

What did he mean by that? Just getting the hang of the job?

Or was he talking about ropes? Real ropes? As in a BDSM scene? *And why did he call me sub? Confusing man!* And what a great start to the evening. Her legs felt like spaghetti, her pussy had dampened and the smoldering heat in her core made her horny. Hot. Needy.

She was glad when the submissive who was supposed to help her entered the reception area. The girl was really nice, and Rebecca was a quick learner. Soon she was completely absorbed in her work.

* * * *

The evening sure went fast. Most people arrived around the same time, and all guests had to be signed in, so that in case of emergency they would know who was inside, and how many people.

The doors closed at ten p.m. Finally, she could catch her breath. That had been quite something. Watching Masters enter with their subs had stirred things inside her. The vibe that radiated off them sure as heck hadn't helped her get on top of the need in her lower belly. If anything, it had made it worse. Clearly the whole Master and sub thing affected her more than she had anticipated. By the time the last couple had gone into the dungeon room, her pussy was very wet.

Many of the Masters and Doms had given her a hard time. Apparently, it took nothing more than a look or a few words to tell them that she wasn't one of theirs, not a Domme. Most had teased her and she had blushed profusely so often that she must have looked like an overripe tomato for the better part of the evening.

One of them hadn't said a word, but had just looked her over with pale blue eyes that gave her the creeps. His gaze had lingered on her breasts, which were pushed up to an almost indecent level by her bustier. His approving smile had made her wholeheartedly regret wearing something so revealing. When he'd lifted his eyes to hers, her clit had throbbed though, and he had smiled a knowing smile.

Damn bastard. Intimidating as hell.

Now that the doors were closed and everyone had gone inside, she wasn't sure what she was supposed to do. Go home? Just sit there like a lemon?

Kyle hadn't told her, and the sub who knew the ropes had left at nine-thirty. The girl had to do a scene with her Master, so Rebecca couldn't ask her.

Maybe she should just ask the bouncer, but he didn't look all that talkative. The man was built like a brick shithouse. No one in their right mind would mess with the guy. And he creeped her out, too. He hadn't said much to her all evening, but he had certainly enjoyed the show when the Masters and Doms had given her a hard time.

She sighed and started tidying the reception desk for the second time. Music floated from the main room. What would it look like? Master Kyle hadn't shown her anything other than the office and reception area, so she hadn't a clue. With her work was done, she got increasingly curious. Could she just go in? *Go into a BDSM club, oh, my goodness.* Yes, she wanted to. She hadn't been in a club for years. And she certainly had never seen a posh one like this. Her heart was racing.

Rebecca's curiosity made her decide to go for it. *What harm can it do?* If she wasn't supposed to go in there, it was Master Kyle's fault, not hers. He could have known that around ten p.m. she would be without work. He hadn't told her what to do next. His responsibility, and his fault, wasn't it? Having to ask her employer what to do next was a perfectly good reason to enter the clubroom.

Now that she had convinced herself, she hoped she'd be able to convince her sexy employer too. If she could find him. What if he was busy with a sub?

Oh, to hell with it. I'm going in.

Rebecca pulled back her shoulders, straightened herself and mustered up all her courage. She walked to the heavy wooden door, opened it and stepped inside.

Wow! This is awesome.

The vibe and smell of the dungeon room settled something deep inside her core. As if she'd been wound up for years and now was finally where she belonged.

Peace inside. Weird.

The scent of leather and the sounds of cracking whips, moans and screams enveloped her. The room was huge, and had a real dungeon look. The walls had brick arches and there was lots of dark wood everywhere, with thick, rustic oak beams on the ceiling. She spotted secluded corners, niches and strategically placed plants and screens, roped off scene areas, a St. Andrew's Cross and lots of other BDSM equipment that she didn't even know the names of.

The lighting was absolutely stunning. Very tasteful, yet enough light in the scene areas to allow for safe play. Some corners had colored lights. The type of music was spot on for this time of night. There were people enjoying it, dancing on the dance floor to the right of the room. Many were scantily clad and some were totally naked. Obviously, those were the submissives. Their partners were mostly dressed in black and leathers, clearly the Doms and Masters. And some Mistresses, too.

Rebecca looked around the room. The place must have cost a fortune to decorate. There was nothing sleazy about it, even though there was a woman in chains, moaning and whimpering as her Dom whipped her ass, and another woman on the St. Andrew's Cross was being seriously flogged and looking totally happy about it. Other couples playing in scene areas and, somewhere at the back, a threesome.

Oh, yeah, baby! Wouldn't mind trying that!

Rebecca giggled. Suddenly, Master Kyle appeared. *Where did he come from? Out of thin air?*

"What are you doing here, Rebecca?" He didn't sound pleased.

"I'm...eeehh..."

Dammit, did the man have to reduce her to a mumbling idiot every bloody time she saw him? She forced herself to stand up straight under his powerful gaze. She even had the guts to look him in the eye. Those unbelievably powerful blue eyes.

"I didn't know what you wanted me to do? Now that everyone is inside," Rebecca said.

He raised an eyebrow and his eyes turned to steel. Cold, blue steel.

She'd forgotten to call him Master. During a play night, in his own BDSM club.

Not good, Becca, not good.

Rebecca's resolve disappeared out the window.

"S-sorry. I'm s-sorry, Sir," she stammered. How had she gotten into this mess? She was here to work at the office and to be a receptionist. Yet, somehow, she had ended up being visually disciplined as a submissive by a Master. A very powerful and sexy Master at that.

All in a day's work, Becca, all in a day's work.

She giggled. Until she looked in his eyes again.

Oh, no. You don't laugh at a Master, Becca. Bad, bad Becca.

"I'm sorry, Sir," she whispered, her gaze lowered.

What am I doing? I'm not a sub! He's not my Master. He's my boss. He has no right to treat me this way.

She dared a quick glance at Master Kyle. He just stood there, his arms crossed over his chest, his eyes on her. Something sparkled in them. Did he think this was funny? She was far from amused. *Nice predicament you put yourself in, Becca.* Being overwhelmed by such a dominant man hadn't really been on her mind when she'd entered the club room. Curiosity killed the cat. And the sub. *Damn!*

Now she couldn't explore the room or leave. Simply walking out on a Master would be weird. Not the done thing.

Rebecca looked up through her lashes. The expression in his eyes had changed. The power in them took her breath away. His looming presence was horribly intimidating. Obviously, she had boldly gone where no receptionist had gone before, and Master Kyle was not amused.

Tears welled in her eyes. Why had she been so stupid as to put herself in this awkward situation? She didn't belong here.

She turned around and stormed out of the dungeon room. Before she had crossed the reception area, there was a strong hand around her upper arm. She was hurled around, and found herself looking at Kyle again.

"Not so fast, little one." His deep voice made her insides quiver. He gently brushed some tears from her lashes. "Come inside and have a drink with me. Please."

Rebecca swallowed against the lump in her throat and looked at him, eyes wide, seeking reassurance, and finding it in his steady gaze. When she gave him a slight nod, he walked her back into the dungeon room, his hand resting on the small of her back. He guided her to the bar and helped her onto a stool. A minute later, she was sipping a nice bourbon and cola.

"So, tell me why you came into the dungeon, Rebecca." His voice was soft, yet the command in it was clear. He obviously wouldn't take any crap for an answer.

"I think…I don't…but…" she stammered.

Way to go, Becca. Back to mumbling idiot again.

"Breathe, sub," Kyle said and held her with his gaze.

"Why do you call me sub?" she spat out, annoyed, yet wanting to know the answer at the same time.

His piercing blue eyes were stabbing, probing, and boring into her very essence.

She couldn't hold herself under his gaze and lowered her gaze, cheeks burning. The corner of his mouth curled up.

"That's why," Kyle said softly. "Sub."

Relief flowed through her, and a sense of coming home. So many years of questioning her contradictory feelings and doubting herself washed away, as if it had all been flushed out of her system. If an experienced Master such as Kyle was so certain she was submissive, who was she to question it? And her gut told her he was right. Something settled in her core, and she sighed with relief.

Kyle chuckled.

How does he know what I'm thinking about? She looked up at him, the question in her eyes. He cupped her face and smiled.

"I'm a Master, Rebecca." His voice smooth and soothing.

She sighed again and leaned in to the hand on her face. *God, that feels good.* She just wanted to sag against him and let him take control of whatever needed control.

No, no, no! You can't. He's your boss.

Quickly, she sat up straight again. As she did, she withdrew emotionally, and the moment was lost.

"Relax, little one," he said. "We're just having a drink at the bar."

Just a drink at the bar? Nothing with this man would be like just having a drink. The power radiating off him was too strong for that. He would always be in control. Like a wild cat would toy around with its prey.

"I asked you a question, Rebecca."

So much for just having a drink. He was still being all Master.

"I...ehh...I was just curious," she said, then quickly added, "Sir."

One corner of his mouth curled up as if to say "Good catch, sub."

Rebecca blushed for the umpteenth time that night. His strong gaze made it even worse.

"Lovely sub," he mumbled. "So...curious about what exactly?"

"Erm..." She couldn't lie under his scrutinizing stare. "I was curious what the room would look like. Sir."

"And? I think there's more to it." he pushed.

Dammit. Damn him. Mind-reading bastard Master!

"I wanted to know how it would make me feel, Sir," she whispered.

Kyle put his hand under her chin and lifted her face, his power forcing her to look into his eyes.

"Rebecca, there's nothing to be ashamed about. There

are thousands and thousands of people who enjoy BDSM. As long as it's safe, sane and consensual, there's nothing wrong with it," he said. "If BDSM appeals to you, and I can tell it does, you're just one of the many others who feel the same way."

"I know, Sir," she said.

He raised his eyebrow.

"Do tell, Rebecca!" he demanded.

Oh, damn. She couldn't tell him she'd been reading erotic BDSM novels and gotten aroused by them. Or that she'd been looking online on BDSM dating sites, reconsidering finding herself a Dom. She could, but she wasn't going to. Too close for comfort. It was way too embarrassing to tell him such private things. Especially since he was a Master. None of his business.

Kyle narrowed his eyes as he observed the woman. *What the heck is going through her?* He could tell she was carefully considering her answer — what to say to him, and what not. But he wasn't quite sure what the dilemma was.

"I had a Dom for a few years, Sir," she resorted to saying. "It, erm… Just for a few years, if that. It turned out we weren't right for each other."

Kyle's intuition told him there was more to it than that. Clearly, there was something that bothered her about it, and he had a sudden urge to find out what. If she needed help, guidance or information, she sure had come to the right place. He smiled and fired another question at her.

Barely five minutes later, she was telling him everything about her past relationship. Totally relaxed.

He knew how to work a sub. *Damn right he did.*

Chapter Three

A few weeks had gone by since Rebecca had started working for Kyle. After their talk, he understood Rebecca's hesitancy toward BDSM. Having had a BDSM relationship with a Dom that had taken off to a great start, only to go haywire shortly thereafter, must have been a confusing and painful thing to go through. It was so important that both parties could fulfill each other's needs. Respect and trust were crucial, and from what he'd heard, her Dom had let her down big time. But that was nothing that couldn't be sorted with the right Dom. Part of him understood why she hadn't gone there anymore after she had left the man, but another part wondered if there was more holding her back.

Her work at the office and reception desk was outstanding. He had heard from other Masters how her first evening as a receptionist had gone. It had made him laugh out loud. He'd expected nothing less from his club Masters and members than to give her a hard time.

Whenever she was working in the office, he was in his own office or doing other things that needed attention. They didn't share the same work space, but they often had a break together, and he found he was growing fond of the woman. She was great to have around. Somehow they just clicked. Kyle had noticed that he needed but half a word with her. Sometimes she'd already done something before he could tell her he needed it done.

During the weekends, he had gotten her to the bar more often after she had finished her work in the reception area. Officially she wasn't a member, and he shouldn't get her in the dungeon, but he couldn't help himself. She was a sub without a Dom, and he wanted to find out about that side of her. And it was much easier to get her to open up about it in the right setting.

After a month, Kyle had suggested that she come into the dungeon as a submissive after she'd finished her work at the reception desk. She had objected profusely, which had only brought out the Master in him. He knew she wanted to be in the club. He had seen the longing in her eyes when she watched couples scene. She wanted a Master — there was just something that held her back. Kyle wouldn't be Kyle if he didn't want to get to the bottom of that and help her out. He had to admit he was interested in her himself. She appealed to him. A lot. But first, he'd need her to warm up to the idea of having a Master.

It didn't take him long to get her to agree with the plan, albeit reluctantly. Her biggest problem had been the steep membership fee. He had suggested she work Sundays instead of paying. Sundays could be busy. The club opened at four p.m. and stay open till nine p.m. There was a buffet so people could eat, which sometimes made for interesting scenes. She could help out in the reception area, and after that serve drinks in the dungeon's bar area.

Kyle had explained that she was allowed to take a bit of time to get used to being in the club as an available submissive, but he had set a limit to it. Two weeks. Which meant four evenings. That ought to be enough for her to get comfortable with the thought. After that, the club Masters could ask her to do scenes. She wouldn't be able to refuse, unless she had a very good reason. Rebecca had looked shocked, and about to change her mind about the whole thing. Kyle had smiled.

"Rebecca, that doesn't mean you have to do things you don't want to do or have done to you," he'd reassured her. "You will have to fill out a checklist, which has all your dos and don'ts on it. Nothing will happen that you really don't want. Masters will play with the things you fill out with a 'Yes' and a 'Maybe'. Things that are a 'No' will be hard limits."

"So, what about that scary sadist?" Rebecca meant Master Luke. Not nearly as attractive as Master Kyle, but a handsome man, nonetheless. But she really wasn't interested in a sadist, or an overload of pain for that matter. She knew from her past experiences she wasn't into that. It was too extreme for her taste.

"Sweetie, a sadist would like to do scenes with a masochist. Since you're not one of them, he won't be interested in scening with you. Master Luke would also have to stick to your checklist, and there'd be very little on there that he'd enjoy doing," Kyle had said. "It's not much different from any other relationship. Attraction is a two-way street. Besides, Master Luke has his own sub."

Rebecca did remember seeing Master Luke play with a woman. She had watched him while he was seriously whipping the submissive. It had sent shivers down her spine. The woman had been in deep subspace though, and had come so violently that, in spite of not liking pain, even Rebecca had wanted to light a cigarette.

"Apart from Master Luke, there's Master Rafe, Master Cal, Master Adam, Master Ian, and a few others who I will introduce you to," Kyle said, "And there's me."

Her heart had done a somersault in her chest. *Do a scene with this overwhelming man? Oh, my God!*

Of course, he had seen her reaction—he was a Master, used to noticing such things. Her cheeks had burned. His low, sexy chuckle had made her nipples bunch into peaks. Kyle had lowered his gaze to her breasts, where it had lingered for a moment. Rebecca had dampened. He had lifted his eyes and the heat in them had started a meltdown of her core.

"Does the thought of scening with me excite you, Rebecca?" His voice had sounded hoarse.

She hadn't been able to lie to him. His piercing blue eyes simply hadn't allowed her to. They had looked right through her.

"Yes, Sir," she'd whispered.

"Thank you for your honesty." He'd cupped her face, bent his head and brushed a kiss over her lips. "Soon, Rebecca, very soon."

And with that promise, he had walked away, leaving her aching for his touch.

* * * *

In spite of some anxiety, Rebecca was happy she'd agreed to Kyle's plan. It was clear to her that she still had an interest in BDSM. She was just a little scared, reluctant. She knew for sure now that she was submissive. Not only from what Kyle had said, but also from her own feelings and reactions to watching scenes. She craved to be one of the subs out there in the scene areas, almost ached to be in their shoes. Okay, most weren't wearing shoes, but that wasn't the point.

Still, actually doing it and submitting to a Master was another step. A big step. At least she got to be in the dungeon as a sub now. She would take her time, see how it would go since club Masters could approach her and ask her to do scenes. Find out how she'd feel when that happened. She could still say 'no', after all.

Rebecca had been told that only the club Masters could play with her, not any of the other Doms. Not yet, anyway. It would be part of her training.

As if she needed training. *Been there, done that.* She had the T-shirt. One stern look from Kyle had reminded her that she had chucked the T-shirt, that her experience was quite some time ago, and she hadn't scened for a long time. Not to mention, it hadn't been particularly great. Training was simply part of the deal. Period.

Rebecca had to agree with him. He'd raised good points. Besides, he was 'Lord of the Manor', wasn't he? She could take it or leave it. And she definitely wanted to take it. It was the chance of a lifetime to explore this side of her, and to find out if she really wanted, or even needed it in her life.

Nevertheless, now that her first possible play-night had arrived, she had the jitters. She knew she looked good. She'd put on a tight blue latex dress. The front had a gold-colored metal zipper from top to bottom that could be unzipped from either end. Having her belly covered made her more comfortable. She had always been self-conscious about her tum, even though it was quite tight. She did have a little bit of extra padding, though, and on her first night as available-to-play sub, she needed every ounce of confidence she could muster. Another thing that slightly concerned her was the scars on her breasts from the reduction she'd had some fifteen years ago. The scars had turned white over time and didn't stand out like a sore thumb anymore, but up close and personal, one could see them. Rebecca had mixed feelings about having to expose her breasts during scenes. She was proud of their shape and firmness, but awkward about the scars when around strange men. Especially around gorgeous men like the club Masters.

Stop trying to be perfect, Becca. Nobody is perfect.

She was sitting at the bar, sipping her usual bourbon and cola. There was a two-drink limit, as it wouldn't be safe for people to engage in scenes when half drunk. Everyone got two tokens for alcoholic beverages at the reception desk. Non-alcoholic drinks could simply be ordered at the bar all night.

Rebecca wanted to keep her head clear, but she needed this one drink. She hoped it would help her to calm down just a little bit. As it was, her hands trembled and her feelings were all over the place. Part of her hoped no one would approach her to do a scene. Another part would have loved to play, to find out how it would feel after all these years.

So far, she'd only had the one Dom, and he used to be her partner. Playing with someone she wasn't all that familiar with would be very different. Rebecca had gotten to know the club Masters a bit over the past few weeks, but it would still not be the same as playing with a man she loved. It could add to the sensation, but it scared her a bit, too. So, she sat on her bar stool, trembling yet excited, hoping Master Kyle would be the first to do a scene with her.

Her bourbon and cola did offer comfort, but when a tall, dark, handsome man sat next to her, she got the shakes. Master Rafe. A bit younger than she, and horribly attractive. Her heart started a triathlon in her chest. Triple somersaults, races, skips and back to somersaults again.

"Breathe, woman," Master Rafe said with a warm smile. "I haven't even spoken to you yet. I just sat down."

She looked into his incredibly dark eyes and breathed in his strength. Somehow it calmed her.

"That a girl," Master Rafe said. "Another breath, good. Now drink a bit."

She complied, and when she'd swallowed the sip, he spoke again.

"I'd like to do a scene with you."

Rebecca almost started hyperventilating.

"Relax, Rebecca, breathe." Rafe's eyes narrowed. The girl was panicking. He'd been informed about her reluctance and past experiences, so he'd make damn sure to go easy on her. He grabbed both her hands and put them on his chest. "Feel my chest move and breathe with me, Rebecca."

He held her with his eyes, aware that she needed his strength and power. Being experienced, he knew that his steadfast calm and gaze would give her just that. Besides, they had a click, she'd accepted his control. And right now, she was absorbing it, drawing strength from it. His chest rose and fell at an even pace under her hands as she was trying to breathe with him. After a few minutes her shoulder muscles relaxed, telling him she'd successfully calmed herself down.

"Good girl," Rafe said softly. He stroked her hair and got a smile. He started a conversation with her, made her finish her drink and ordered her a cola. No more alcohol. She could have her second drink after the scene he'd planned with her.

While Rafe was talking with her, he started touching her. Nothing intrusive, just light caresses to let her get used to his hands on her body. A hand briefly on her shoulder, running his knuckles over her cheek, a tickling finger over her forearm. She began to relax under his touch. He sensed she was starting to like it. Rafe casually put a hand on her leg, just above the knee, and she didn't jerk away. He let it rest there, drawing slow circles with his thumb over the tender skin.

A smile pulled at his lips. She was getting used to being touched by him, and even held up her part of the conversation as he continued to do so. Then he moved his hand up a bit more, and her breathing got faster. He let his fingers tickle the tender inner side of her thigh and saw her nipples bloom under the latex. Rafe kept talking to her, even though she had stopped replying. His lips curved in a smile. The woman wasn't even aware she had stopped talking, and was totally enjoying his touch and the warmth of his hand.

Oh, my God, that feels so good! Please don't stop! Thoughts raced through her head. *This is so wrong, so totally wrong, to sit here and let yourself be touched by an almost stranger.* Another voice was arguing. *But it feels so good!*

Could she do this? Sit at a bar in skimpy clothes and let this man put his hands on her like that? Of course, she could. She was in a BDSM club, not the local diner.

Master Rafe moved his hand up again and came really close to her pussy. Her clit throbbed. A soft mewl broke from her lips. Her face flushed. Rafe groaned his approval. He leaned forward, and cupped her face. His dark brown eyes held her pinned.

"I want to kiss you, Rebecca," he said softly.

Her heart skipped a beat.

Yes, please!

He bent his head and took her lips, the pressure just right. Gentle but firm. Wonderfully tempting to open up for him. When she did, he swept in and started a sensuous dance with her tongue and she passionately participated. The man sure knew how to kiss. Her insides began to melt and her pussy dampened. She wanted more. Then, without releasing her mouth, he put his hand on her left breast and fondled it. He took her nipple between his fingers, pinched it to hardness, and rolled it. She moaned in his mouth as pain sizzled straight to her clit. It throbbed to live and the sting turned to pleasure. She pushed her chest toward him in an unspoken plea for more. He pulled at her nipple, hard, and she squirmed on the barstool. Her head was spinning, her pussy wet, her nipple aching.

Oh god, yes! Don't stop!

Her breathing was ragged when he released her. He gave her a sexy smile before he dropped his gaze to her breasts. The way he looked at her breasts was highly arousing. The heat in his glance made her nipples strain against the latex.

"Lower your zipper for me. As far down as still has you feeling comfortable," Rafe commanded.

Her hand trembled when she pulled it down a tad, revealing a fair bit of cleavage. Her gaze rose to meet his, hoping he was pleased with what he saw.

Rafe's eyes were dark and unreadable when he traced his fingers over the swell of her breasts, dipping into the tight valley between them. Then up and up, teasing and tickling over her collarbone and the sensitive side of her neck. She tipped her head to the side. Slowly, he ran his fingers down the upper curve of her breasts again. Her chest was heaving.

"Nice," he said softly, "I want to see more. Unzip until they almost roll out."

Her eyes widened.

You can do this, Becca, you can do this! Don't be a wuss!

Weird how this could feel so intimate, too intimate, while she used to hang out topless on the beach.

She sucked in a breath and slowly pulled down the zipper a bit more, hoping he would say it was enough when most of her breasts were exposed. He didn't. Rebecca stopped before the lapels of her dress could reveal her nipples.

"Very nice, Rebecca," Rafe said softly. He cupped her head and leaned forward to take her lips. Gently at first, then he took her deeper. She hadn't been kissed like that in years. It was mind-blowing. She clung to him for dear life. Her fire ignited in her core. When he finally pulled back, her head was spinning, and her pussy throbbing and wet.

"Stand in front of me, sub."

Rebecca complied. He got up, leisurely sauntered around her while tracing his fingertips over her body. Her skin burned under his touch. He moved down in erotic circles, gently squeezed her ass, slid up her spine, and tickled her sensitive neck. Her breath caught as she waited for what he'd do next.

Please hold my neck! Or my throat. I so love that!

A shiver of joy ran through her when he did put his hand around her nape. She leaned into it, overwhelmed by the sudden submissiveness that welled up from deep inside her belly. She could barely keep herself from moaning.

Rafe whispered, "Such a beautiful subbie." Without releasing her gaze, he took the zipper pull between his fingers and ever so slowly started lowering it.

Her chest was heaving as it came undone, a tooth at the time. Any moment now her breasts could spill free. She found that she wanted that, to have his hands on them, have him toy with her nipples.

Just pull the damn thing down!

A corner of his mouth curved up, telling her he knew exactly what was she was thinking. Yet he didn't go any faster.

Tick.

Tick.

Tick.

Tick.

Finally, the parting sides of the dress started to give way under the pressure of her full breasts. The latex tugged at her nipples as it ripped free, and she sucked in a breath as the tiny pain sent an electric current to her clit. Her breasts spilled out, swaying slightly. He didn't look at them. Instead he kept her pinned with his dark eyes. A roller-coaster of emotions raced through her. Shame, lust, need, impatience.

Why doesn't he touch me? Why doesn't he even look at my breasts? Doesn't he like them? Oh, my God, the scars!

Rafe smiled into her eyes, then dropped his gaze to her chest.

Goddamned nice rack! Fucking gorgeous tits! His cock strained against his leathers. Too bad he couldn't play with the nipple clamps tonight.

"Very nice tits, Rebecca!" he said, his voice hoarse.

Her shoulders relaxed. The insecurity in her eyes turned into desire.

Her areolas puckered tighter under his gaze, as did her nipples. Delicious, pink, slightly large. Firm nipples in the middle.

Rafe weighed her breasts in his large hands, cupped them. A nice handful. He fondled them, drew soft circles around the hard peaks, then squeezed them. Tugged. She whimpered. Rafe played with her breasts and nipples until they were swollen in his hands. Arousal had turned her cheeks a delightful pink.

She keened a protest when he let go of her breasts. He smiled. *Lovely, needy woman.*

"Pull up your dress so I can see your pussy." He made sure he put enough command in his soft-spoken words.

Rebecca didn't comply, though, she just stood there.

"Now!"

The sharp edge to his voice almost made her jump. She complied and pulled up her skirt a bit, revealing her black thong.

"Take it off."

No hesitation this time — she quickly got rid of the flimsy piece of material and put it on the barstool.

A tremor went through her legs as he looked at her pussy. Thank heavens she had shaved. But his gaze on her bare pussy was so intimate. Way too intimate. The fire in her core flared up, made her wet. And confused. How could being vulnerable and exposed arouse her this much?

Rafe stepped in, cupped her mound and a breast and brushed his lips across hers. She almost melted in his hands. Her legs wobbled.

"Sit down, pretty sub," he whispered against her lips. He grabbed a small towel from a stack on the bar, draped it over the barstool, and helped her get onto it.

As she sat, her dress rode up, exposing her entire ass. She frantically started pulling it down.

"Leave it!" Again, he spoke softly, but the power in his voice could not be ignored.

Rebecca quickly let go of the dress.

"Good girl," he said, letting her know he was pleased with her. "Turn around so you face me."

Oh, my God, no! Please don't make me sit with my naked pussy toward you.

She dared look at him, begging him with her eyes not to do that to her. The set line of his jaw told her he wouldn't relent.

She complied hesitantly.

"That wasn't all that bad now, was it?" he said in a soothing voice.

"No, Sir," she whispered, although she wasn't sure.

Her shoulder muscles were tight. Him looking her over didn't help much. Nothing seemed to escape his piercing gaze.

"Sweetie, don't lie to me. Tell me how you feel."

"I-I'm sorry, Sir," Rebecca stammered, "I feel…awkward. I don't know you that well." She lowered her gaze and mumbled, "Maybe this is just not for me."

She swallowed a sob, tears pooling in her eyes. She was so disappointed in herself that she couldn't do this. And he must be disappointed in her, too.

Damn, my first night, and I already let down a Dom. No, worse yet, a club Master. She couldn't do this to him. She was supposed to please him. Yet, all she really wanted to do now was go home, curl up into a ball and cry.

A tear fell from her eyes and he lifted her of the barstool, her size and weight not a problem for his strong arms. As Rafe crossed the room to a more secluded area, she started crying.

"I'm...so...sorry, Sir," she sobbed. "Please, let me try again. Please, don't send me away!"

He held her close and mumbled into her hair, "I'm not going to, sweetie."

Hearing that helped her to calm down a little bit. At least she hadn't completely screwed things up.

"I do need to know what happened, Rebecca." He spoke softly, his deep voice soothing her.

That didn't make answering him any less awkward. She found out within thirty seconds that beating around the bush with a Master was not an option. It resulted in him firing questions at her in a tone that demanded an honest reply. She had no choice but to give in and tell him all he wanted to know. While she talked, he kept stroking her. His gentle touch helped her to relax and open up. She finished her story with a sigh, relieved she had told him everything, yet uncertain how he'd react.

"Rebecca, you didn't let me down. I don't expect a full-blown scene on your first night." Rafe smiled in her eyes. "I might next week, though."

A longing shiver ran up her spine. Her resolve started to come back. And with that, hope that he wouldn't leave her hanging like this. She still wanted more. If she was honest, she craved it. Her entire being longed to be pushed, to have all the glorious sensations of submission flow through her veins.

She looked up at him, praying he would know she wanted to go on. The look in his eyes and the way he smiled made her heart skip a beat. *Of course, he can tell.* Why had she even questioned it?

Then something changed in his gaze. It got stronger, piercing. Dominant.

Oh, dear. Master is back!

"Go to the bathroom and freshen up a bit," Rafe said. "Then return to the bar. Same position as before."

"Yes, Sir," Rebecca said, glad he was going to continue their…thing. Whatever it was they were doing. Could it be called a scene? She wasn't sure.

Her breasts and lower body were still exposed and she started to pull down her dress. He stopped her with firm hands, and wrapped an arm around her waist to keep her from stepping back.

"I like seeing you like this."

How could such dark eyes be so hot, make heat sear straight to her pussy?

His piercing gaze kept her glued to the floor. A corner of his mouth curved up as he put one strong hand on her breast, kneading it until it swelled in his palm. He rolled her nipple, tugged. A soft moan escaped her. Without breaking their visual connection, he turned his attention to her other breast and fondled it until it was equally sensitive and swollen. He pulled at her nipple, then pinched and held it. She yelped and tried to jerk away from the stinging pain. His arm lay like a steel bar around her waist that held her in place.

"Breathe through it, sub," Rafe said softly. "That's it, good girl."

The sting from her nip raced over her nerves to her pussy and poked up the fire in her core. Her clit throbbed with need, yearning to be touched, rubbed.

He let go, captured the swollen, aching bud in his mouth and pulled.

"Aaahh!"

Rafe slowly released her, turned her around and gave a soft push.

"Off you go, sub."

He swatted her ass. She yelped, and quickly sped off to the bathroom, his soft, husky laughter still ringing in her ears.

Inside the bathroom, she leaned her head against the wall. *Damn, that was intense.* She was quite shocked that Master Rafe had gotten her so aroused. Just thinking of his firm touch sent a jolt through her core. She knew she was wet. Awfully wet. Rebecca pushed herself off the wall and glanced into the mirror.

Wow! She looked...hot. Needy. Her breasts were still swollen. They felt so full, as if the skin had gotten too tight around them. Her hard nipples ached from being manhandled. She wanted more. Much more.

She dropped her gaze to her lower body. *Oh, my goodness, I look like a slut.* Her pussy was clearly in need, too, her swollen labia slightly apart.

Shit. She had to go back to him like this in a minute. *Oh, my God, I don't know if I can do that!*

Rebecca crossed the short distance from the door to the full-size mirror to see what she looked like when she walked.

Damn. Her breasts jostled and her ass jiggled. Way too sexy. Too slutty. Oddly enough, the sight made her even wetter. Excitement bubbled up inside her. She could do this. She would go back out there with swaying hips and bouncing breasts, and sit on her barstool facing him so he could see her pussy. She could do it. She would show herself and Master Rafe that she had what it took.

Rebecca hauled in a breath and opened the door.

* * * *

She had done it! She was proud of herself. Master Rafe had been proud, too, and that had filled a void inside her lower belly. It had warmed her from the inside out. She'd found that she wanted to please him.

They had done a scene. Master Rafe had told her what the limits would be for that night, so she wouldn't panic or get the wrong expectations. No sex, no orgasm.

She had known her disappointment showed when he had laughed his slow, sexy laugh. After thoroughly kissing her, he had told why there would be no sex and orgasms that night.

"I want you to get used to scening in public before you come in public," he had said. He had gone on to explain that vanilla and self-pleasuring related orgasms could be tame compared to BDSM-induced ones.

"It can be quite shocking when you're not comfortable with public scening."

Rebecca had understood. She really had. It made perfect sense that anticipation, lengthy arousal, pain, teasing and mind games could trigger overwhelming orgasms. And she was glad he was concerned about her well-being. But she still hadn't liked the no-orgasm part. He had patiently waited for her consent. It was a take-it-or-leave-it deal. She took it. His eyes had glinted with... Amusement? The realization that he had known what she'd chosen had made her blush.

Master Rafe had taken her by the hand to scene area, where he had done a flogging scene with her. He had gotten her even more aroused than she had already been from walking around half naked. Not being made to come had been utter torture. And he had forbidden her to get herself off. Her only pleasure and release were to be given by the Masters at Serenity. Or not.

Rebecca sighed. Her ass was still tender from his flogging. A constant, low heat simmered in her core. She was so happy that she could go to the club again tonight. She hoped the Master who would play with her — whoever that may be — would allow her to come.

For God's sake, please don't make me suffer like that again.

Kyle had kept an eye on Rebecca when Rafe had been playing with her. He had deliberately chosen not to be the first Master to play with her. It had been a tough decision, as he'd sure as hell wanted to. Yet something had made him hold back. And Rafe was a great choice, a good Master to work with relatively new subs.

Kyle had thoroughly enjoyed what Rafe had done to her. She had a wonderful body, breasts that could drive a man insane, and she was very responsive. But she had not submitted. She had enjoyed everything, had clearly loved the flogging, but somehow the woman had managed to stay in control of her mind and body, no matter what Rafe had done. Sure, she had gotten very aroused, to the point where she likely would have accepted any cock. But that wasn't submitting to a Master. She hadn't even gotten close.

The next night, Master Adam had scened with her. The same thing. Extreme arousal, pleasure. She had done all the right things, had learned to kneel properly and had obeyed commands well, most of the time. She'd had her first public orgasm when Master Adam had put his mouth on her pussy. And she had come beautifully, jerking on the chains. But no sign of submission.

Kyle was thinking what he could do for Rebecca. He knew, sensed, and had seen that she craved to submit, needed to submit to be happy and whole, but none of the available Masters and Doms seemed to be a good fit for her. The right Master for her would have to be strong, quick-witted, smart, intelligent and above all strict. All his club Masters fit that description, yet so far it hadn't worked. Something was missing. That tiny little click that would make her let go of her control. Make her *want* to let go of control and submit to a Master, wanting to please him. Her desire was there, but somehow she couldn't. Wouldn't. Her defense mechanism was blocking her. She needed someone who would barge through that mechanism without scruples. Someone ruthless. Someone like Cal.

Kyle grinned. Cal would scare the hell out of her, but

when the setting was right, he would trash her walls. From the rubble, they could build a bridge of trust, allowing her to blossom into the beautiful flower she longed to be.

Chapter Four

Cal had been without a regular sub for over two years. Cal's last one had been his partner in day-to-day life, as well, but she hadn't been truly submissive. For her, it had just been a kinky game, and she had lost interest after the novelty had worn off. Their love had simply faded away, and in the end, they'd split. Not a really bad breakup, but it had affected Cal. Hell, anyone with a heart would be affected by a separation, bad or not.

Kyle had known his friend was over it when he'd started visiting the club again, ready to do scenes. But none of the available subs could hold his interest for longer than a couple of scenes, if at all, and his visits had gotten scarce. The last time Cal had been at the club was just before Rebecca had started working for Kyle, so the two hadn't met yet.

Cal hadn't been too enthusiastic when Kyle had phoned him about Rebecca. But his interest had piqued when Kyle had explained the situation and what was needed. He knew Cal liked a good challenge. Kyle had managed to get him to attend a play night to see for himself. Kyle would do a scene with Rebecca so Cal could watch her, see how she'd react before, during and after a scene. They agreed he'd come over early, so he wouldn't have to get in via the club entrance and meet Rebecca prematurely.

On the night, Kyle reserved the scene area with the spiderweb. When he'd told Rebecca he wanted to play with her that night, her eyes had lit up. Clearly, she was as excited about scening with him as he was. He told her to be at the spiderweb scene area at ten-thirty sharp. That would give her half an hour to finish up after work and to have a drink.

He was sauntering through the dungeon, really looking forward to the scene. But for now he was watching other couples, checking how things were working out. He knew he could rely on his DMs—Dungeon Monitors—but he liked to keep an eye on things just the same. Watching club members play, talk to people who were sitting in the niches here and there, the submissives who were waiting for their Doms, helped him to stay in touch with his club and its members. He instinctively knew when people were right for one another, if the vibe of a scene was good or not, and sometimes Doms asked his advice. He would never interfere, unless something was wrong, like a rope being too tight, cutting off the blood flow.

Tonight he saw nothing but happy people. Moans and cries of pleasure and pain floated through the air, and were music to his ears. Most play areas were being used, the submissives in subspace and Doms in topspace a sight for sore eyes. Other people were discussing a scene and some were getting the necessary care after a scene.

Kyle took his time. He wasn't in a hurry. He deliberately got to the spiderweb area ten minutes late.

Rebecca was waiting, kneeling, hands on her thighs, head slightly bowed. He could tell she was nervous that he was late. It had made her unsure what to do—wait longer or get up and go look for him.

Kyle didn't see Cal, but he knew he'd be there, watching. *Time to start.* He stood in front of Rebecca, aware that with her gaze lowered all she'd be able to see were his boots and leathers. His Dom-radar zoomed in on her and, in spite of the music, he picked up a soft of relief. Then her breathing fastened a bit, and he smiled. The woman was excited. So was he.

He didn't say a word, just took her in. Her long brown hair was loosely put up on the top of her head. A few shiny curls spilled down. Earlier he had seen her in a tight, black dress, but she was wearing a different outfit now. One that stirred his dick to life.

"Get up, Rebecca. Eyes down," he said softly.

Gracefully, she stood, her feet slightly apart, wrists crossed on her back, eyes lowered. *Beautiful sub.* He looked her over, circled her. *Gorgeous. Stunning.*

She had gone for a white off-shoulder top and a red leather waist corset with buckles and rivets. The corset pulled the top tight over her full breasts, emphasizing them beautifully. Her round ass in black, frilly burlesque hot pants made his mouth water. The hot pants had suspenders that held up black back-seam stockings.

As Kyle stood behind her, he tickled the undercurve of her ass, leaned forward and kissed the crook of her neck.

"Woman, you look delicious," he whispered.

"Thank you, Sir." Her voice soft and husky. The undertone of anticipation sweet and arousing.

He reached around her and cupped her breasts, her nipples jutting hard into his palms. He pressed another kiss to the sensitive curve of her neck, then nipped it. A soft moan came from her lips. Kyle pulled her back against his chest and her breath caught when his hard erection touched her bottom. He rubbed his thumbs over her nipples, circled them, and they puckered tighter. He played with her breasts until they were full and swollen in his hands.

Kyle walked around her and pulled the top down over her breasts. Her velvety nipples were poking out, begging to be teased, licked and sucked. His gaze caught hers, taking in what he saw. Desire with a pinch of insecurity. That typical helpless sub-look he loved so much. Without releasing her eyes, he pinched one nipple and held it. She whimpered. He bent his head and captured the other nipple in his mouth, circling over her areola. Then he sucked hard. She arched her chest and her moan made his cock jerk.

Damn, he could play with her nipples and tits forever. She was so responsive. He let go of her swollen nipple and switched to the one he had pinched. He circled his tongue around it, lapped over the hard bud and sucked it into his mouth.

Her movements and soft mewls turned him on. He hadn't touched her pussy, but he was quite sure she was very wet. She seemed every bit as aroused as he was.

When Kyle had had his fill of her breasts, he took a step back to look at her. One overheated, needy sub, panting, legs wobbly, breasts swollen. *Beautiful!*

He stepped forward, fisted his hand in her hair, pulled her head back and took her mouth. She willingly opened for him and he swept in, teasing and caressing. A wonderful, deep kiss, yet somehow something was lacking. It was all right, nice. A good kiss. But it didn't trigger any of the sparks that normally shot through him when he kissed someone he was attracted to. His cock was throbbing nonetheless, responding to the vicinity of a hot, sexy woman.

He let go of her mouth and nipped the curve of her neck.

"I'm going to blindfold you, Rebecca," he said softly. "And I want to play with ropes. Are you willing to let me tie you up?"

"Yes, Sir, I am," she said then hesitated.

Kyle cupped her face and looked in her eyes.

"Talk to me, sweetie. If you're not sure, I won't use ropes."

"I want to try the ropes, Sir, but I don't like to be suspended," Rebecca whispered.

Kyle narrowed his eyes as he assessed the woman in front of him. Fumbling her fingers, doubt and guilt showing on her face.

Years of experience and intuition kicked into gear and told him what was going on. A sub fearing to let a Dom down.

He smiled at her.

"Rebecca, it is important that I know what you don't want. For now, I'll consider suspension a hard limit." He kept his voice soothing. "You may use your safe word at all times. If you aren't sure, but don't want to stop, you can use 'yellow'. Understood?"

"Yes, Sir, I understand. Thank you," Rebecca said softly.

"Good. Now, I want you to strip for me," he said.

She looked up, shocked, all puppy eyes.

Kyle chuckled. Obviously, stripping wasn't one of her favorites, either. But since it came with the territory, and she hadn't marked it as a hard limit, he was not going to budge on this one. Besides, watching her go from shock to resistance to compliance was way too much fun, and also part of the game. A part he thoroughly enjoyed. It was endearing, sweet, lovely to see and incredibly arousing to have a sub give in to his command.

So, he waited as if he had all the time in the world, knowing that his aura of power would contradict that sense of freedom of choice. He loved causing a clash of emotions in his sub, as long as it added to their mutual excitement.

Then she looked up at him, begging him to not make her strip, and he got hard. The way her eyes widened, and the disbelief in them as she realized he wouldn't relent, almost made him groan. Her expressive face showed all her contradicting emotions. Doubt, desire, embarrassment, need, then finally surrender. His cock jerked again in response.

He watched as she nervously stripped for him, which was somehow sexy as hell. It turned him on far more than a femme fatale act could have done. Her fingers trembled as she undid the buckles on her corset and let it drop to the ground. The top followed. Then she undid the suspenders and carefully got out of the stockings. Now, the sexy burlesque hot pants were all that kept her from complete nakedness. She hesitated again. He eagerly waited for her to lose the garment, sensing it was the last threshold of her submission to him.

After what seemed like forever, she slowly wiggled out of the hot pants. His dominance zinged through him and he took a moment to feast his eyes on her body.

"Beautiful, Rebecca," he said, softly touching her cheek.

He brushed a kiss over her lips, picked up her clothing

and draped the garments over a chair, then walked to his toy bag to get a blindfold and ropes. He put the blindfold on her, a soft, black shawl, and tied it at the back of her head. Having robbed her of sight, he let her know he was still there by caressing her face, shoulders and breasts.

When her muscles relaxed, he started playing with his ropes. He teased her with them, softly dragging them over her shoulders, her breasts and the side of her neck, so she could get used to the feel. After a few minutes of sensory play, he began working the ropes, a red and a black one. Carefully pulling them around the back of her neck to the front, tying a decorative knot at her breastbone, just above the swell of her breasts. He worked with sure hands, gently touching her skin, tying knots and winding the ropes around her, forming a beautiful corset. Ropes around her breasts, her waist, down over her belly and hips, the knots a neat row in the middle. As he was working, he kept touching her, feeling her, hearing her every breath and gasp. When he was done, both her legs had ropes around them as well, like stockings with knots going down the middle.

He had sensed and seen that she loved the ropes. Her soft mewls and moans were delightful. She had gone into subspace before he was even done, overwhelmed by the sensations of being bound and restrained, the tight rope corset like an embrace.

Kyle gently pushed her back until she was against the spiderweb. He fastened the wrist cuffs to it, her arms raised in a vee, making her breasts arch forward. Next he moved her legs apart and tied them to the spiderweb. He took a step back. *Gorgeous!* Spread-eagle, her breasts and pussy swollen with need. The black and red ropes were a work of art on her lush body.

He took a step forward, his body inches from hers, and ran his knuckles over her cheek.

"Are you all right, subbie?" he asked softly.

"Yes. Yes, Sir," she mumbled.

Kyle brushed a kiss over her lips, and put his hands on her

breasts. He fondled them, toyed with her nipples and sucked them into his mouth, loving her moans. He slipped a hand between her legs and cupped her pussy. She tilted her hips in response. Kyle groaned, slid a finger between her labia and circled her clit. More moans. His cock was throbbing. He wanted to feel her wetness, yet he hesitated. He loved Rebecca's responsive body. He really liked the woman, enjoyed doing this scene with her. Part of him longed to play with her slick pussy, to thrust his finger into her cunt. His cock was certainly eager to go there. But something in the back of his mind started screaming again. Something wasn't quite right. There sure as hell was attraction, but somehow, it just didn't seem okay for them to get sexually involved. His cock begged to differ, but his brain won the argument with ease. He was an experienced Master, after all, and he could control his urges. He shouldn't go any further than this. Couldn't. He had reached the limit of what he could do, of what they should do together. The ropes had been an act of intimacy and trust, a bond and connection, which was congruent with the vibe between them. Sex, however, wasn't. If he went further, he'd come to regret it, and so would she. They would cross a delicate line if he made her come. He sensed it would ruin something precious between them. Something he didn't really understand, but instinctively knew he could not neglect. Unfortunately, they had started the scene with the promise of more. Both had somehow misjudged what was between them.

Fucking great, Kyle. Get a woman in subspace, completely aroused and needy, then realize you can't continue. For a minute, he wasn't quite sure what to do. He had never had this happen to him before. He couldn't go on, but he couldn't leave her hanging like this, either. Not when she was all worked up. That would damage their relationship just the same, and more importantly, her self-confidence as a sub.

Damn. Nice fucking mess, Kyle.

Rebecca started to stir. He had to do something before she

sensed something was off. He had to act now.

Kyle looked up and saw Cal, his eyebrow raised. Clearly he had noticed something wasn't going according to plan. Kyle motioned for him to come over. Being able to go with the flow was a quality a good Master needed when the situation called for it.

Hell, it calls for it now!

He remembered Rebecca was interested in doing a threesome. *So, be it.*

Cal slowly walked to the scene area and waited near the edge. Kyle was touching and caressing his sub. The girl's whimpers and mewls made it painstakingly clear she was in need. Cal also noticed Kyle wasn't doing anything to get her off. He was fondling her breasts and playing with her pussy, but not in such a way that the girl would come. What the hell was he doing?

Kyle quickly walked around the spiderweb and put his arms around the woman.

"Sweetie, do you trust me?" Kyle asked softly in her ear.

"Yes, Sir."

Kyle glanced at Cal and jerked his head for help, a plea in his eyes. Cal narrowed his eyes and they sprayed fire. He did not like this unexpected turn of events and he sure as hell would demand an explanation later. *You better come up with a real good one, pal!* Right now he couldn't leave the woman hanging. He was too much of a Dom for that, and obviously, Kyle wasn't going to help her out, for whatever reason.

He got on his knees before the woman and gently ran his fingers over her legs, stopping just an inch short of her swollen pussy. The woman gasped as she realized there was a second pair of hands on her body.

Cal bent his head, licked the tender inner thigh, felt her quiver, and nipped. She whimpered. Cal looked up and saw that Kyle was whispering in her ear, soothing her, while playing with her breasts. At least the asshole was looking after the woman.

He focused on his own unexpected task. *Not unpleasant at all.* He had watched the whole scene, and the way she'd reacted to the ropes and being tied up had aroused him. He loved Shibari, especially if the submissive was as beautiful and responsive as this one.

Cal licked up over her inner thigh, getting closer and closer to her wet folds. A moan escaped her and she bucked her hips. He curved his fingers over her buttocks and opened her pussy with his thumbs, exposing her swollen clit. He blew over it, sending a tremor through her. Her breathing was shallow and fast. For a brief moment, he did nothing, deliberately building up anticipation. Fully aware that she was hoping, waiting, to receive his wet mouth on her pussy. She instinctively moved her hips and her impatient mewl was music to his ears. He smiled, then gave her the pleasure and put his lips around her clit. A husky cry filled the air. He slowly lapped over the sensitive nub, feeling it swell even more, and took great pleasure in hearing her whine. A sweet song of need that made his cock throb. Cal would have loved to free her legs, cup her ass and fuck her to paradise. Instead, he thrust a finger inside her. He groaned when her cunt clamped down on him. He finger-fucked her while he licked one side of her clit, then the other. *Time to make this baby scream.* He bent his finger and rubbed her G-spot. Nice and swollen. She writhed and jerked on the web. When he sucked her clit into his mouth, he felt everything in her tighten. Her leg muscles tensed as her orgasm neared. Another rub over her G-spot and she exploded against his mouth.

"Ooohh, yesss! Ooooh, God! Yesss!"

Damn, she came beautifully, jerking and spasming on the spiderweb, screaming. Cal kept his mouth on her pussy, licking every aftershock out of her. When her body got soft, he started working her up again. The woman deserved a bit more pleasure and he didn't mind giving it to her.

He thrust two fingers deep into her pussy, earning himself

a gasp. As he drew circles around her nub with his tongue, she tried to move away. He knew full well her clitoris was still overly sensitive so soon after her climax, but he kept lapping and circling.

"No...please...too much," she said with a thick tongue.

Cal chuckled and forced her to hold still with his fingers inside her, pushing them deeper. He slowly moved his fingers in and out while licking around her clit. When he nipped her labia, she yelped. Encouraged by her reaction, he did it again, and her pussy clenched around his fingers. *Hot little subbie.* He nipped her opposite labia, held it between his teeth and tugged. A wail from her. A groan welled up in his throat. The woman aroused the hell out of him. He thrust his fingers into her, hard and deep. Her hips bucked and incoherent sounds and begs broke from her lips. He captured her clit in his mouth and started licking and sucking. As he sensed her orgasm approach he pulled back, and stopped fucking her with his fingers.

"Please, ooohh...please, don't...stop!" Rebecca sobbed.

Her trembling body and quivering legs told him she was hovering on the delicate precipice. Just where he wanted her. Nothing pleased him more than a begging sub, especially if she was as hot as this one.

He moved his fingers again and put his mouth on her clit, licking. She squirmed. *Needy little thing.* His cock pulsed in tune.

"Oooh, God...please, don't...stop! Please!"

He thrust deeper into her tight pussy and sucked her clit hard. She came violently, shocking and spasming. Cal growled as he kept working her pussy, licking over her throbbing clit. Her cunt grabbed his fingers, sucking, clenching.

Cal took his time to ease her down, gently lapping and moving his fingers until he'd drawn out all the afterwaves. He got up and looked at the sub, completely sated, hanging on the cuffs. He grunted, tangled his hand in her hair, pulled her head back and took her mouth. She moaned as he ruthlessly plunged in. When he finally released her, she was panting, her lips swollen and red. He gently ran his fingers over her face and stalked away, leaving her into Kyle's care.

* * * *

When Rebecca regained her senses, she was on Kyle's lap, wrapped in a soft blanket. She looked up at him.

"Hi, sweetie," he mumbled.

"Hey," she said. "What happened...? Who...? Why...?"

He didn't immediately answer and she could tell he was off-kilter, which made her a little nervous. She shifted on his lap, not certain what to do or say, except that she wanted to know what had happened. Kyle gently tucked an escaped curl behind her ear.

"Becca," he started, his eyes on hers.

"Something was off, wasn't it?" Rebecca asked. She was a smart woman, and subspace or not, she had still known that their scene hadn't been right.

"Yes, Rebecca, it was off," he said softly. "There is something between us, but it's not sexual. It's almost..."

"More like we are good friends," she whispered.

Kyle's eyes warmed. "Yes. Really good friends. And taking it further would have been...wrong."

She nodded, understanding him. She had known it when he'd kissed her. It had been a good, but somehow, it hadn't triggered her usual response to an attractive man. Normally a hot kiss was like oil to a simmering fire. It would send flames searing through her and make her very wet. That hadn't happened. She had gotten turned on by the ropes and the touch of his hands sensitizing her skin and nerves. And in the end she had been very needy, aching for sweet release. But she hadn't wanted it from him. It just wasn't right to have sex with someone who was so close, too close almost, like a soul mate. A soul mate should be a close friend, not a sex partner.

Rebecca took a deep breath and rested her head against his strong chest, happy he was there for her now and grateful he had not pushed her further.

Kyle held her close, and mumbled, "I'm glad we're okay."

After a while of peaceful togetherness, he stirred.

"Off you go, sweetie." He lifted her off his lap. "You may put on the waist corset and the sexy hot pants."

"What?" She glared at him. "I can't…"

Suddenly he was looming over her, and Rebecca swallowed hard. Master Kyle was back, taking full charge of the situation.

"You can, and you will." The power in his voice cut through her like a knife. She cringed under his unyielding gaze. No way could she be comfortable around him half naked. Especially after what had just happened. It would be a helluva lot easier with all her clothes on. His eyes told her he begged to differ and without further ado he pulled the blanket from her body. Suddenly, she felt very, very naked and vulnerable. Kyle put his hand under her chin and tilted her face up.

"We may not do intimate scenes, but I will not hesitate to discipline you." He cupped a breast and fondled it. "I have no problem spanking your naked ass or putting some nipple clamps on you if you get ornery with me, sub."

"Yes, Sir," Rebecca whispered. She quickly put on the waist corset and hot pants. He hummed his approval, then told her she could go have a drink.

As she quickly walked away, she could still feel his gaze on her skin.

* * * *

Cal had listened when Kyle explained what had happened. The man had seemed glad when he understood. And he did. He wasn't a rookie and he had seen, sensed, that somehow the chemistry hadn't been right. When Kyle thanked him for helping out, he said, "Glad to have been of service."

Then he stated what he wanted in return. Not a request, a clear demand.

"I take her on as my trainee. She will not scene with other Masters or Doms for as long as I'm training her."

A 'take it or leave it' deal. Kyle had taken it. Cal had nodded. He knew how to get what he wanted, and he had an interest in this woman. More than that, he was intrigued. For months, he hadn't played with a sub, any sub, for more than one evening. For some reason, this one stirred something inside of him.

Kyle grinned. As if the bastard had known this would happen.

"Wipe that smug look off your face," Cal growled. He was a bit shocked himself that he had demanded the woman as his trainee. That he wanted her even. A sub. *Trainee, Cal.* After what Kyle had told him about her, he was rearing to go and take down her defenses. To have her submit to him, to hear her beg him to fuck her. To taste her again. *Damn, she tasted good.* Both her pussy and her lips. His cock throbbed at the thought. He'd have her under his command, train her, take her, prep her for the right Dom and let go of her.

They discussed how they'd tell Rebecca about their plans. Kyle had been sure that if Cal simply walked up to Rebecca, things weren't going to work out. She would pull up her defenses. So, together they came up with a plan.

Chapter Five

It was Saturday night, early still, before opening hours. Kyle, the Masters and DMs would have their weekly meeting. They'd discuss existing and new club members, and anything else that needed to be addressed.

Rebecca had been ordered by Kyle to attend, as well, which was highly unusual. She hadn't a clue why he wanted her there, and that made her nervous. The other Masters and DMs would no doubt raise their eyebrows when she entered the room. The thought of having their powerful eyes on her made her shiver. One on one with a Master was almost more than she could bear. Having to face a room full was daunting. She could only hope that Master Kyle had told them she'd be joining them. Maybe then it would be a little less awkward for her. After all, they all respected Kyle. No one in their right mind would question him. Or so she hoped.

Rebecca was in a hurry. She was late for the meeting. She rushed into the room and barged into a solid wall of muscle.

Ooophh! What the hell?

Someone's strong hands curved around her upper arms like vises. She tilted her head up to look the wall in the eye and give him a piece of her mind for blocking the entrance. She had to look up and up and up.

Damn, this man is really tall. When she finally met his gaze, she sucked in a breath. Eyes black as coal, merciless, lethal. A predator, holding his prey — her — with the power in his gaze. Her knees got weak. Her spine took a leave of absence. She wanted to melt in a puddle at his feet right then and there, and beg him to forgive her, to spank her, to…

What was happening to her? Why had her pussy suddenly dampened?

She couldn't drag her eyes off him. His face seemed chiseled. A ferocious warrior god. Square, broad shoulders, rippling muscles, solid chest. Black hair with a hint of gray at the temples, a perfect straight nose, full lips that were pressed into a thin line, a masculine, strong jaw. And those black eyes... He was no god—he looked like the devil himself.

After long minutes, his eyes released her and she sighed in relief. A short-lived relief, as his dark, smoldering gaze dropped to her breasts. Her body reacted instantly. Her nipples tightened into hard peaks and she could barely keep a moan from escaping her lips.

His eyes met hers again and a tremor of need shook her body. A corner of his mouth curved up and his devilish smile made her heart do a triple somersault. He put his hand in the hollow of her back as he ushered her to a chair at the table. His touch made her skin burn and tingles sparked straight to her pussy. When he removed his hand, she almost whimpered at the sense of loss. He gallantly pulled back a chair, gave her a wicked smile and sat next to her.

Does he have to sit right next to me? Dammit! Rebecca suppressed the urge to bolt from the room. She was totally out of her depth, so close to this powerful man. She didn't know where to look, so she simply kept her eyes lowered. She'd always thought Master Kyle was intimidating, but one piercing gaze from this guy was enough to send anyone running for the hills, while screaming bloody murder. He put the 'I' in intimidating. All four of them—in capitals.

Then why was she turned on? Feeling his black eyes on her, probing her, had made her wet. And needy.

Who the hell was he, anyway?

She found out a minute later, when Kyle introduced him as Cal, one of the club Masters. Rebecca just nodded her acknowledgment. No way was she going to look at this Cal dude. It was bad enough he was sitting next to her. He had moved his chair over so he was close to her. So close that he was invading her personal space. Their thighs had touched and she pressed her legs together. He took the opportunity to spread his legs a bit farther so his knee brushed her thigh, then left it there to rest against her leg.

How rude! Normally, she would simply ask the person to move over a bit. But the thought of facing him and speaking to this…this giant predator numbed her brain and turned her spine to mush.

The heat that was radiating off his body was almost palpable. Her entire left side was on fire. Oddly enough, she wanted to lean in to him. That didn't make sense. She should be trying to get more distance between them.

His arms were resting on the table and she couldn't help but stare. Muscular forearms, strong wrists. Masculine hands, long fingers.

How would they feel on my breasts?

A soft mewl broke from her lips. Cal looked at her, one eyebrow raised. Heat crept over her face. His low, sexy laugh made her wish the ground would open up and swallow her whole. She'd never been this awkward in her entire life.

A warm, calloused hand covered hers.

"Relax, little subbie," Cal mumbled. "Breathe. That a girl!"

Oddly enough, she did relax. A sense of being safe and cared for came over her. *How the heck does he do that?*

She needed to get away from this man. He was way too dangerous. He barged through all her defenses with an ease that was frightening.

Rebecca tried to focus on the meeting. She mentally shook off her feelings and looked up, straight into Master Kyle's eyes. Amusement flickered in them and he had a smug look on his face. The asshole was certainly enjoying her discomfort. Suddenly aware that Cal's hand was still on hers, she jerked it out from underneath his. He didn't say anything, didn't look at her, either, but she still caught the smile that grew on his face.

Asshole!

When the meeting was finally over, she fled from the room.

* * * *

After the awkward meeting, Rebecca welcomed the hustle and bustle of a busy Saturday night. She needed the distraction after her collision with that dark, scary man.

It was well after ten-thirty before she was ready in the reception area and could finally go into the clubroom.

Rebecca desperately needed a break, and to get off her feet for a bit. She walked over to the bar, sat on a stool and ordered her usual drink. She glanced around to make sure she was nowhere near that intimidating man. She didn't see him anywhere. Not in the scene areas, nor at the bar. Maybe he'd gone home. *Thank God for that.*

"I think it is about time you start doing scenes again."

Rebecca almost choked on her drink, turned around and found herself looking into Master Kyle's piercing blue eyes. Very unyielding blue eyes.

Was he going to put his foot down now? Master Kyle had let her get away with not doing any scenes the last two nights, even though she was supposed to be getting trained by the Masters and finding herself a suitable Dom. So far he hadn't made a problem out of her reluctance, but it looked as if his patience was wearing thin.

If she wasn't going to do scenes, would he ban her from the clubroom? Rebecca didn't want that. She really liked being in the club. It helped her relax and it allowed her to simply be herself. To let out this kinky side of her. Even though she hadn't done a scene after the one with Kyle, she felt at ease in the dungeon. She just hadn't met the right Dom yet.

Bullshit, Rebecca! You're scared, you wuss!

"Rebecca, the idea is for you to find yourself a Dom. Doing scenes in a safe environment is a great way to get there," Kyle said. "Sitting at the bar every night isn't going to get you anywhere."

"I know, Master Kyle. I am sorry," Rebecca whispered.

"Now, put that drink down and dance with me." Not a request.

She slid of the barstool and let him walk her to the dance floor. He took her in his arms and they swirled around. He was a good dancer and she had no problem following his lead. Her muscles relaxed and she enjoyed herself. She wished she could fall for him. He was truly a gorgeous man, and a great Master.

The next song started, an upbeat rock song. Master Kyle made her twirl and twist and turn. Rebecca laughed. *This is great.* Kyle held her hand, swung her out and spun her back against him. He made her twirl again, but instead of holding her, Master Kyle let go of her hand. She cried out, about to lose her balance, when two muscular arms enveloped her, steadying her. She looked up and up and up into a pair of black, smoldering eyes. Rebecca whimpered. The predator! Master Cal gave her a devastating smile, bent his head and took her mouth, hard and demanding. He forced her to open her lips, and when she did, he plunged in, taking all she had to give and more. She moaned into his mouth.

He cupped her bottom with his strong hands and yanked her against him, his hard erection pressing against her lower belly. Her body reacted immediately — her pussy dampened and her nipples bunched into tight points against his chest. Rebecca clung to him for dear life and kissed him with a hunger she hadn't known she had.

After long, delicious minutes alarm bells went off in the back of her head. She remembered those lips. The demanding, possessive mouth that had taken hers after the scene with Kyle. This was the man who had put his mouth on her pussy. She froze in his arms, ready to break away. He fisted his hand in her long hair to hold her in place, and took her deeper, and she lost herself in the kiss again. *Damn, the man can kiss!*

The realization of what was going on sank in. Master Kyle and Master Cal had set her up! *Assholes!* She pushed against Master Cal's chest, trying to get away from him, but his arms were like solid steel bars that just wouldn't budge.

She started to squirm, getting angry that he wouldn't let go of her. She considered kicking him, but with her bare feet, she'd likely only hurt herself.

She bit his bottom lip instead.

Master Cal growled. For a second, he looked at her in shock, then his ruthless eyes were shooting fire.

Oh, my God, what have I done? Run, Rebecca, run!

But her body refused to work. She stared up at him, feeling like a rabbit caught in a trap, about to be devoured by a wolf. Master Cal's merciless eyes told her he was going to have her for breakfast. Three times over. Tremors of fear shook her legs and her bottom lip quivered.

Biting a Master is so not smart. Biting an ominous one like Master Cal was a death wish.

She swallowed hard. His cold, unforgiving smile sent shivers down her spine. He moved so fast that it seemed like a blur, and before she could even blink to clear her eyes, he had slung her over his shoulder. The world moved upside down around her and fear of crashing to the floor numbed her brain. Rebecca shrieked and pounded her fists on his back.

"Let me go, you bastard. Put me down! Put me down, dammit!"

He didn't bat an eyelid and sauntered toward a chair in a niche with her over his shoulder, as if she was nothing more than a sack of potatoes. It infuriated her and she kept shrieking.

A few seconds later she was dangling facedown over his lap. He put his leg over hers to keep her in place. Her skirt was pulled up, baring her bottom.

No, no, no! This is so not right!

"No, let me go! I don't want this!" Rebecca yelled, trying to get up, but he pushed her down with a hard hand between her shoulder blades. As he let his hand rest on her upper back he slapped her ass with the other.

Smack!

"Oowww! Let me go, you —" she started.

Smack!

Rebecca tried to squirm off his lap, but he easily held her in place with a leg and his left hand, while he walloped her ass.

Smack!

"Goddammit! No! I don't want to! Let me go!"

Smack!

He slapped her even harder now, and again, and again. She started sobbing.

"I'm sorry, I'm so sorry!" she cried, as tears dropped from her eyes.

Smack!

"I'm sorry, Sir! Please, stop!"

Cal caressed the skin of her already bright pink bottom.

"I'm not convinced, sub. You will take six more for me, and count them." The steel edge in his voice reverberated through her. "And thank me after each one."

Six more? Six! Thank him for it? No way!

Rebecca started to squirm. She'd had just about enough of this.

Cal sighed. "All right then, have it your way."

Smack!

Rebecca yelped. That had been a really hard swat. And another one to her other ass cheek.

"Oww! You...you...monster!" Rebecca sobbed uncontrollably now. Her body shook on his lap and tears fell to the floor.

Cal waited. "Anytime you're ready, sub."

Rebecca sensed he was simply not going to relent. No mercy.

Something inside her gave way, as if a veil had lifted deep

in her core, torn to shreds by the slaps to her ass and his unyielding demeanor. The stronghold deep in her belly crumbled, collapsed, and her core opened. Sweet release washed through her, astounding her, the sense of freedom so strong it made her head spin. The soft 'Ooh?' that escaped from her lips expressed her wonder.

He felt her submission when her body went soft on his lap and her muscles relaxed. Cal smiled. Smoldering heat flowed from his core. He loved when a sub surrendered, especially if it was her first time. From what he'd been told, this baby had never really submitted to any man before. Knowing he was the first whipped up every bit of dominance and possessiveness he had in him. And it woke his dick. His now hard cock was throbbing.

Cal focused on the luscious curves of the woman on his lap, who had just submitted so sweetly to him. He gently stroked over her back, tickling her spine.

"Ready to count, sub?" His voice sounded gravelly. Oh hell, he had just taken her submissive virginity. He was allowed to be a bit emotional, wasn't he?

"Yes, Sir." Her voice was a mere whisper, but steady.

Smack!

Rebecca gasped. "One, Sir. Thank you," she breathed softly.

Smack!

"Two. Thank you, Sir." Immediate reply this time.

Smack!

Rebecca cried out and started sobbing again. "Three, Sir." A pause as she sucked in a breath. "Thank you, Sir."

Her world narrowed and became hazy. All that remained was the pain in her ass, his steady thighs under her belly, his hard hand and his low voice as he mumbled his approval to her. The deep timbre of his voice was the only thing that cut through the haze in her head, her life-line. In spite of the stinging pain, his voice somehow calmed her, made her feel safe. Each hard slap softened the funny spot in her belly, overwhelming her, freeing her.

By the time she had thanked him for the sixth swat, her head felt weird. Dizzy. Foggy. And her ass hurt like hell.

"You may thank me for the lesson now, sub."

"Thank you, Sssir…for the lesson, Shir." Her words came out slurred.

Suddenly, a devastating urge to cry rose from the newly discovered place in her lower body and raged through her. Her shoulders shook as she broke down in tears.

Cal quickly lifted her and turned her around. She immediately burrowed against him while bawling her eyes out.

He put his arm around her, holding her close, and accepted the subbie blanket that Kyle handed him, and wrapped it around her.

A female submissive on waiting duty rushed over with bottles of water, chocolate and a tube of cream that would alleviate the pain.

Rebecca vaguely heard some people around them, and Cal mumbling to someone. Not that she cared. All she needed was to be close to him. The way he gently rocked her and made soothing sounds. Nothing else mattered right now. He had wrapped an arm around her and cupped her head with his other hand, holding it in the hollow of his shoulder. It fit perfectly. They fit perfectly, her soft body against his hard muscles. It felt incredibly good to be held by a strong man. A dominant man who kept her safe and stable. He rested his cheek against her hair and the scent of his aftershave drifted up her nostrils. A masculine, musky scent with a hint of citrus and amber. Powerful and mysterious. Totally befitting him. Something inside her clicked into place. For the first time in years. No, for the time *ever*. That made her more emotional, and she started to cry even harder.

"It's okay, sweetie, let it all out," he mumbled into her hair.

And she did. Her inner barriers had tumbled down,

leaving her vulnerable and exposed, and all the stuff that she had kept bottled up for years came out. Had to come out. It was so liberating. Fears, control, need to let go, the inability to do so—it all spewed forth.

Finally, the worst was over and only the occasional sob escaped.

"Good girl. You've done well. I am proud of you," Cal said softly, and he tilted her face up with his hand and looked her in the eyes. His intent gaze seemed to go straight through her.

Rebecca jerked her head out of his hand, and lowered her eyes. She didn't want him to see her like this. She had been bawling her eyes out for what seemed like forever. Her entire face felt swollen and had to be puffy. Embarrassment washed through her. Doing a train-wreck act on a guy she didn't even know was not her idea of a great evening.

"Don't you go play hide and seek with me now, subbie. Look at me!" His commanding voice cut through her awkwardness. Knowing he wouldn't let her slip back into that stronghold in her gut filled her with joy. He was there for her. But she felt so weird. Scared.

"Look. At. Me."

She complied, feeling naked and vulnerable.

"That's it, my girl," Cal said, holding her steady with the intent gaze in his black eyes.

"Wolf Man," she mumbled.

"What?" Cal looked puzzled. His eyes narrowed, boring into hers. Intense shyness flooded her. Rebecca's face heated.

Did I have to say that out loud? Damn it!

"Talk, subbie!" A clear command. No leeway whatsoever, not in his voice, not in his gaze. She had no choice but to answer.

"Wolf Man," she whispered. "You…you…are a Wolf Man."

The fine lines at corners of his eyes crinkled, a smile pulled at his lips, then his full, deep laugh filled the air.

Cal's face changed entirely when he laughed. *Damn, he's attractive!* His eyes were gleaming with laughter when he looked at her again. She couldn't help but smile back at him. He simply took her breath away.

"Woman, I'm going to thoroughly enjoy spending time with you." The promise in his low, smooth voice swept through her. That, and the heat in his eyes, made her pussy tingle with need.

Rebecca's eyes widened as proof of his excitement pressed against her hip, and her cheeks flushed. His chuckle rumbled inside his chest.

"Don't worry, subbie," he said softly. "Not tonight."

Disappointment spiraled through her and she quickly lowered her head. By now, she had a pretty good idea that he could read her face like an open book. She knew she hadn't been quick enough when he put a finger under her chin and lifted her face up.

"Don't hide from me, sweetie," he said. "You're one hell of an attractive woman and I'm totally hard for you. But you've had enough excitement for tonight."

Her thoughts and emotions flashed over her face. *Attractive?* She knew she always looked horrible after bawling her eyes out. *And who are you to decide what's enough excitement for me? You don't even know whether I want you or not. Arrogant asshole.*

His lips curled up.

"Let me explain a few things. First of all, you are very attractive. Even when you've cried. I am a Master and I love seeing the real, authentic sub. You look beautiful, sweetie." Cal said, his voice low and husky. "Second, you want me, and you want me to fuck you. Real hard."

Rebecca gasped at his crude words. Her already warm face burned now, and she shook her head in denial. He just smiled his devilish smile.

"Shall I check your pussy?" He slid his hand up her thigh.

"No, please!" she begged.

He raised an eyebrow. The power in his eyes — *damn those*

black eyes — got to be too much for her and she lowered her gaze.

"Sir?" she whispered.

"Do you want me to fuck you? I want either physical or verbal confirmation. Now."

Her innate stubbornness kicked in. She couldn't tell him that. She didn't want to tell him that. He had no right to ask such questions. She couldn't, wouldn't submit. *Not to anyone, dammit!* No one would walk over her. No one would fucking bully her. Never, ever again.

The portcullises of the stronghold deep in her belly began to drop down. Tears pooled in her eyes and her vision blurred. *No, no, no!*

Cal lifted her chin again, forcing her to look at him.

"Rebecca, what's going on? Talk to me, sweetheart. Don't go back hiding in that dark place now." Cal's soft voice enveloped her. He caressed her cheek with his warm fingers. "Talk to me, Rebecca."

Her gaze rose, and when she saw the warmth and care in his eyes, the portcullises started clanking up again. She sighed her relief.

"I don't want to go back there, but I'm so scared!" Tears rolled down her cheeks. "Please hold me."

She burrowed close when he drew her into his arms, held her close to his chest and let her cry. Glad that he bore with her even though she was on an emotional roller-coaster. Happy she'd met this man, scary or no. Even as she cried, she thought, *Please be the one for me!*

* * * *

Cal had no clue how long it would take her to calm down, nor did he give a toss. He was a patient man and this beautiful, warm woman was worth his time. Right now, she needed his aftercare. And he needed to give it, had to be there for this newborn, fiery sub who had surrendered so beautifully under his hard hand.

He'd have to look after her red ass too, put some cream on it to ease the pain and soothe the skin. But it would have to wait. Her emotional needs were more important right now. Even though her ass was red, even if she'd gotten a few bruises from the harsh spanking, her ass would recover. Her vulnerable sub-heart wouldn't. Not without him salving it.

So he just sat there, stroking, soothing and holding her, slightly surprised that he'd managed to break through her barriers in such a short time. That was quite something. He hadn't expected it. Not this fast. She pulled at his heart. She moved him. He wanted her. All of her. And damned if he wasn't going to get it.

After a while, Rebecca stopped crying. Her breathing became regular and deep and Cal could tell she was doing a lot better. She stirred in his lap.

"Thank you for holding me, Sir," she mumbled against his chest.

"You're welcome, sweetie."

Rebecca rubbed her cheek on his wet shirt, and giggled.

"What's that, subbie?" Cal demanded.

"I wet your entire shirt. I'm so sorry. Maybe you better take it off."

A husky giggle. *Damn, the woman bounced back fast!*

"So you want me half-naked?" he whispered in her hair. "But you don't want me to fuck you?"

She stiffened for a second, then melted against him again. "I do," she whispered.

He had no clue which question she had answered, and his lips curled up. *Cheeky little thing, playing mind games!* He'd play along. He liked mind games. Especially as he was the one winning them. Always.

"Which one, subbie? Me half naked or me fucking you?"

"Both." Her voice was barely audible.

His cock stirred to life. Impossible for him to hide his erection, impossible for her to not notice it. He didn't mind. Nor did she. Her soft laughter floated toward him, a tell-tale sign she enjoyed arousing him.

Cal tangled his hand in her hair, pulled her head back and looked her in the eye.

"Are you playing mind games with your Master, subbie?" His voice was hoarse. He used his Dom-gaze, daring her to defy him.

A smile pulled at her lips. "Maybe, Sir." She looked at him from under her eyelashes.

The woman had spunk for sure. He would have his hands full with her. He was looking forward to it.

Cal bent his head to take possession of her mouth and kissed her passionately, demanding a reply. She yielded completely to his hard kiss and he groaned. He loved kissing her, loved how she reacted to him, surrendered to him. When he released her, his breathing was ragged, and his dick was pulsing. The dazed look in her eyes didn't help. The pressure in his balls turned up a notch. *Damn, did he want her!*

"Rebecca, do you want me to be your regular training Master?" Cal asked, his intent gaze on hers.

A myriad of emotions showed in her eyes as she pondered the question. Shyness, eagerness, and mild fear alternated with vulnerability and a hint of playfulness.

"Do I have to sit at your feet?"

Cal leaned forward, nibbled her bottom lip and whispered against her mouth, "If that's what you need."

A soft moan escaped her. She whispered against his lips, "I do!"

Amusement trickled through him. Which question had she answered? Damned tease!

"Do what? You want me to be your training Master or sit at my feet?"

She gave him a sultry look.

"Both."

That one word set his core alight. He groaned, pulled her head back by her hair and kissed her. She opened her mouth and he swept in. Rebecca wrapped her arms around his neck and rubbed her breasts against him. Without releasing her lips, he pushed his hand between the two of them and cupped her right breast. She moaned into his mouth. He tugged at her nipple, and felt a shock go through her.

Damn, she's passionate! His cock throbbed. But not tonight. The emotional roller-coaster ride had been enough.

Reluctantly, he let go of her sweet lips and drew her against him.

"Enough for tonight, baby," he said, his voice husky. "And, yes, I get to decide, because I am your Master."

"Wolf Man," she mumbled.

His chuckle put a smile on her face. She closed her eyes and yawned.

Yep, the woman was shattered.

* * * *

"Rebecca. Rebecca. Wake up!"

"Mmm... Whassup?" she mumbled, keeping her eyes closed, unwilling to open them.

"Rebecca."

"Go 'way!" She flapped with her hand as if to get rid of an annoying bug.

A low laugh rumbled under her ear. *Huh? A laughing mattress? Warm. Solid. A chest.*

Her eyes flew open. *Cal! Oh, my God I fell asleep on top of him! And who had put my ass on fire, dammit? Cal!* He was to blame for everything. He had scared her, made her cry, had hurt and exhausted her. Had just taken without mercy, and given to her by doing so. He had freed her.

"Rebecca, you with me?"

That wasn't Cal. She turned her head to where the voice had come from. Kyle. His intent eyes on her, assessing her. He smiled.

"Hi, sugar. Welcome back," Kyle said. "You with me? Good. Rebecca, you cannot stay alone tonight. You've been through a lot, and chances are you will get sub-drop. You know what sub-drop is, sweetie?"

Rebecca nodded. She'd done enough research, and she'd been there in the past. The thought of sub-drop didn't appeal to her. She knew she had been in subspace during the spanking. Not very deep maybe, but with the emotional upheaval and breakthrough after that, sub-drop could happen. She shivered.

"Have you got someone you trust who can stay with you tonight, Rebecca?" Kyle asked.

She shook her head. Her friends would either be out drinking or they hadn't a clue about subspace and sub-drop.

"Then you will stay with me, and tomorrow you're not working," Kyle said.

Rebecca knew it would be the logical thing to do, since they had gotten to know one another quite well. There was trust between them, and he knew what to do if she dropped. It wasn't what she wanted, though. She shook her head ferociously and burrowed closer to Cal. Kyle grabbed her hand.

"Sweetie…"

Without looking up, Rebecca shook her head again.

Cal held her tighter, and she reveled in his possessiveness as it enveloped her.

"Well, I guess that's that sorted then." Kyle chuckled.

"Rebecca, Master Kyle is right. You can't stay alone," Cal said softly. "Are you sure you don't want to go with him?"

Rebecca nodded as she clung to Cal. Right now, she was so deeply connected to him, the Master who had freed her. All she wanted was to be with him. After what she'd been through, what they had shared, she needed to be near him. To absorb his strength and to be safe in the arms of this powerful man. It didn't seem to matter that they barely knew each other — she had bonded with him.

"Sweetie, do you want to stay with me?"

She nodded.

"Rebecca, look at me." Kyle again. She complied.

"Are you really sure?" he asked.

"Yes. Yes, Sir," she answered. When Kyle nodded his approval, she snuggled up against Cal again.

She realized Kyle wasn't leaving and turned her head to see what was going on. The men had locked eyes and tension was almost palpable in the air between them. Rebecca's shoulder muscles tightened. *What on earth is going on?* She looked from Cal to Kyle and back. Two Masters in a non-verbal cockfight? Over her?

"You best take good care of her," Kyle said. The warning in his voice could not be missed.

"Fuck off and stop worrying," Cal replied, sounding equally strong.

Rebecca watched as Kyle's lips curled up. He gave both Cal and her one last look, turned around and sauntered off. With a smile on his face.

Men.

After Kyle had walked off, Cal handed her a bottle of water and fed her bits of chocolate in between. She drank half the bottle in one go and gratefully took the chocolate from his fingers with her lips. She closed her eyes, savoring the delicious flavor.

"Mmm…wonderful!" she purred, licking her lips. "More, please, Sir."

Cal grunted. Would she look like that if he fed her his cock? Beg for more, as well?

He broke off another piece of chocolate and teased her with it, traced the wonderful curve of her upper lip with the chunk and watched as she darted her tongue over her lips to lick them clean.

Their eyes met. The lust in his set her core on fire. So did the growl that came from him.

"Very hard indeed." He didn't have to say more. She got the referral to him fucking her hard. Her cheeks burned.

"Please, Sir!" Her voice came out a husky whisper.

"You want it now?" Cal's eyes narrowed.

"Yes, Sir." She giggled, and he lifted an eyebrow.

"The chocolate, please, Sir." She laughed now.

Cal leaned in, his face barely an inch from hers. "We're going to have a lot of fun, sub. A lot of hard fun!"

"Yes, please, Sir," Rebecca replied, thinking of him on top of her, taking her hard.

"I was thinking about your rear end, sweetie," he whispered. Wolf Man was back. Dark eyes, devilish smile and all. "I love spanking a hot piece of ass."

Now that Rebecca was reminded of her sore bottom, it suddenly seemed to hurt more. *Time for a little payback!* She grabbed the next piece of chocolate with her teeth, deliberately nipping his fingers.

"Feisty little bitch, aren't you!" He fisted his hand in her hair and pulled her head back, exposing the sensitive curve of her neck. He nipped it. Hard. It hurt, made her insides quiver. His eyes met hers and she gasped as the power in them swept through her. All predator again, merciless.

"If you ever pull a stunt like you did tonight, show disrespect for your Master like that again, I will not let you get off as easy." Cal's low, rumbling threat made her bones rattle. "You understand, Rebecca?"

Genuine trepidation flowed through her. Shivers ran down her spine. No way would she ever rile this man that way again.

"Yes, Sir. I'm so, so sorry, Sir," she whispered, her eyes brimming with tears, ashamed that she had actually bitten his lip.

"I know you are," he growled. "No more waterworks now, woman. Get up and lie down over my lap so I can take care of your ass."

Oh, damn, she didn't want him to touch it, nor even look at it.

Please, leave my ass alone!

But she dared not cross him. Not when he was in full Wolf Man mode. She got up as quickly as her sore ass would allow and draped herself over his thighs. Cal moved her into position so he could reach her bottom and pulled up her skirt.

When he started rubbing cool cream on her skin, she whimpered softly.

"I'm sorry, sweetie," he muttered. "But I really have to do this."

When he was done, he pulled her skirt down, lifted her off his lap and got up. Rebecca sagged against him, totally exhausted.

"Are you sure you want to come home with me instead of going with Kyle?"

"Yes, Sir, I am sure," she mumbled.

Cal asked another submissive to collect Rebecca's bag and clothes from the dressing room. When she got back, he put the bag's strap over his shoulder, wrapped the blanket around Rebecca, lifted her in his arms and carried her out of there.

"Time to take you home, baby."

Chapter Six

When they got to his place, he carried her in and walked straight to his bedroom. A few minutes later, he had her undressed and blushing profusely. She had objected to being undressed by him, to being treated like a child. It had taken just one look from his dark eyes to shut her up.

Cal put a bunch of pillows against the headboard and made her sit in bed. His bed. How intimate to be there, his most private place. Yet, it seemed natural. As if she belonged there.

"Stay right here, girl," he said, giving her a stern look before he left the room.

As if she would go anywhere. She was stark naked to begin with, and she was too tired to even move. And...she didn't want to leave. Master Cal was intimidating as hell and managed to instill fear in her at regular intervals, but in spite of that, she felt oddly safe with him. The constant need to submit to his every whim was overwhelming, and it scared her. Maybe she had lost her marbles. Maybe she should get the hell out of there instead of sitting in his bed, hoping he'd take her. Maybe her hormones and desire to be submissive were impairing her judgment. But, right now, she didn't really care. There was no place she'd rather have been than here with him.

Cal came back with a glass of red wine for her and a whiskey for himself, and sat down next to her on the edge of the bed. She thanked him as she accepted the glass, and took a sip. She was stuck for words. Intimidated. His eyes were unreadable and she had no clue what to expect. Was he going to sleep here, too? Did he want to have sex with her? The thought of lying under him as he thrust into her got her excited and wet. Her nipples tightened into hard peaks. Thankfully the duvet covered her breasts so he couldn't see.

"Becca, look at me," Cal said softly.

She complied. His probing gaze made her uncomfortable. As if he could read her thoughts and feelings, her fears, her excitement, her anticipation. Rebecca blushed.

"I will let you hide," he mumbled as he ran his fingers over her cheek. "For now."

With difficulty, she dragged her eyes away from him and took another sip of wine. Her hand trembled slightly as she put the glass on the nightstand.

He caressed her face. "I am not going to jump you, Rebecca."

She looked at him again, confused. She was indeed scared he'd do just that, that he'd take her against her will, yet part of her *wanted* him to take her.

He leaned forward, cupped her face and held her gaze. Fire lit his almost black eyes when he said in a husky voice, "When I take you, I will take you without mercy, Rebecca. But…you will want me to, maybe even beg me to."

She swallowed. *Oh, my God. Is that a threat or a promise? Or both?* And why did it make her even wetter?

He reached for her head and she raised her hands in a reflex, ready to push him away. Mild fear put a knot in her stomach. His dark gaze told her to put them down, and when she did her upper arms touched the bare flesh of her chest. *Oh, no!* The covers had slid down. Heat rolled up over her face. *Please, don't look at my naked breasts!* Her nipples were poking out, and she so didn't want him to know just how excited she was. The smile that tugged at his lips told her he already knew.

Cal brushed his fingers through her long brown hair and groaned. He pulled her head back by her hair, exposing her throat. Feeling utterly vulnerable, she moaned softly. Little tremors shook her as he bent his head and pressed soft kisses on the side of her neck. His eyes were heavy-lidded when he raised his head. The heat in them seared her. Made her hot and wet, needy. Then he kissed her, so intense and deep that her head swam. She wrapped her arms around his neck and ran her fingers through his hair, needing to feel more of him.

When he finally pulled back, they were both breathing quickly, raggedly.

"Drink your wine now, sweetie. Soon, very soon, you'll be mine," he said with a hoarse voice.

As he got up, the thick bulge in his jeans came into her line of sight. She stared at it like an idiot. Why didn't he take her? Clearly, he wanted to, as did she.

He didn't say a word. Instead, he turned around and walked out of the room.

Rebecca took a deep breath, trying to get her head straight again, which wasn't easy with all the mixed emotions that raced through her mind. Her submission to him, mild rejection that he hadn't taken her. Insecurity about not being attractive enough for him to simply fuck her. Oddly enough, she was glad he hadn't done that. She craved a real connection, something deep. Being someone's fuck toy wouldn't fulfill her. Her pussy didn't agree, though.

She sighed and drank some more wine, hoping it would douse the fire that was raging through her core. After she'd finished her drink, she curled up under the covers, only to find she couldn't sleep. She was still awake when Cal came back. He walked to the other side of the bed, undressed and got in beside her.

"Relax now, Rebecca," he said softly. "Sleep. It's been quite the night."

Within minutes, she was sound asleep.

* * * *

Rebecca woke up crying on his chest. He held her close and stroked her hair while making soothing sounds.

Within a split second, she remembered where she was and she tried to get a hold of herself. Breaking down on a guy twice within a few hours was not good.

Way to go. How to push a guy away. Dammit! Instead of calming down, the thought made her cry even harder.

When she finally stopped, he demanded to know what was going on. Rebecca hauled in a breath. She had dreamed about her ex. Being rejected by her ex. Whenever they had done a scene, she had craved to be taken by him, and he hardly ever did. She couldn't begin to count the number of times he had left her hanging, all wound up, in terrible need, with no release. She had never understood why he didn't get aroused from their scenes. All she knew was that she had begun to feel utterly rejected as a woman, and as a sub, and had ended up wondering why she had been so repulsive to him. It had made her question herself. Maybe she was too fat, too tall, too ugly, too something.

"And n-now you..." she stammered, "you don't want me, either. So he was right after all."

Rebecca sobbed again.

He sat up, reached around her and swatted her thigh, snapping her out of her misery. She gasped and looked at him in shock. Cal pulled her up onto his lap and forced her to look at him.

"No more crying now, Rebecca," he said. "Your ex was an asshole if he didn't appreciate you. You are a very attractive, beautiful woman, and there's nothing I want more than to take you."

"But—" she objected.

"Silence!" he said with a snap in his voice. "There is no but. I have wanted to fuck you ever since I tasted your pussy and made you come with my fingers deep in your tight cunt."

Rebecca inhaled sharply. Her entire face was burning and she tried to avert her eyes, completely embarrassed.

"Look at me," he ordered, deliberately not forcing her head up. She had no choice but to willingly obey, and as she did, his gaze kept her restrained more than any ropes or cuffs could have done. His eyes told her that he would not accept her hiding anymore.

"You looked stunning on that spiderweb, Rebecca." He sounded husky now. "And the honor of making you come was entirely mine. As was the pleasure of getting you to submit. As will the pleasure of fucking you be. But I'll do so when I am ready to do so, and when I am, you are going to be, too. I will not take you because you need someone to prove a point. Am I clear?"

Rebecca nodded. He raised an eyebrow, and she realized her mistake. "Yes, Sir," she whispered.

"Good girl," he mumbled. "I choose when, how and where, not the other way around. I don't mind walking an emotional minefield with you, but I will not walk on eggshells because of it. Whenever we get to a mine, I will stand by you while you defuse it."

His unrelenting gaze told her that he would not shy away and wasn't going to allow her to, either. She swallowed hard, sensing that with each and every mine she'd disarm, he would break down her defenses, brick by brick, until all her walls had been torn down. And she'd be exposed and bare and vulnerable. Then he'd take her. He'd take everything she was and had, and some more.

* * * *

The smell of fresh coffee woke her. Rebecca quickly got out of bed, then realized her clothes were gone.

Dammit. I can't face him naked! Why did things always seem to be different in the morning? It was as if daylight illumined even her brain differently and brought back all her awkwardness about her bodily flaws. She stood in front of the large mirror and watched herself. Her hips, the slight curve of her belly, the scars on her breasts. They all seemed so much worse in the harsh light of day. And she really should have spent some time in the gym to work on her triceps. She did not like her upper arms. They weren't too bad, but lacked muscle tone, and they always made her awkward about wearing sleeveless clothes.

She suppressed the urge to throw something at the mirror, as if trashing it would alter her body.

Now what? She didn't dare rummage through Master Cal's wardrobes for a T-shirt. She grabbed the duvet and wrapped it around herself, feeling totally ridiculous with the thick, king-sized cover around her. Mustering all her courage, she walked into the kitchen as if she was wearing a queen's robe with a train instead of a large duvet that dragged over the floor. Cal blinked as she saw her, then burst out laughing.

"Woman, you are a piece of work," he said with amusement in his voice. "Wait here."

A minute later he came back with a red T-shirt. "Lose it."

Feeling very self-conscious, Rebecca hesitated, until her eyes met his. Unyielding, very cold eyes. His aura of power enveloped her, steeped her in it. A shiver ran down her spine, and her fingers obeyed his command and simply let go of the duvet. It pooled around her feet and she felt very much like joining it, suddenly craving to please him.

His gaze ran over her naked, quivering body.

"Very nice, sweetie." Cal's eyes had warmed again and his approval flooded her core, melting her insides. "I'd like a good-morning kiss now."

Rebecca stepped forward until her body almost touched his. She looked into his unreadable eyes and need welled up in her lower body. She rested her hands on his chest, got on tiptoes, and gazed up at him, her lips almost touching his. He hadn't moved, appearing calm, but his breathing had sped up nonetheless. Her soft lips touched his, a featherlight kiss. She pulled back, and whispered, "Good morning." She leaned closer again to kiss him, nibbled his bottom lip and licked over it.

He didn't move, didn't wrap his arms around her, didn't open his lips. Insecurity washed through her like a tidal wave. *Why doesn't he react?* She instinctively withdrew, both literally and emotionally.

"Touch my dick." Even though he had spoken softly, it was a peremptory command.

Her hand trembled as she touched his erection through his jeans. He covered her hand with his.

"I am not rejecting you." A simple statement.

She felt the caress in his voice, saw the controlled power in his eyes. He did want her, he was hard for her. He wasn't turning her down. In spite of his obvious arousal, he had control over his needs, the situation and her. Enough control to work on her rejection issues, forcing her into a place that triggered her insecurities, then replacing the old memory with a new one. One that told her he did want her, without giving in to what she needed to feel reassured, which right now would have been kissing her, holding her and taking her.

That would have worked for a bit, but not in the long run. He was guiding and supporting her, making her find confidence within, not without, and refusing to let her take control by making him do things that would make her feel more confident. He was a Master, after all, and he would not be manipulated into doing what she wanted. Rebecca remembered what he had told her the previous night. *'I choose when, how, and where, not the other way around.'*

She realized that statement wasn't just about his control over her, but would allow her to grow and become more self-assured. And it would help to build trust. Trust that he would not leave her hanging. Ever.

His lips curved up. "Thank me for the lesson, sub."

"Thank you for the lesson, Sir," she whispered.

"You're welcome, Rebecca." He smiled at her. "Now let's get breakfast together. I'm hungry."

Rebecca blinked. She hadn't even been awake for twenty minutes and the man already had her off-kilter. From laughing and smiling one minute to totally dominant the next, then back to normal again. As if he could simply flick a switch. She realized he probably could.

He handed her his red T-shirt and told her where she could find the oven gloves so she could take out the croissants.

After she'd put them in a basket, she carried them to the table. As she walked past him, he slid his hand under the T-shirt to stroke her ass, reminding her that he could — and would — touch her whenever he wanted.

* * * *

Breakfast had been nice. It hadn't taken her long to relax, and she had enjoyed chatting with him. He had asked her about her work and she had told him about her coaching practice, and her other passion, painting. Since he'd seemed genuinely interested, she had shown him some photos of some of her paintings on her cell phone. At some point she realized she was babbling. "I'm sorry. I shouldn't have... I got carried away." She'd blushed and lowered her gaze.

"Don't apologize. I like listening to you," he had said with a lazy smile.

"But I didn't ask you anything about you," she'd objected.

"You'll get to know me. Eventually." The promise in his deep voice had made her acutely aware that she wasn't talking to just any man, but a Master. Her trainer.

You're not on a date, Rebecca. Don't get too caught up in this man.

For a minute she hadn't known what to say, but he'd lightened the mood by handing her a croissant.

"Eat a bit more. I'll make us another coffee." He'd smiled at her before walking off to the kitchen. A sigh of relief had fled her lips. She liked Cal for sure, and it was good to be around him, but somehow he always put her on edge. And she had a sense that he enjoyed the hell out of doing that. Oddly enough, she did too, even though it could be terribly awkward.

Let it go now. Eat, go home, analyze later.

After breakfast they cleaned up together, and when all

was done, she asked him to take her home. Or rather, back to the club, as that was where she had left her car the night before.

Cal pulled her into his arms, forcing her to tilt her head back to be able to look into his eyes. Immediately overwhelmed, she wondered if she'd ever get used to being so close to a man who was so incredibly tall.

"Do you have to go home for work, pets, children?" he asked.

Kyle had given her the day off, and Cal knew that, too. Maybe she should lie. Tell him she had to walk her dog or something. But she couldn't lie. Not when he gave her that intimidating, masterly look.

"No, Sir," she answered.

He hummed. "That's that sorted, then. You're staying here. Tonight I'll take you back to your car. Consider today part of your training, lil' sub."

The set line of his jaw made her swallow the protest that had welled up in her throat.

"Yes, Sir."

"Smart choice. I'm going to have a shower now and you're going to wash me." He had spoken casually, yet desire rushed through her. She'd be touching him, seeing his strong muscular body. Naked. And his dick.

Oh, my!

Her cheeks were burning. His low, sexy chuckle made it worse. She felt like an overripe tomato ready to explode. He guided her to the bathroom.

"I like my sub naked before she undresses me," he said softly.

She kept her gaze lowered as she pulled the T-shirt over her head and tossed it onto a cupboard. She glanced up to meet his eyes and she sucked in a breath when the fire in them seared her. Her nipples hardened and her pussy got wet. Her hands were trembling when she started to unbutton his black shirt.

"Woman, I'm not going to eat you alive." His voice

sounded rough. Husky.

She avoided his gaze and kept working on the buttons, getting more and more aroused by each piece of skin she bared. His chest had a sprinkling of crisp, dark hair, and typical flat nipples with small areolae. She undid a few more buttons, revealing a treasure trail that disappeared under the waistband of his jeans. The delicious trail that would go all the way to his...

"Sweetheart, I had planned to shower today."

She blushed and quickly undid the last buttons. When she slid the shirt off his arms, she stood in awe, mesmerized. He was gorgeous, muscular, statuesque. She wanted to touch him, had to feel him. How could she resist? She moved her fingers over the beautiful planes of his chest, the crisp chest hair tickling and tantalizing as she explored. His skin was warm and soft, the muscles underneath hard and solid. She rested her palms on his pecs. They seemed to fit perfectly. His nipples hardened under her touch. She slid her hands up and over his wide shoulders, the firm deltoids, tracing over the curve of his biceps and his equally muscular forearms. Slowly she moved to his abs, continued over his treasure trail toward the button of his jeans and undid it. Her fingers trembled as she tugged the zipper over the thick bulge, and he groaned. She shoved his jeans down, revealing his long legs with hard, muscular thighs and calves. He stepped out of them, leaving him in his tight black boxers. Carefully, she pulled the boxers over his erection, and her eyes widened. He was huge. Larger than average, and much thicker. The mushroom head made her mouth water. She helped him step out of the boxers and got up, not knowing where to look. Only by great effort could she keep herself from staring at his manhood, but when she glanced up, she found herself ogling his strong chest. *Drooling like a schoolgirl. Ridiculous!* The alternative was his eyes. When they met hers, he drew her into his arms and took her mouth with a possessive hunger that made her knees buckle. She put her arms around his neck and brushed her nipples over his chest hair. Jolts of pleasure shot straight to her clit and she moaned into his mouth.

He released her lips, his gaze holding her, the fire matching the one that was raging in her lower body.

"Sod the shower," he growled.

He swung her up in his arms, walked straight to the bedroom and tossed her on her back on the bed. Before her brain could register what he was doing, he had her wrists tied with cuffs and ropes on the headboard. He shoved her legs apart and swirled his fingers through her wetness, then pushed a finger in her pussy. Rebecca bucked her hips as he pumped in and out a few times, desperate to get more. For him. He quickly put on a condom and positioned himself on top of her while keeping his weight on his arms.

He nipped her neck. "I'm going to fuck you hard, subbie."

His rough words sent a jolt through her clit. He fisted his dick and started pushing inside her, slowly, his gaze on her face. She began to whimper. He was so big, and stretched her to the point of pain. Panic rose from her gut and she jerked on the ropes.

"Cal, no! Please, I can't…it hurts."

He stroked her hair, kissed her lips. "Yes, you can, and you will, take me. All of me," he said with a certainty that made her relax the muscles in her lower body.

She moaned as he slowly pressed farther into her. When he had sheathed himself completely, he stopped moving. She kept her gaze glued to his, using him as her anchor, still not sure about his huge cock inside her. He slowly pulled out, and thrust back in again. Relief washed through her when she realized he would not simply hammer into her to take his pleasure and hurt her tender tissues in the process. The feeling of trust mingled with the sweet sensation of his shaft sliding in and out of her pussy. Her body started to adjust to his size and her pussy got even wetter as need took over. She'd never felt so full. The pressure was breathtaking, the friction in her lower body mind-boggling. She wanted more.

"That a girl," he mumbled, and slammed his cock into her.

Rebecca's shrill cry bounced off the bedroom walls. The brutal invasion had fire roaring through her. Her mind blanked and her vision blurred as he hammered into her, again and again. Her world, her entire existence, narrowed down to the excruciating pleasure in her pussy and her increasingly throbbing clit. He nipped the sensitive curve of her neck. The sting shot straight to her core, and his next hard thrust sent her over the pinnacle.

"Wrap your legs around me," he groaned.

His command cut through her orgasmic haze, and she complied, realizing it allowed him to get even deeper. She whimpered as he hit her cervix, the pain turning into instant pleasure, making her want even more. Another climax started to build at the speed of light. Incoherent words escaped from her mouth.

"No...no...too much. Cal...ooohh, my God...pleeease!" she begged, rolling her head back and forth.

Her pussy was on fire. The heat in her core tightened, the pressure almost unbearable. She was hovering over the precipice, on the zenith of desire. Her clit was pulsing, her cunt clamping down on his shaft and her nipples ached, her need to plummet over the edge so incredibly high. Something had to give.

He groaned and thrust hard and fast into her. Hearing his need, sensing he was about to come inside her, took her head off. The fireworks in her core exploded, outwards and up. Sizzling-hot waves of pleasure washed through her, and her entire body shook and spasmed in glorious joy. His roar bounced off the walls when he came and he fucked the last aftershocks out of her as he gave her all he had to give.

A moment passed, the after-orgasm haze wore off and Cal stood to dispose of the condom. With the fire doused, Rebecca started to feel insecure again, and oddly shy. When he came back into the room, his gaze traveling over her body, she wished she could hide. Or cover her body.

Both would be good. She hoped he wouldn't notice what was going through her mind. She hadn't a clue how he did it, but the man always seemed to pick up on that sort of thing.

Relief washed through her when he didn't say a word. But he had an odd glint in his eyes. *Will he know? Damn him and his mind-reading skills.*

Cal untied her wrist and swung her up into his arms. Her entire body tensed. She couldn't help it. Nor could she stop her brain from screaming.

I wish he wouldn't pick me up. I'm too heavy!

She looked at him and opened her mouth to blurt out the words verbatim, but the power in his eyes shut her up before a sound could even come from her lips. A hint of rebellion at being dominated shot through her, as well as guilt about him having to carry her weight.

A corner of his mouth turned up and amusement sparkled in his eyes. "Rebecca, I'm a big man. I can carry a big woman," he said.

She winced at his words and hurt stabbed her.

Cal sighed, and as he put her down. He curved his fingers around her chin, forcing her to look up. "You're tall, so you're not a small woman. You're curvy, meaning you have the right assets in the right places." He touched her breasts and moved over her belly and hips as he spoke. "You're soft where a girl should be, and with just enough muscle underneath."

He kissed her and nibbled her bottom lip. "Your lush body drives a man crazy. It drives me crazy," he mumbled against her mouth. He made her open her lips and swept in with a groan. His erection pressed against her, and knowing he was hard for her again, barely ten minutes after steaming hot sex, filled her heart with joy. He did find her attractive and did want her, in spite of her height and padding. Something inside her started to settle. A tiny spark of light in the dark pool of rejection and insecurity.

"Thank you," she whispered against his lips.

Cal smiled into her eyes. "Now, you can either offend

your Master by walking to the bathroom, or trust that he can carry you."

He swung her up again and when she relaxed in his arms, he made a sound of approval. Rebecca wrapped her arms around his neck and rested her head against him.

God, this feels good! Utterly feminine and desirable. She couldn't remember ever having been carried by a past lover or partner. And certainly not with the ease with which Cal did. His arm muscles flexed, and as she looked at his corded neck, she couldn't resist pressing her lips on it.

"Don't distract me, woman," he murmured. "I'm hard enough as it is."

She giggled, nibbled his neck, and whispered with a husky voice, "I know. Everything about you is hard. I like it."

"You're obviously feeling a lot better, cheeky girl!" he said with a grin.

As they got to the bathroom, he gently put her down, and she pouted, wishing it had been a bit farther away.

They spent quite some time in the shower, hugging, kissing and touching. When they finally got out, Cal allowed her to put the red T-shirt back on, but no underwear. He took her into his garden and they sat on his patio with cappuccinos. They talked and flirted, getting to know each other a little better.

Rebecca was at ease, until Cal told her he wanted to go through the checklist with her. And go through his after that so she'd have an idea of what his likings were.

"But I already filled out a checklist at the club," Rebecca said, somewhat confused. She was wondering if he hadn't seen it, which didn't exactly inspire trust. She'd thought and expected he would have read it, especially her *Noes*.

Cal smiled reassuringly. "I know, sweetie, and I have perused it, don't worry," he said. "I would just like to know if something has changed. You filled out that list a while back—maybe you feel different about some things now. And it's good for a Master and his sub to discuss it together."

Rebecca seriously doubted that something would have changed, but agreed to go through it.

Cal gave her the list and a red pen, so it would be clear what would be different or not.

It would take some time to go through the entire list again, and Rebecca was glad he wasn't breathing down her neck. It was difficult enough to focus with him sitting on the other side of the table. He couldn't read what she was doing, but she sensed his eyes were on her. Then she got to a threesome question. That interested her, but checking it and discussing it with him, not so much. She nervously shifted on her chair, trying to make up her mind. She knew she had to be open and honest, but wasn't sure if she had the guts to do it.

What do I do? Decisions, decisions.

She cursed under her breath when Cal got up, circled her and looked at the list. Of course, the mind-reading bastard had picked up on her discomfort. Rebecca suppressed the urge to put her hand over what she had just changed. Her heart was pounding in her chest and her cheeks were burning.

"A threesome. In public," Cal read out.

Rebecca dared not look at him. *Will he be offended? Maybe think he won't be enough for me? Men can have such fragile egos.*

"So you want sex with another woman and a man," Cal stated.

Now she looked up at him, her eyes wide. "No! I don't! Not a woman, no way!" she said. "I…maybe…never mind. I'm sorry."

Cal chuckled.

"Rebecca, you do not have to apologize for anything. This is about you and what you are interested in," Cal said softly. "There's no reason whatsoever to feel awkward. You have to be honest, so I don't do anything you don't really want."

He stroked her hair and gently touched her cheek. She closed her eyes and leaned in to his touch, enjoying it.

"But, Rebecca," he began.

"Yes, Cal," she mumbled.

"You've checked the wrong option." Cal gently tapped the tip of her nose and she opened her eyes and looked at the list.

He was right. She'd checked the threesome with another woman option, not the threesome with another man. She quickly corrected her mistake.

"You better pay attention, subbie, lest you end up with things in or on that gorgeous body that you don't want!" Cal said, sounding amused.

"Yes, Sir!" she whispered.

When she'd finished revising her checklist, she was surprised to see that indeed some things had changed.

"Enough for one day. We'll go through it later on." Cal pressed a kiss to the top of her head. "I'm hungry. Let's find out how good you are in the kitchen."

She followed him indoors and they prepared lunch together. Cal fried eggs and made toast, while she whipped up a really nice salad.

They had lunch outside, simply enjoying the food and each other's company.

Rebecca had just put the plates and cups in the dishwasher when Cal's phone rang. He answered. "Well, hello, Kyle. Yes, she's all right. For now." Cal chuckled. "No, don't worry. No, you don't need to come over to check."

Silence as Kyle was speaking again. Cal growled. "She's been fed, pleased, fed and will get pleased again. Extremely pleased. Emphasis on extremely."

Cal burst out laughing when Kyle's voice got loud.

"Stop worrying, mate. She's fine. You're embarrassing her. And me." Cal handed Rebecca the phone. She gave him a puzzled look.

"Please tell him that you're okay, so he won't drop in on us," Cal said, not looking too pleased.

After Rebecca had reassured Kyle that nothing was wrong, he gently took the phone from her hand, said "Goodbye now, Kyle!" and simply hung up.

Then his eyes were on her, a glint sparkling in them.

"Now, where were we?" he asked.

She shook her head, desperately trying to recall what they had been doing. Nothing came to mind, other than cleaning the table.

"Lose the shirt."

Rebecca blinked. *What? I don't want to be totally naked!* But when he raised an eyebrow to show his impatience, she quickly complied. She held it in front of her naked body, trying to keep both her breasts and her pussy out of sight.

"Woman, I've seen every inch of your body. Drop it."

The command in his voice made her obey and she let the shirt fall to the floor. The sizzling heat in his eyes made her skin tingle as he looked her over. His gaze lingered on her breasts and made her nipples bloom. Her breathing sped up a bit. Damn that man and his ability to arouse her with a simple look.

His gaze seemed to caress her entire body. He walked around her, gently ran his fingers down her spine and tickled her behind. He curled his hands around her hips and leaned in to kiss the sensitive curve of her neck.

"So beautiful, so soft, all woman." A whisper in her hair. The words were bewitching, the admiration in his voice arousing. Then he cupped her breasts, lifted them a bit and started kneading. A husky mewl came from her lips. He started playing with her nipples, circling them so they puckered even tighter, then gently pulled. A moan welled up in her throat and she put her head back to rest it against his chest.

"You love that, don't you? Such sensitive, gorgeous breasts," Cal said, his voice husky. His erection pressed against her bottom. "I love playing with your tits. It turns me on."

Cal let go of her, quickly took off his shirt and drew her into his arms. Without further ado, he kissed her, and when she willingly opened her lips for him, he swept in with a groan. Their tongues met in an intimate caress and Rebecca instantly became wet. She pushed her pussy against his hard erection and rubbed her breasts over his chest. The friction of his coarse chest hair was wonderful on her sensitive nipples and little sounds of arousal broke from her.

When he let go of her lips, they were both panting.

"Gorgeous, hot woman," he said, bent his head and took one of her hard nipples into his mouth. Jolts of pleasure washed through her as he circled his tongue around the hard peak, teasing and tickling. Then he sucked, strongly, and she threw her head back on a whine.

God, the things that man could do. Whether it was her mouth, her pussy or her breasts, he always knew exactly how to turn her on. This had to be heaven.

Her brain shut down. She was completely enjoying the pleasure he was giving her. Sweet sensations shot from her nipples straight to her pussy, and her clit pulsed in reply, and she yearned to be touched there. The sweet expectation of more, knowing that this was just the prelude and she would ultimately get him inside her again—it blew her mind.

She crash-landed when she realized he was tracing the point of his tongue over the scars on her breasts. In broad daylight they had to be horribly visible. Sudden insecurity overwhelmed her, and she instinctively wanted to take a step back. Cal's arm was around her before she could do so, and he continued to lick over all the scars, including the ones on the undersides of her breasts. Those scars had damaged the nerves there, so the touch of his tongue was odd when it ran over them. There was a vague sense of something moving over her skin, but that was about it. Thank God all the other scars were thin. And her nipples were every bit as sensitive as they had been before the breast reduction. All the scars had gone white with time, so they weren't too obvious. And the larger ones were at the undercurve, and not in full sight when she was standing. So, all in all, it wasn't too bad. Maybe. Hopefully. But still...to have a man trace them with his tongue made her incredibly insecure.

Rebecca wasn't sure if she should tell him about the numbness of the skin under her breasts.

Cal cupped her face, his gaze on hers. Probing, assessing. Too close for comfort, and Rebecca swallowed nervously. She didn't want him to see the mixed emotions that were going through her. Relief that he didn't find her breasts and scars repulsive, and didn't even shy away from touching them with his mouth. And insecurity, as if the physical scars had scarred her very femininity.

"Woman, I love your breasts," he said softly. "I don't care about some scars. Your breasts are perfect. They are full and sensitive, and you have delightfully responsive nipples. You love having your breasts played with, and I love playing with them. Don't ruin it for yourself with your insecurities."

"But..." she started.

He gently put a finger across her lips. "No buts. I am the one looking at your breasts. I am the one playing with them. And I want to," he said. "You're sexy as hell, and the way I see it, the scars are part of you. Learn to see it that way yourself, Rebecca. Accept."

Cal took her hand and put it on his dick. He was rock-hard.

"That's what your breasts do to me." The heat in his gaze zinged across her nerves and warmed her heart.

Tears welled in her eyes. "Thank you," she whispered.

He just smiled and brushed a kiss across her lips.

"Good time for a cappuccino," Cal said.

Rebecca was grateful for the break. She needed a moment to find her emotional stability again. Then he said, "You may serve it outdoors on the patio. Off you go."

She pouted.

"I said no to the role-play waitress thing," she objected.

"I know, Rebecca. That's why I didn't give you a sexy pinny to wear," Cal said with a grin. "This is called 'Pleasing your Master'."

With a "Humphh," she stomped off to the kitchen to make the cappuccinos, almost wishing she had filled out that option with a 'Yes', so at least she'd have had a pinny to cover some of her body.

A few minutes later she walked out onto the patio. The way he feasted his eyes on her naked body was nerve-racking. She knew her breasts were swaying, her nipples were hard and her labia slightly swollen. Walking around skyclad had gotten her unbelievably excited.

She managed to put down the cappuccinos without spilling anything, even though her hands trembled slightly. His gaze seared her skin, which added to her excitement.

Rebecca didn't dare look him in the eye. She didn't want him to see that she was incredibly turned on, although she suspected he'd know, anyway.

Being scantily clad in the club was quite arousing. Being naked in the club with so many other people there was almost scary, which made it even more exciting to her. But being naked in someone's home was worse. Much, much worse. The societal norms and values kept screaming in her head that she shouldn't be walking around naked in a home during the day, with the curtains open at that. It was naughty, perverse and wrong. Yet it turned her on tremendously. Her pussy had gotten wetter and wetter as she had made the cappuccinos, and the idea of making herself come right then and there had crossed her mind.

I'm a naughty girl, she thought, as she sat down opposite Cal. *A bad girl. A slut!* She almost moaned out loud. Why did the idea of being a slut turn her on even more? She realized she'd made some sound, because Cal raised an eyebrow and asked, "What's that thought, Rebecca?"

She blushed profusely and started stammering.

"Look at me and tell me," Cal demanded.

Oh, dear, Wolf Man is back. His face looked chiseled and his black eyes were unreadable. They seemed to cut through her, penetrating her very core. It made her heart pound and her clit throb. She swallowed hard and shook her head a bit as if to clear the haze from it. She knew if he had to ask a third time, she was going to be in trouble.

"I...I was thinking... That..." She looked at him. How could she tell him? It was awkward to reveal such intimate thoughts and emotions. "I was thinking that walking around naked...is odd."

She kept her fingers crossed he'd accept that explanation and not know she was not being upfront. His lips curved. Not a friendly smile. Her breath hitched.

"I think lying deserves punishment. As does stomping off when your Master tells you to do something," Cal said casually. "Did you know that some Masters put their subs in a corner when they need punishment?"

Rebecca swallowed again. *Not that!* She'd hate that.

"Now, I don't really fancy that at all," Cal continued, and she let out a sigh of relief. But when he got up with a glint in his eyes as he walked over to her, she was quite ready to run to a corner and stand there for an hour. Before she could object—if she'd had the guts to object—he'd dragged her into the garden, to the middle of the lawn. He made her put her hands on her back, feet apart and her head up.

He walked back to the patio, sat down and took a sip from his cappuccino.

"Hmm...excellent cappuccino," he said. "Excellent view as well. I like it."

Rebecca felt horribly exposed. He didn't have any neighbors close by, so no one could see her. Yet, standing there totally naked in an open space, while that intimidating, sexy man was ogling her, was humiliating. Awkward. She would have preferred staring at the bricks in a corner.

Asshole. How can he do this to me?

Her mouth dropped open when she saw him unzip his trousers and take his erection in his hand. Heat crept over her face when he slowly started to pleasure himself. Quickly she averted her eyes. Too much, too intimate. Too...something. Embarrassing?

"Look at me, Rebecca." The steely undertone in his voice made her comply without a thought. Her breathing sped up as she focused on him. His wide, naked chest, the smoldering eyes, and how he moved his up and down over his shaft. She didn't want to look at it. But the urge was too strong. She couldn't help herself. She had to see. When her eyes dropped to his dick, she inhaled sharply. A smothered sound came from her lips when she saw the swollen tip. She desperately wanted to have him inside her. She was so wet that she was surprised her juices weren't running down her inner thighs.

"What are you thinking, Rebecca?" he asked softly.

"This is…so…so wrong," she stammered.

"Why?" He kept moving his hand.

"I…I don't know." A mere whisper.

"What were you thinking earlier?" he asked again.

Her brain ceased working. Blood rushed through her body and her core was on fire. All she could think of was lowering herself on him, feeling his strong chest against her swollen breasts, being filled by his large cock.

"I am a bad girl." Her voice sounded husky. "I…I…this is all wrong!"

"Does it turn you on to be naked?"

"Yes," she moaned. "I think…does that mean…that I'm a slut?"

"Would that bother you?" he asked softly.

"Yes! No! Yes. Maybe. I don't know," she cried out and finally looked up, needing some mental support. She found it in his eyes. As he took in the delicious mix of lust, desire and confusion, he put his cock away, and walked over to her.

"I love a naughty woman." Cal tugged a strand of her hair as she looked up at him. "Men want a cook in the kitchen, a lady in the parlor and a slut in the bedroom."

"Not going to work," she said defiantly. "I don't like cooking."

Cal snorted a laugh.

"Mouthy woman," he said, as he slid his fingers through her pussy. A tremor shook her as he brushed over her clit, toward her entrance, and dipped into her juices. "You'll learn to cook all right. In the meantime, you can make up for it by being a slut in the garden."

She sucked in a breath. "But, Sir…" she started.

"On your knees, sub, and show your Master how slutty you can be." His voice sounded hoarse as he pushed her down. She unzipped his jeans with trembling fingers, pulled them off his hips and freed his manhood. With a soft mewl, she put her lips around the head of his cock and earned a loud groan from him.

"That's it, baby, make that mouth work."

She licked his entire length, sucked the tip into her mouth, tickled the frenulum with her tongue and thoroughly enjoyed the sounds of pleasure he made as she did that. She slid down over his shaft and tried to get his entire manhood into her mouth while sucking as hard as she could. Soon she completely lost herself in pleasing him, her Master. His groans, the movement of his hips and the throbbing cock in her mouth drove her wild.

Then he fisted his hand in her hair and gently pulled her head back, forcing her to let go of his dick. She groaned , not wanting to stop.

"Do you like being a slut, Rebecca?" he asked, his voice thick with lust.

"Yes. Please, Sir, I want to please you." She begged him with her eyes.

He groaned his approval.

"Suck me. Drink my cum. Every drop of it."

Rebecca looked at him, and the sheer lust in his eyes melted her insides. A longing sigh escaped her.

"Yes, Sir," she said huskily.

He let go of her hair, and she pleased him so much that when he came even his distant neighbors must have lit a cigarette. She didn't give a damn.

* * * *

They were still outdoors, sitting in the shade on the patio. After their cappuccinos, Cal had gotten fresh juice and some snacks for them to nibble. They talked about everything and anything, mostly lighthearted conversation.

They agreed that she would stay for dinner and that he'd take her back to her car around ten p.m. They had plenty of time to enjoy each other's company.

But Rebecca found it difficult to focus on their conversation. Cal hadn't allowed her to get dressed, and talking to an attractive man while being naked wasn't easy. Apart from that, the heat in her lower body was still smoldering. Cal had done nothing to make her come, which had her off-kilter and horribly disappointed. He didn't even seem to notice she was naked anymore. It made her increasingly insecure and awkward about being skyclad.

Part of her wanted to tell him to sod it, get dressed and go home. Another part wanted to seduce him, to make sure he'd notice her naked body. What better way to do that than by arousing him? Then make him enjoy her body, giving her the satisfaction and reassurance she craved. She was torn between the two and she was starting to get moody.

"Come here," Cal said softly.

Clumsily, she got up from her chair and walked over to him, still not sure whether to give him shit or start bawling her eyes out.

Cal pulled her onto his lap, wrapped his arms around her and held her close to his chest. He gently stroked her hair.

A sob welled up from her throat. She was completely lost and confused, and even though he was the one who had triggered it, the comfort he offered did her good. His embrace was a safe haven. Tears rolled down her cheeks, and as she clung to him, she started to cry.

He made soothing sounds and simply let her shed her tears.

When she calmed down, and just the occasional sob came

out, he lifted her head and smiled into her eyes. He softly ran his knuckles over her cheek and pressed a kiss to her lips.

"Feeling a little better now, Rebecca?" he asked.

She gave him a shaky nod. He gently kissed her again.

"As a sub, you don't get what you want whenever you want it. You will have to trust that your Master will give you what you need, though," he whispered in her hair. "If he doesn't do that, he's not the right Master for you."

Rebecca nodded in agreement when he paused.

"You do have to give someone the chance to give you what you need, Rebecca," he continued. "Getting cranky when it doesn't come when you want it is not a sign of trust."

"But...we don't know each other...how can I know—?" she started.

"Indeed, we don't know each other all that well yet. But the chemistry between us is strong, and I think we both want very similar things," Cal said with a slow smile. "But you've got to allow things to develop. If you keep trampling on it with your insecurities or impatience, it's not going to work out for us."

Rebecca lowered her eyes. She knew he was right, and she didn't want this thing with Cal to be over before it had even properly begun. What he'd given her in the few hours they'd known each other was already so much better than what she'd ever experienced before.

"I'll try," she whispered.

"No, you won't." The steel in his voice cut like a knife and a tremor ran through her body. "You have to make a choice. You either want this or you don't. If you want a guinea pig, you'd best find someone else to experiment with."

Rebecca swallowed, then nodded. She looked up through her lashes and read in his eyes that he wanted her answer now. *Damn it. Pushy Dom.*

She wanted to speak, but when she opened her lips, nothing came out. Tears brimmed in her eyes. *Why does he have to be so intimidating?*

Cal sighed.

"Go get some more drinks, take a few deep breaths, and when you come back I want your answer," he said in a level voice. "That means you've got two minutes to think it over."

Rebecca quickly jumped off his lap and had only reached to the patio door when he called out to her.

"Oh, and Rebecca, if you had an unsightly body, I wouldn't want you naked around me. That's all the reassurance you're going to get. It should be enough. Trust, Rebecca."

Her cheeks warmed, both from shyness and from joy.

"Yes, Sir," she whispered, then rushed indoors.

When she came out onto the patio, she was walking tall. She'd made her decision. She put her drink on the table, sashayed to him with his, gracefully knelt in front of him and looked him in the eye.

"I want to stay, Master," she said as she handed him his drink.

For a minute, he didn't speak, and she tried to read his eyes, but failed. Those piercing eyes seemed to penetrate her very soul. She could barely hold herself together under his intense gaze, but she found she couldn't look away either. When he finally took the drink from her, a sigh of relief came from her lips.

"Thank you, Rebecca," he said, sounding a bit hoarse.

Joy washed through her. She knew they'd just overcome quite an obstacle. The thought of losing their budding connection, whatever it was or would turn into, had twisted her stomach into a knot. This would likely not be the last time this man would make her choose. He wasn't going to force her, which would be so much easier for her. She'd have to face her inner demons herself. With his help.

Rebecca wasn't sure if she was looking forward to it. But for now it was okay. She rested her head on his thigh, totally content. And when he gently put his hand on it, she smiled happily.

* * * *

They were in the kitchen prepping dinner. Cal had given her a button-down shirt to wear.

"I don't want your lovely body to get burned by greasy spatters when we cook, sweetie," he had said, and the caress in his voice and the look in his eyes had melted her insides.

As their eyes locked, the vibe between them suddenly changed. Heat shimmied in the air, and Rebecca's breathing sped up. Cal yanked her against his solid body, tangled his hand in her hair and pulled her head back a bit. A soft mewl of anticipation escaped her, then he kissed her with firm lips, demanding that she open for him. When she eagerly complied, he swept in, taking full possession of her mouth. He caressed her tongue with his, dueling and swirling, and she wrapped her arms around his neck and clung to him for dear life. Her head was spinning, and when he gyrated his hips so that his erection rubbed against her pussy, she moaned in his mouth. He cupped her ass and she wrapped her legs around him.

Cal let go of her lips.

"Do you trust me, Rebecca?" His voice sounded hoarse.

"Yes," she said without hesitation.

"Then let's skip straight to the main course. I want to fuck you right now." The rude word and his low, husky voice sent heat spiraling down her spine, straight to her pussy.

He carried her into the bedroom, draped her on a bed and cuffed her wrists to the headboard. With the swift movements of a man who knew what he was doing, he put cuffs around her ankles and attached them to ropes that ran through eyebolts on the ceiling. He pulled on the ropes until her legs were spread up in the air, slightly angled toward her shoulders. The only things she could move, apart from her head, were her fingers and toes.

Cal grabbed a condom and quickly sheathed himself. He groaned as he looked at her wet, wide-open pussy. He bent his head and she felt his hot breath over her wet tissues.

"Beg me to fuck you, Rebecca. Beg for your Master's cock to fill your cunt."

Her pussy clenched and flames shot up from her core. "Please, Cal, please!" she begged. "I need you in me."

Cal swatted her thigh and she yelped.

"Try harder, sub!"

"Please, Sir. Please, fuck me!" she panted.

"You can do better." His voice was thick with lust. "Beg!"

Before she could comply, he lowered his head and put his lips around her clit. Her husky cry filled the room when he started lapping at her nub.

"Oh, yes! Please, yes! More!" She tilted her hips to push against his mouth and the tongue that gave her so much pleasure. A groan escaped her when he lifted his head and swatted her thigh again.

"Focus, sub. Beg for your Master's cock to fill your juicy cunt." Cal's deep voice cut through her haze and she tried to focus on the words. She really did. But when he moved up and tore her shirt apart, she lost all sense of reality. He sucked a hard nipple deep into his mouth.

She arched her chest in an attempt to counter the sweet pain that shot from her nipple straight to her core. Her brain stopped working when he put his fingers on her other nipple and started to toy with it, milk it. Her clit was throbbing happily.

When he'd taken his fill of her nipples, he moved down toward her pussy again.

"Focus, sub, say the words," he said, and immediately went down on her again, sucking on her clit until it was hard and swollen.

"Oh, yes! Master, yes, please. Take me. Take me hard!" She got more and more turned on by her own begging, and the hot mouth on her pussy.

Her legs started to quiver and the fire in her core was about to explode. She wailed when Cal drew back seconds before she could orgasm. He moved up again and forced her to look at him. His eyes were like smoldering black coals that sent heat surging through her.

"Now!" he growled. "Punishment for disobeying will be hard."

The tip of his cock against her wet entrance distracted her. She struggled to form the words. "Please, Master. Fill me with your cock," she slurred. "Please, make me yours!"

Possessiveness fired from his eyes as he buried himself to the hilt inside her, and she wailed.

Her pussy desperately tried to accommodate the large intrusion. Hovering over the delicate edge of pain and pleasure melted her brain. The sensations that shot up from her lower body made her beg for more.

Cal gave her what she wanted and slammed into her. She couldn't stop a moan as the sweet pain mingled with sparks of joy.

"Damn, you feel so good," he groaned. "I love your tight, slick cunt."

She started rambling incoherently and kept begging him for more. Her pussy walls clamped down on him as if to try to get him even deeper into her hot wetness.

"Yes, please fuck me, Master. Ooohh!" She was delirious with passion and lust.

A deep rumble welled up from his chest as he started plundering, taking her mercilessly. Her husky shrieks of pleasure sounded through the room.

One hard thrust and she came violently, riding the heatwaves that ripped her apart. Sparks exploded in her head as her body spasmed in ecstasy.

"Fuck, yesss!" he groaned, and rammed into her as he came as well.

His merciless hammering, and the sheer lust that oozed from his every pore, made her come again. Her scream accompanied his groan as they each took all that the other had to give.

Chapter Seven

Cal was thinking about Rebecca. Why the woman kept fussing so much about her body, he did not understand. She wasn't skinny, but he didn't want a skinny woman. He preferred softness under him, not someone with bones sticking out everywhere. He'd just never been completely comfortable with small women. He was always afraid he'd break them in half with his sheer strength or weight. He didn't have an ounce of fat on his lean body, but his height and muscles definitely put him out of the lightweight category. He'd simply never liked petite women. He preferred them on the taller side, with padding and lush curves.

Rebecca was exactly how he liked to see a woman. A lush figure with nice round hips and ass, soft belly and a great rack. Her full breasts were more than big enough to fill his large hands. Her legs were long and muscular with full thighs, not the skinny mannequin legs he disliked so much, and nice slender calves and ankles.

Yet the woman was uncomfortable being exposed. In private, things had improved, but they mostly played in public in the club, and that seemed to remain difficult for her.

He'd work on all that, one step at the time, to make her feel more comfortable about her own body. *And why not start right away?* It was Thursday — not a regular club night, but occasionally Kyle organized a special themed event. Rebecca had the night off. The woman didn't know it yet, but tonight he'd put her to work at the dungeon, as his sub.

Your trainee, Cal, not your sub.

He was going to pay her a surprise visit to pick her up to take her to the club. He got to her place just after seven p.m. He rang and waited. Nothing. Knocked on the door. No answer.

Cal walked around to the garden. He was tall enough to look over the fence.

There she was, on all fours, bent over, scooping soil out of a hole. She had to bend over quite far. Clearly it was rather deep. Her knees were apart to keep her balance, her ass up in the air. Just the right position to get on his knees behind her and thrust into her. Her breasts would shake back and forth as he hammered his cock home. He'd take her so hard and deep, she'd cry out in pleasure and pain.

Damn. His jeans got uncomfortable.

"Very nice, subbie," he said softly, knowing his deep voice would easily carry across the garden to her.

She froze, her head and arms still in the hole, ass up in the air. Then she turned around so quickly that she lost her balance and landed on her bum, legs bent and spread, her arms behind her for support, which pushed her breasts up under the unsightly top. He looked straight at her crotch.

"Keep going, subbie. I like the show. Very tasteful!"

Rebecca scrambled to her feet. "What the hell are you doing here?"

Cal chuckled when he saw that she was acutely aware of what she looked like. He could read her like a book, and it was painfully obvious to him that she just wanted him to leave. Leaving was the last thing on his mind. Instead, he took his time to look her over. She was wearing old jeans with paint stains all over them, and worn-out boots. One had a broken zipper, so she had wrapped a piece of string around it to keep it from falling apart. The icing on the cake was a shapeless, long-sleeved top with paint stains all over it. Her hair was a mess, she was sweaty and she had muddy streaks on her face.

Amusement trickled through him. This woman was totally unpredictable. She looked stunning in her club outfits, sexy

and attractive in her daily jeans and tops. This outfit was...
amazing. Barely more than rags. He'd never seen a woman
dressed like that and felt so damn attracted to her. This was
the real Rebecca. He throbbed for her. Wanted to take her.
Bad.

"Open the gate."

Anger fired through her, and she almost screamed, 'You
are not king of my castle!' This was her home, dammit,
he couldn't just tell her what to do. The power in his gaze
didn't falter, instead it got darker still. Predator eyes,
instilling fear in his prey. Succeeding. Rebecca swallowed.
He'd probably simply barge through her fencing if she
didn't comply. He'd chase her through her own garden.
She was no match for him. He'd take her down in seconds,
rip her clothes off and...

She got wet. And needy. The sudden heat in her core
matched the fire that burned in his eyes. It turned her
nipples into hard points.

Pathetic, drooling over a fence.

Rebecca went to the gate and unlocked it, her heart racing
in her chest. She stepped back as he entered her garden and
closed the gate behind him. Her home. Her domain.

Not anymore, Rebecca.

She was fuming, yet yearning for him to take her. Right
then and there. How did he do this to her? Take over her
home, make her spine melt?

"Because I'm your Master," he said, answering her
question. *How did he know?*

Rebecca eyed him nervously as he stood in front of her,
taking her in. Then her awkwardness turned to anger.

"Sorry, I'm working in the garden, and... Why am I saying
sorry? It's my home. You expect me to wear high heels and
stockings when I'm working in my garden? Dammit!"

"High heels would be sexy. Right now I'll take the boots
with the rope." Cal's husky voice made her feel even more
needy. "A sub who plays with ropes in her spare time.

Kinky."

His soft, low laughter made her blush.

"I'm...I...best change clothes," she stammered.

Cal stepped closer, cupped her face and caressed her cheek with his thumb.

"Sweetie, I love seeing the real, authentic sub. This is the real you, a gem, unpolished, raw. Beautiful." Cal's voice was a whisper on her face.

Rebecca saw nothing but open admiration and hunger in his eyes. Then he kissed her, so intense and deep it made her legs quiver. He pushed his tongue into her mouth, taking complete possession, plundering. Would this man ever be gentle? She hoped not.

When he released her, her legs were shaky and she had to hold on to him for stability. His dark eyes were smoldering, burning her. Need zinged across her nerves.

"I'm going to fuck you, Rebecca. Right here."

Reality kicked in and her mouth dropped open. "What? Now? Here? No! You can't!"

She quickly stepped back, her eyes large. *He has to be kidding!* One look in his eyes told her he wasn't.

Oh, my God. No! Not here in her garden. Her neighbors... She wasn't clean...

"No way!"

"Way!" His growl made her gasp. She took another step back, and when he started moving forward, she turned around and ran. She couldn't really go anywhere—there was just the one gate. But maybe if she could get him deeper in the backyard, she could make a run for it. He would be faster, but she had the advantage that she knew her garden. It was nowhere near done and there were obstacles everywhere. There were cobblestones and rocks on the unfinished paths here and there. She knew where they were and he didn't. Maybe he would trip and...

But I don't want him to get hurt! her heart yelled. Her brain screamed, *But I don't want to get taken down and fucked in my own garden!* Yet the thought of Cal taking her, just taking her, whether she wanted or not, had fire searing through her body.

She veered around some bushes and stopped behind the vine-covered trellis. Cal stopped on the other side of the trellis. He couldn't get to her.

Rebecca grinned at him.

See if you can get me, asshole!

His smoldering eyes sent a shiver up her spine.

"I'm going to enjoy taking you down, sub," he said, his voice thick with lust.

The promising chuckle that rose from his chest made her breath hitch. She instinctively knew that defying him would only rouse him more, would make him more intent on fucking her hard. But even though sassing him scared the bejesus out of her, she couldn't stop herself. She wanted this. Badly.

"If you can catch me," she breathed, raising her chin.

"When I catch you, babe, not if." Cal grunted. "The only question is where. Behind some shrubs or in the middle of your garden."

She gasped. *No, no, no! My neighbors will…*

Cal moved to the right to veer around the trellis.

Damn, he's fast. Like a cougar.

Rebecca went left, and he suddenly turned left too — *smart bastard* — and grabbed her arm. She yelped, jerked her arm free and ran like hell. His deep, soft laugh told her he wasn't running after her, yet. The asshole seemed to enjoy toying with her. When she did hear him chase after her, she took the path down the middle, the one with the scattered cobblestones and rocks. *Sod him, let him twist his ankle!*

She ran around the small pond at the end of the path and started toward the path to the left of the garden. He was still chasing her. *Dammit.* He had probably seen the stones and simply jumped over them. She took the last path. She was quickly running out of options. Her garden was quite large, but not that large. And now she was in the far corner, nowhere near the gate. *Damn, damn, damn!*

She ran across the path along the back of the garden, toward the trellis again. From there she could sprint for the gate. Rebecca heard Cal close in on her. Fear washed through her — the nightmarish fear of being chased after.

No, I don't want this!

Yet her pussy was throbbing. His breathing sounded from somewhere behind her, getting closer. *Oh, my God, no!* Adrenaline pumped through her veins. She raced past the trellis and decided to make a run for the gate.

Cal jumped over the hole she'd been digging and she barged into his solid body, knocking the air out of her lungs. He wrapped one arm around her like a solid steel band and curved his other hand around her throat, forcing her head back. A funny thing inside her took over and she gave in. Her body and mind yielded completely to his will.

He growled.

"Beautiful sub!"

He grabbed her waist and flung her around, put her on her knees, forearms on the lawn, ass in the air. Before she could react, he shoved her knees apart with his foot then groped her. Rebecca arched her back and moaned.

"Silence, sub!"

Even though she was still dressed, she felt utterly naked when he began fondling here everywhere with hard hands, fondling, exploring, kneading and rubbing over her labia. He pushed a finger over the seam of her jeans through the middle of her pussy, found her clit and moved from side to side. Shocks shot through her core and legs. There was nothing gentle about his touch. It was almost painful, but the crudeness of it turned her insides to molten lava. It wasn't enough. She craved for him to take whatever he wanted from her. She needed him to take more, everything, anything.

He grabbed her breasts, and squeezed them hard with his strong hands. She sucked in a breath.

"Oh, yes, we like that, don't we?" Cal mumbled.

He slid his hands under her top, yanked down the cups

of her bra and, when her breasts dropped like ripe fruit into his hands, he fondled them roughly. Rebecca's clit was throbbing. Her entire pussy was swollen and aching with need. When he pulled her nipples hard and held them, she almost came. Tremors shot through her legs and a long whine broke from her lips.

Cal pulled back and slapped her ass. "Silence!"

When he had finally taken his fill of groping and fondling, he stood behind her. Rebecca's heart was racing, her breath ragged.

Please, please, take me! I need you to take me!

She wiggled her ass and earned herself another slap. A hard one.

Cal's throaty groan sounded in her ears. A deep longing to submit to him welled up inside her. She craved to do so, fully, without holding anything back. And after the chase, she needed it, and her sub-instinct told her he needed that too. For her to submit, to control her, possess her, make her his. And she knew that he would. It was undeniable, unavoidable. Her submissive cravings and his dominance shimmied in the air, enveloped them both.

"How are your knees?" he asked.

"Knees?"

"Yes. I don't want to fuck you in the middle of your own garden in broad daylight," he said, sounding hoarse. "Fucking you in the back of the garden however…"

He slapped her with open hand between her legs, on her mound.

"Ooohhh!" She almost climaxed.

"Crawl." He growled. "Crawl to the corner at the back and get down again, ass in the air."

She complied, no hesitation, even though she felt humiliated, knowing he was walking behind her, watching her. She couldn't not do it. Because her Master had commanded her to do this. *I so want – need – to please him!*

As she crawled, her breasts dangled underneath the baggy top, and the sensation aroused her tremendously.

"I like the view," Cal said with a hoarse voice. "I wonder how you'd look naked."

Oh, yes, please! No, wait, no! The neighbors. I can't! I won't!

Cal's soft laughter filled her ears. Her Master was aware of her predicament.

"Let's get a feel for it. On your knees." The softness of this voice didn't undermine the power in it. It seemed to enhance it, like a dangerous animal might softly growl right before attacking its prey.

Rebecca complied, her bottom on her heels, thighs slightly apart, her hands on them, eyes lowered.

A minute later, her top was gone. He'd left the bra on, the cups under her breasts, her nipples poking out proudly. Thank goodness they were behind some bushes so no one could see her. The cool breeze that wafted over her skin made her acutely aware that she was half naked in her own garden. It made her nipples tighten so hard they ached.

"Crawl." Barely audible. Had he actually said that or had she thought it? She was so tuned in to her Master that she might have simply picked up his thoughts.

A soft grunt came from behind as he watched her crawl. Her now naked, dangling breasts swelled when he mumbled, "Fucking gorgeous tits." His rough words shot through her core, and a soft mewl broke from her lips. She craved his hands on her again, groping, kneading, squeezing, arousing. Taking.

Finally, she reached the piece of grass behind a large bush and got into the position he'd ordered. Her heart was thumping against her ribs.

Even though she couldn't see Cal, she knew he stood behind her. Then his boots and clothes landed in a pile on the lawn right next to her.

"No barriers, skin on skin, total connection, total touch," he said, his voice thick with lust.

Oh, yes, yes! Finally, please!

The thought of her Master naked behind her, about to take her, made her core melt and her brain shut down. She couldn't help but move her hips, aching for the friction of his thick manhood inside her.

"Absolute silence. Use your arm or hand."

Even as she put her forearm against her mouth, his hands were on her. Strong, calloused hands, kneading, squeezing, pinching the soft flesh of her belly and hips, pulling her nipples. Rough and hard touches. The feel of his solid, warm chest over her back, the coarse chest hair tickling and tantalizing. Her moans were muffled by her arm. Her brain had left the building. She could only feel, take whatever he gave her, whatever he did to her.

More, oh God, more!

He gave her more. He slapped her mound with his open hand. And again, and again. She jolted as flames licked over her nerves. She wailed her need against her arm as he slapped her pussy again, until she was hovering on the burning precipice. One more slap and she'd go over. She almost started to cry when he didn't. Instead, he removed one boot, not bothering with the one with the rope around it. He reached around and undid her jeans, pulled them down over her ass, along with her panties, and got them off her legs. He pushed her thighs farther apart, fully exposing her.

He got on his knees behind her and thrust two fingers to the knuckles into her slick pussy. She arched her back and muffled cries sounded in the air. He pumped his fingers in again, then pulled back and licked them clean.

"Darling, you taste so good!" His voice was thick with lust.

Knowing he was licking her juices off his fingers made her pussy clamp down on…nothing. Being empty hurt. She made a protesting sound.

He slapped her bare pussy, his middle finger hitting her swollen clit. The sting set her core alight. The next one sent her over the edge and the molten lava in her core exploded. She could barely smother her screams as heatwaves seared through her body until even her hair seemed to be on fire.

Her vagina was still rippling with delicious aftershocks as he thrust two fingers in her soaking-wet pussy. She clenched around them, making him groan. He alternated finger-fucking her with strokes around her still very sensitive clit. When she tried to move away from his fingers, he simply smacked her on her ass and continued what he was doing. Each time he touched the sides of her hotspot, quivers ran through her legs, turning to shocks when he rubbed over it. So sensitive right after orgasm, it was almost painful. Yet he worked her without mercy until her clit was hard and engorged. When her entire pussy was swollen and throbbing, inside and out, and her need to come started to build again, he aligned his chest with her back. His hard cock dragged over her pussy and clit and she gasped. He rested his weight on one hand, cupped her breast with the other, fondling, kneading. He rolled her nipple between his fingers.

Please, pull! Ooooh, yesss!

Rebecca arched her chest when he did tug her nipple hard, and held it. When he moved his hand away, she keened a muffled protest. His low, husky laugh somehow seeped through her hazy brain. He toyed with her other nipple, pinching and rolling, then pulling it even harder. She hissed and pushed her hips back against his cock, needing him to take her so badly to counter the pain that zinged from her tormented nipple to her clit. Having his hardness against her wide-opened pussy but not getting him inside her was utter torture, and it added to her need.

Cal let go of her nipple and instead played with her swollen clit. Rebecca was almost delirious with desire and couldn't stop a constant wail of need. He pinched the swollen bud, and growled "Come for me now!" as he thrust his cock to the hilt inside her. He pulled out completely the moment her world shattered into a thousand pieces when she came. Excruciating waves of pleasure rolled through her, as well as disappointment when her vagina clenched and found nothing. Her pussy ached to feel him, and a sob broke from her, tears pooling in her eyes. She couldn't take much more.

Then Cal rammed his full length inside her while she was still spasming. A smothered cry broke from her. Joy filled her entire being, as did his cock. Her cunt clamp down on him, welcoming the thick intrusion. He closed his strong hands on her hips in a merciless grip. Her need was unbelievably high. Sensing his was too roused her even more. He yanked her onto his cock each time he thrust his hips forward, impaling her.

Her pussy was pulsing inside and out. Everything inside her coiled tighter and tighter in a matter of seconds, the sensations overwhelming. Her body so ready for glorious release, aching to plunge off the precipice.

"Yes, oooh, Cal, yess!"

When he slammed into her again, the white-hot ball in her lower body exploded. She screamed as heatwaves raged through her. Tongues of fire melted her brain and seared her skin, licking up and out. Jolt after jolt shot from her pussy that convulsed and sucked on the hard cock that kept pumping in her. His low growl added to her joy and she moaned as he came.

An odd sense of satisfaction and possessiveness filled her being while he fucked the aftershocks out of her. When he finally sagged on her, a sigh of contentment escaped her lips. She was completely happy and totally sated.

* * * *

Rebecca turned her head up in the shower, enjoying the warm splatter of water on her face. Cal had washed her body, gently sponging the soil from her knees and elbows. After he had done a thorough job, even between her legs, making her blush, she had washed him. She loved touching his body as much as he seemed to like touching hers. She had squirted a large blob of shower gel onto her hand and enjoyed washing his manhood, feeling his balls. Large balls.

Yummy! She'd gotten on her knees and sucked him in her mouth. Even when not erect, he was still quite a mouthful.

"Woman, you're stirring up things, and we have plans for the night," he'd said, and pulled her up.

"Plans?"

"A surprise," he answered, giving her no more clues. Just a grin.

As the water hit her face, she was thinking about their chase through her garden. It had basically been a rape game. She had loved every minute of it. Okay, not so much so when an almost paralyzing fear had washed through her when he had closed in on her. But still, even that had added to the excitement of finally being taken down, and taken hard. She knew rape fantasies weren't uncommon at all and she'd had them for years. But she had learned that afternoon that getting turned on by the fantasy and craving to try and undergo it was absolutely not the same as being a participant. Despite knowing lots of ins and outs when it came to psychology, she was off-kilter after the experience. Her brain told her she was sick. A sick pervert. Yet the thought of what had happened turned her on again.

"What's up, sweetie?" Cal asked, a concerned frown on his face.

"I... I am... I... Cal, I d-don't k-know," Rebecca stammered. Tears welled in her eyes as she looked up at him. She was so confused and really needed him to hold her, to keep her safe, to comfort her. To simply be her Master and hold her steady when she wobbled.

He pulled her into his arms, gently stroking her back, her hair, soothing and calming. Wolf Man could be gentle. She sighed against his chest and wrapped her arms around him, lost in the moment of his strong, yet gentle embrace.

"You're feeling confused and upset because you enjoyed what we did." Not a question. He knew and understood. She sighed again and relief washed through her.

"Yes," she mumbled.

"Rebecca, rape fantasy comes in many forms. Some

111

people go as far as wanting—and asking—mere strangers to rape them. Sometimes in their own homes even, when they don't expect it. That comes very close to actual rape. What we did is quite different." Cal paused. "Becca, there is serious attraction between us. You want me as much as I want you."

Rebecca looked at him, her eyes big. She hung on to his every word. She gave a slight nod, yes, she wanted him. All the time. Her cheeks warmed and he smiled into her eyes.

"You know me…" he started, and paused.

"And I trust you," Rebecca whispered, finishing his sentence. Cal's eyes warmed and he kissed her soft lips.

"Yes, you trust me, lil' sub. You know that I would never hurt you or do anything you really don't want," he continued. "And I trust you to tell me when you've reached a hard limit."

"What do you mean?" she asked.

"That I would have stopped the second you'd let me know you wanted to stop. Verbally or physically. I read body language, sweetheart. I'm an experienced Master," Cal said with a faint smile. "But I still need to trust my sub to let me know if I've reached a hard limit. That's why Doms don't like playing with subs who don't use their safe word when they should. Too much of a risk, even when the Dom is experienced. No matter what, we're not mind readers."

"Then how did you know…?" she started.

"That you wanted it?" Cal grinned. "I can tell the difference between a sub in heat and a truly scared woman. And as it so happens, I can read you quite well, lil' one."

Rebecca blushed. A sub in heat sounded so…wrong. Cal's deep, full laugh filled the shower cabin.

"Becca, if you wouldn't be a sub in heat, I wouldn't be able to do scenes with you. It comes with the territory. Nothing to be ashamed of," Cal said softly.

Yeah, yeah. Rub it in, asshole!

She snuggled against him, her face in the hollow of his shoulder, arms still around his waist. The amazingly hard muscles of his back intrigued her, and she traced them with her fingertips in admiration. They were like steel cables.

Cal rested his chin on her head and said, "What I did to you triggered your fight-or-flight response. There's more to that than most people know. Some people freeze, and another possible reaction is sexual surrender. That's why women who get raped for real can get wet, even though they do not want it. In your case, you are a submissive, Becca. You know me, you trust me, you want me and you want to submit to me. So when I trigger your fight-or-flight response and play with that, it's quite logical that you'd want the rush of sexual surrender when your Master is chasing your sexy hiney."

She laughed huskily and he smiled. Sensing she could really trust him, she plastered herself even closer to his hard body. When his cock stirred to life, she sniggered.

"Oh, yeah, just watching your ass jiggle when you run would be worth doing it again." The desire was clear in his voice. "Maybe this time I'll chase my naked, dripping sub through her house!"

A quiver ran through her. The thought, and the pressure of his erection against her lower body, sent a jolt through her clit.

"Rooms with slippery floors are off-limits. That narrows down your choices quite a bit, doesn't it?" Cal's voice was hoarse. "But we're both wet, and we do not take risks, Rebecca, understand?"

Rebecca nodded. *Oh, my God.* Adrenaline rushed through her veins.

Cal tugged a strand of her hair. "I'll count to twenty. Run, girl!"

She lost two precious seconds as her legs refused to work. Then she carefully walked out of the shower cabin and bathroom and put the speed on, racing through the carpeted hallway. Leaving easy to follow, wet footsteps on the carpet.

Where do I go? Damn, why is my house so small?

She ran downstairs, into the living room, and went behind her sofa to hide. She heard Cal walk through the room, and his low laugh when he came toward her. Mild fear washed through her. Stupid, silly fear of being chased and captured.

More adrenaline. Would he turn to the right or the left of the sofa?

She held her breath and tried to listen to where he was going, but she didn't hear anything other than the pulse of her own heartbeat. Suddenly a hand grabbed her over the sofa and she screamed. He missed, and she lunged away and raced through the living room. Her breasts bounced painfully as she ran to the dining room table and stood behind it, panting.

"Such great tits. Damn, woman, you're fucking hot!" Cal came toward her, slow, threatening and graceful at the same time. Fire lit his dark eyes. His lips were pressed together, yet slightly turned up at the corners. A predator taking pleasure in the hunt and toying with his prey. Her nipples tightened into hard points and her pussy got amazingly wet. His gaze dropped to her breasts and his lips curled up more. She almost gave up running, wanting to melt into a puddle at his feet, to offer herself to him. Still, when he suddenly lunged toward her, she yelped and sped off, back upstairs.

Where to go, where to go? Damn!

She went into the bedroom, rounded the bed and turned to face him as he walked in. Cal gave her a wicked smile and leaned his shoulder against the doorjamb.

"Now that's a bit easy, ain't it?" Despite his nonchalant posture, his voice sounded thick with arousal. "What a shame!"

Rebecca snorted. "You haven't got me yet, have you?"

Cal pushed himself off the doorjamb and stalked toward the bed, his eyes pinning her. "I bet you are totally wet and ready for me, lil' one. Why not get on the bed and offer your hot cunt to me?"

His language shocked her, and he used the momentum to

jump onto the bed and reach for her. Rebecca shot off again and she giggled when he cursed.

"Serves you right for distracting me!" she yelled while running down the stairs again.

He got her in the hallway — *how did he get down the stairs so fast?* — grabbed her left arm and yanked her against him. Rebecca looked at him and tilted her head back, offering him her vulnerable throat.

"Please, Master," she whispered, her voice raw with a sudden overwhelming need to be dominated, controlled.

He curled his fingers around her throat and her body got soft, yielding completely to him. Time seemed to come to a halt when Cal held her, his hungry eyes on hers, possessiveness firing from them.

Finally, he let go.

"I'm going to enjoy taking you." His voice sounded raspy, lustful.

He grabbed hold of her, swept her feet out from under her, laid her on her back and positioned himself on top of her. A moan fled her lips when he fisted a hand in her hair, forcing her to look at him.

"Eyes on me," he growled.

Rebecca swallowed. Nothing could be hidden if they kept eye contact. He was demanding everything from her. He would take her mind, body and soul, and she was willing to give him anything and everything.

She spread her legs, wrapped them around his hips, and he thrust balls-deep into her. He groaned.

"So fucking tight and wet," he panted.

He pulled back, and gave her his full length again.

"Ooohh, yess!" Rebecca bucked her hips to meet his next thrust. He hammered into her, hard and deep, and she climaxed, screaming his name. He kept thrusting into her and a new fire ignited in her core. As he took her, she saw care, possessiveness and sheer dominance in his eyes, and...something. His gaze was so intense, searing, the eye contact so intimate, that she wanted to look away, but found she couldn't. She was mesmerized. His dark eyes filled her world as his large, thick cock filled her pussy. He took her completely, hard and ruthlessly, no room for holding anything back.

When his groan filled the hallway, drowning out her shrieks as they came simultaneously, he had taken her mind, body and soul. And her heart.

Chapter Eight

Cal and Rebecca entered the club room and Rebecca's mouth dropped open. The dungeon looked completely different.

The usual plants had been replaced with large pink bougainvilleas and pots with pink, white and red roses. The arches on the walls held beautiful red velvet and satin drapes. The St. Andrew's crosses had large metal arches with roses over them. Rebecca couldn't work out if the pink and red roses on them were real or not. The piles of subbie blankets were replaced with red, pink and white ones. So were the cushions that could be used for submissives and slaves to kneel on.

The place looked beautiful and the decorations seemed to clash with the sounds that came from the different scene areas.

"It's romantic BDSM night tonight," Cal said with a smile.

Rebecca giggled. Moans, cries, screams and whimpers, clanking chains and cracking whips were not really her idea of romance. The scent of roses, leather and sex, combined with the sounds of pain and lust, were absolutely arousing though. Her nipples had hardened the minute they'd walked in, and now her pussy dampened as if to get in tune with her breasts.

Cal turned her around so she faced him and got a box out of his leather toy bag. He opened it and took out a beautiful red rose on a golden clip. He gently put the flower in her hair at her right temple and hummed his approval.

"Now you're ready for the evening," he said softly. "You're the most beautiful sub in the room, babe."

Her cheeks got as red as the rose. "Thank you, Sir. And thank you for the dress."

Cal cupped her face and rubbed his thumb over her bottom lip.

"It is my pleasure, Rebecca," he mumbled. "Enjoy it while you can."

Rebecca gave him a puzzled look. "Sir?" she asked.

"The rose I gave you is the only thing you will be wearing the entire evening." His dark eyes held her pinned. "And the pretty cuffs, of course."

Suddenly her knees felt weak. Naked but for a rose in her hair? *No, no, no!* He couldn't do that to her! The dress was revealing enough, but at least it gave her the illusion that her breasts and the scars, her belly and her upper arms were covered.

The dress was really beautiful, even though she had gasped when Cal had given it to her. He had handed her the tight red dress that fit around her body like a second skin. Unfortunately for her, the dress was nothing more than a scattering of fabric hearts some three inches wide that were attached to one another with thin, red straps. Through the many openings in between the hearts, her skin showed. The off-the-shoulder neckline and the hem were strips of beautiful red lace some four-inches wide. The dress was so short, it barely covered her ass. Cal had given her a red lacy thong and matching arm warmers to go with it. Her legs and feet were bare.

A dress with hearts was definitely a good choice for tonight's romantic theme, but she had expected, and hoped, to wear the excuse of a dress the entire night.

Hang on, he said, 'pretty cuffs'. What cuffs?

"Cuffs, Sir?" she asked.

Cal smiled. "That took you some time to work out," he said. "Yes, cuffs. Now, let's begin your striptease."

Striptease? No freaking way! Panic rose and knotted her stomach. If he wanted her to strip for him, in the middle of the room, she was going to…she would…

She didn't really know what she'd do. Run away? Burst into tears maybe? Kneel and beg? Get angry?

Her heart was racing as she glanced up at him, feeling like a deer caught in the high beams of a car.

"Breathe, Rebecca." The power in his voice snapped her out of her panic. She hauled in air, not even aware she'd been holding her breath. "Again."

She looked into his steady eyes, felt his control and self-confidence, and she breathed it in. As she took in his strength to find her inner balance, her heart rate and breathing returned to normal.

"Do you trust me, Rebecca?"

"Yes, Sir," she said, her voice shaking slightly.

"Take off the arm warmers, Rebecca," he said softly.

Just the arm warmers. She could do that. After she handed him the thin items, he told her to hold out her hands. She complied, and he put red lace wrist cuffs on her. They had shiny ribbons dangling off them that he tied together.

Cal put his hand under her chin and tilted her head up.

"Trust, Becca. Remember you have your safe word, and you may use 'yellow' if things get too overwhelming," he said. His voice got husky when he continued, "I won't make you do a striptease here. Not tonight."

Not tonight? Does he mean… No! She was shocked.

He caressed her cheek with his thumb, his scrutinizing black eyes pierced right through her.

"Oh, yes," he murmured, "you will strip for me, right here in the club with everyone watching, but you will dance only for me. Strip off layer by layer until your beautiful, sexy body is naked for my touch. You'll finish with offering me your breasts. Then I will bend you over and fuck you hard until you come, screaming."

Rebecca swallowed. That sounded so exciting and hot. Slutty. But she didn't want to do that here. *No way, Jose!* She shook her head.

"No, Sir, no," she begged.

Cal's slipped his hand under her dress and pulled down

her thong. He slid his fingers through her folds to her entrance and circled her wetness.

"I think the correct answer is 'Yes, Sir'. You are very wet, girl," he said, amusement clear in his voice. He pushed a finger inside her pussy and slowly moved it in and out. He leaned forward, his lips almost touching hers. "Would you like to strip for me, Rebecca, seduce me, arouse me, make my cock throb?"

The idea was bedazzling. Sexy as hell. Her breathing got faster and her pussy clamped down on his finger. A corner of his mouth turned up, and heat crept over her face. The damned bastard knew the thought excited her.

"I'm waiting, girl," He leisurely kept thrusting into her. There was no point denying it, since her body had already given him her answer. But that didn't make her any happier about being forced to admit to it.

"Yes, Sir," she said, and glowered at him.

"I do not like that look, trainee." How could such softly spoken words hold so much power? He suddenly seemed to loom over her, intimidating her. Dominating.

"I'm sorry," she hastened to say.

He held her pinned with his powerful black eyes while he kept thrusting into her with his finger. His controlling, merciless gaze a stark contrast with the intimate thrusts. Why did that arouse her so much? She got even wetter and a heady need flared through her body. If he kept looking like that she might come right then and there. His lips curled up at the corners, telling her that he knew exactly what effect his control had on her. Her vagina clamped down on him and a soft mewl escaped her.

Heat lit his eyes and he pushed two fingers inside her, ruthlessly finger-fucking her. When he started talking again, his voice rough and husky, he emphasized his words with deep, hard thrusts of his fingers.

"You will strip for me" — thrust — "and offer me your gorgeous tits" — thrust — "and I will fuck you" — thrust — "while everyone's watching" — thrust — "and you will scream" — thrust — "and scream" — thrust — "and scream" — thrust.

Her pussy clenched around his fingers. Her clit throbbed and she was soaking wet. The controlled power in his smoldering eyes melted her spine and set her core on fire. Full blast. A surge of clawing need shot through her.

"Come for me now, trainee," he ordered. He crooked his fingers and pressed against her G-spot, while he stroked the sides of her swollen clit with his thumb. The pressure on her clit from the inside and the rubbing over it on the outside ignited a fire so hot that it seemed to fry every nerve in her body. When he moved over her clit, pressing hard, she exploded and came violently, riding the heatwaves that rose from her core. Wave after wave raged through her body as he kept thrusting and rubbing her G-spot and clit, demanding every last spasm from her.

When her eyes focused again, she was grateful to have his strong arm around her waist, holding her up, as her legs had turned to jelly. She had sagged against his hard chest, and had wrapped her arms around him for stability and comfort.

He pulled his fingers out of her pussy, licked them off and held her close. He let her snuggle for a few minutes, then pushed her away a bit and took her mouth. She tasted herself as he swept in to take complete possession. He dueled with her tongue, demanding a response. She moaned into his mouth and completely surrendered to his will.

When he released her, her eyes locked with his black ones. The message was clear. "I can make you do whatever I want, whenever I want, and I will take what I want, when I want."

Rebecca inhaled sharply as she realized he could and would. He had made her come right here near the entrance of the dungeon to teach her that lesson. Her cheeks flushed. They hadn't even gotten to a proper scene area. He didn't care, he'd take her whenever and wherever he wanted. It made her insides quiver with fear and need. Fear as she knew that she couldn't stop him—he'd barge straight through all her defenses and objections. And fear because she wanted him to barge right through them. And now that she had fallen for him, she'd allow him to take even more. Her legs started to tremble and her bottom lip quivered.

God help me, I love him, and it scares the hell out of me!

* * * *

After he'd pulled up her thong, Cal had guided Rebecca to the bar and set her on a stool. He had ordered a beer for himself and juice for her. No alcohol—he wanted her to keep her head clear. He wouldn't allow her to fully find her bearings after that public orgasm. He would continue to shake her up, a little bit at the time. He didn't want alcohol to soften the impact.

He had seen the anxiety in her eyes, warring with need. And he'd seen her feelings for him too. It had made his heart skip a beat. He really liked the woman, cared for her. A lot. But he wasn't looking for love. Love equaled a relationship, and he wasn't in the market for one. He knew feelings could easily flare up between a Master and his sub, as such bonds always ran deep. But that still didn't mean it was the kind of love that could forge a lasting romantic relationship. He also knew subs could get hung up on their Masters, and he was quite sure that was the case with his beautiful trainee. So, he'd ignore it, as well as the way she often tugged at his heart. For now, they had a deep connection as Master and sub, and after her training, he'd let go of her and help her find the right Dom. A stab of jealousy ran through him at the thought of Rebecca, his Rebecca, with another Dom. Another man, even. He put the emotion in a vault and locked it.

Their drinks were put in front of him on the bar, and he untied the ribbons on her lace cuffs and tied them together on her back. The posture made her breasts arch forward. He slowly ran his eyes over her body and sounded his pleasure when her nipples spiked under his hot gaze.

He stood behind her and pulled her against his hard chest with one arm, wrapped it around her waist. With his free hand, he picked up her drink and put the glass against her lips.

"Drink, lil' subbie."

She opened her lips and he slowly tilted the glass so she could drink.

Cal put the glass on the bar and curved his left hand around her throat. A solid, steel grip, yet he didn't cut off her airflow at all. He groaned when her body yielded instantly to his control and she melted against his chest, leaning heavily against him.

He made her turn her head sideways and back so he could look in her eyes. Dilated pupils. Her lips slightly apart. His cock pulsed.

"So beautiful," he mumbled. He held her with his gaze as he ran his hand down over her collarbone and the swell of her breast. He rolled a nipple between his fingers and pinched it. She whimpered. Without further ado, he pulled the lace neckline of her dress down over her breasts, making her gasp. Before her brain could react and object to being exposed, he found her nipple again, and tugged on it. She squirmed on the stool.

As he watched her intently, he slid his hand down and splayed it over her abdomen. Insecurity flashed in her eyes.

"I love my women soft, Rebecca," he said, his voice hoarse. "Nothing like a soft, squirming woman under me when I hammer my cock into her slick, hot cunt."

Cal laughed softly when she blinked at the crude words, and a brief expression of shock appeared on her face. Then she blushed. The words could have affronted her, but it was clear to him they turned her on. *Fuck, she is sexy!* He held her with his gaze, not allowing her to lower hers, no matter how much she wanted to hide from her shyness. He chuckled, and her already pink cheeks turned a bright red. The corners of his mouth kicked up.

"Oh, yes, my baby loves some dirty talk," he said softly in her ear. "I'll put that on the menu for tonight."

The way she glanced at him, all puppy-eyes, almost made him groan. The delicious mix of embarrassment and excitement that oozed from her poked up the heat in his lower body.

"Open your thighs for me, subbie."

As she complied, he stroked down over her belly, over her tender inner thigh to her knee, then up again. He tickled her skin, inching toward her pussy, and anticipation sped up her breathing. She tilted her hips, aching for his touch. All the while he kept her pinned with his gaze, so intimate, almost too intimate. The heat in his eyes seared through her, poked up the fire in her lower body even more. When he stroked over her swollen nub, she jolted. He slid under her thong and found her wet entrance, her inner labia swollen and puffy.

"Pleeease," she moaned, needing pressure on her most sensitive part.

Ever so slowly, he slid up through her folds, toward her clit. He drew figure-eights around her sensitive nub and entrance. Too slow and light for her to get off, yet enough stimulation to make her tissues swell even more. He played with her until her entire lower body was aching and pulsing.

Her eyes had glazed over, and she was leaning heavily against him. His cock throbbed and his balls were so tight they ached. His dominant heart thumped hard at the sight of her trust, her need, the soft mewls that came from her sexy red lips. His breath caught when he saw love in her eyes. A sensational mixture. A groan escaped his lips. The gorgeous creature squirming under his hands lit a blazing fire in his core—and in his heart and soul.

Dammit, Cal, not love. Not fucking love.

Yet, the vault cracked open as he looked into her hazel eyes. She roused a hunger in him that he couldn't control. A burning desire that seared through every cell of his body. He had wanted all of her, everything. How could he forget it was a two-way street? With every little bit he'd taken from her, she'd taken him, slowly but surely. The sexy vixen had gotten under his skin. He didn't want her there, but he couldn't stop it. She was like an addiction—a Rebecca addiction. He couldn't just bite off a mouthful and treasure the flavor. He needed more. And more. And more. He wanted the whole goddamn pie. Everything she had to give and allowed him to take. The urge to possess her, completely and totally, surged through his veins. He had to, even if it meant she would get as much of him in return.

Her 'Please, Master' pulled him back to reality. He softly stroked her throat with his fingers, before he tightened his grip again. Seeing how she yielded to his complete control when he put his hand around her vulnerable throat woke every ounce of dominance in him. He loved the wonderful feeling of her submission when he took it. He held her with his eyes and hand, and used the other to work her pussy harder and faster. He pressed against the sides of her swollen nub, found the oh-so-sensitive spot high up on the right side of her clit, then rubbed over it. It engorged against his finger, and his cock jerked.

"Come for me, Becca," he whispered, his voice rough with emotion. He took her hard clit between his thumb and index finger, then pinched.

Her leg muscles became rigid and she bucked her hips. Her shrieks filled the air and her head thumped against his chest. His cock throbbed and his balls ached with need as he watched her come. *Gorgeous woman. Absolutely stunning when she comes.* He held her spasming, climaxing body stable until she sagged against him.

Cal kissed the top of her head and swung her up in his arms. He sat on the barstool with his back against the bar and her on his lap. With one hand, he undid the lace cuffs so she would be comfortable, and held her close. Rebecca snuggled against him and put a hand on his chest, over his heart. As she let out a sigh, seemingly happy and sated,

125

something inside him shifted into place and he was totally content.

I am so Goddamn fucked!

When they had both had finished their drinks, he got up and lifted her off the stool.

"Take off your thong," he said.

She wiggled out of the flimsy thong and handed it to Cal. A rush of excitement washed through her. To stand there with her breasts exposed and her pussy bare under the scant dress got her juices going again. It turned her on so much she didn't really care about the scars on her breasts anymore. In public, she was still somewhat awkward about it, but the club was reasonably dark. And knowing he was okay with it had helped her a lot.

But when he traced his fingers over her breasts, followed by his tongue, she remembered she still hadn't told him about the numbness of the skin at the undercurve.

Damn. Why hadn't she told him sooner? Or written it down on her checklist? This was so not the right moment to start talking about that. But she didn't know what he'd have in mind to do, and he needed to know.

"Cal…" she said softly.

He raised an eyebrow.

"Is this about your surgery again?" he asked softly. The look on his face told her clearly, that for him, that discussion was closed.

"Yes, but…I have to tell you…" Rebecca swallowed. Damn, this was awkward, telling a hot guy — her Master — about yet another flaw. Then she blurted "I don't have full sensation on the underside of my breasts." She didn't want to see his reaction, expecting disgust, and dropped her gaze to the floor.

Cal put his fingers under her chin and tilted her face up, forcing her to look at him.

"Thank you for telling me, sweetie." His eyes were warm, with no sign of disgust. "Quite important to know when we play. You should have told me before, love."

Her heart skipped a beat when he said 'love', then he ruined it all when he continued, "When your training is over, and you do scenes with other Doms, you will have to tell them upfront. Understand, Rebecca?"

Other Doms. I don't want to play with other Doms! I only want you!

The hurt in her eyes tore at his gut. He recognized it as it was the same pain he felt at the thought of her with another Dom.

He pulled her against his chest and held her close. For a moment he didn't quite know how to react. He wanted her, ached to possess her all the way, but he was supposed to train her. And let go of her.

Damn this shit! It had all gone too fast. His feelings for her were so strong, and had come up so fast, that they'd hit him like a brick in the face. He was not going to make any promises until he had sorted out the turmoil inside him. And telling her how he felt would be like a promise. A promise for more, exclusivity, a relationship. He wasn't ready for that yet. Not out of the blue like this, in the heat of the moment. If he was going to tell a woman he loved her, he wanted to be damn sure that it was love, and not infatuation and lust.

"Let it slide for now," he murmured in her hair, as much to himself as to her.

Rebecca sucked in a breath, pushed herself away from him and gave him a tremulous smile. He smiled back, but knew it didn't reach his eyes.

Cal shook the feelings off himself, put his hand on the small of her back and guided her into the dungeon. They just walked around, stopping at scene areas to watch. He chose carefully, only taking her to scenes he knew would turn her on.

During the third scene, he moved behind her and started playing with her breasts. Her cheeks got red. He wondered if she'd ever get used to being touched in public.

"Red becomes you, sweetie," he said with a laugh in his voice. "I love to see you hot and bothered."

He cupped her breasts, enjoying how they filled his large hands. "I love a handful of tits." He rubbed his erection against her round ass and she gasped. "I'm going to fuck you so hard tonight. I want to hear you scream when I bury myself inside you."

A soft mewl broke from her and her cheeks got warm again. From lust, not embarrassment. Her nipples were taut and she longed for him to play with them. She arched her chest, pushing her breasts in his hands. He started kneading and squeezing again.

God, please, yes!

She squirmed against him, and in doing so she rubbed her ass over his erection.

"Woman, stop moving that soft, sexy hiney over my cock," he groaned.

Her husky giggle made his lips curl up. Rebecca wiggled her behind against him, and he cursed under his breath. He abandoned her breasts, ignoring her soft protests, and moved her dress up over her behind to cup her ass cheeks. Without warning, he pulled them apart a bit and held them open.

"My cock seems to like your ass. Maybe I'll take you there tonight," he growled, and pressed his erection against her bottom. Her breath caught and her heart started racing. No way did she want his thick dick in her ass. Way too big — he'd tear her apart. Yet her clit started throbbing, as if it wanted to tell her that her body would welcome the invasion in her most private place.

"Your body betrays you, Becca," he said softly, "It wants me to take your ass."

"No, no, it doesn't. I don't want it," she said, sounding breathy.

Cal put a hand around her throat and she immediately

yielded, her body soft against his chest. "Do not lie to me, Rebecca." The sudden ice in his voice seemed to freeze the air in her lungs. She was surprised she couldn't see her own breath when she exhaled.

"I'm sorry, Master," she said, her voice shaking.

"Don't lie to me again, ever." The threat did nothing to warm her frozen blood. "If I had prepped your back hole, I'd bend you over and demonstrate how much you want me there, right here, right now."

Rebecca swallowed. If it wasn't for the hand around her throat, she would have dropped to her knees to beg him to forgive her.

"Yes, Master," she whispered. "I'm sorry."

His approving sound started to melt her blood again, and she sucked in a breath.

"We will leave your ass exposed, as a reminder," he grumbled.

He released her, set his hand on her back and started guiding her through the dungeon. Rebecca kept her eyes lowered, ashamed she'd lied to him, and acutely aware of her naked ass. And with the back of her dress pulled up over her bum, the front started to ride up as well. Each step she took pushed it up higher, until her pussy was in sight.

Damn! Now that the dress only covered her belly and back, she might as well be naked. Although she was grateful that her belly wasn't exposed, she doubted anyone would have looked at it. Her breasts were jostling, her ass jiggling, and her labia were slightly swollen. She sensed people looking at her, eyes glued to her breasts, ass and pussy. Heat washed through her and she got wet. Her nipples had tightened so much, it was painful.

"Stop here, trainee," Cal ordered.

She immediately complied.

"Sir?"

"Hold up your breasts for me, please."

Her hands were trembling slightly when she cupped them under her breasts and lifted them a bit. Some people stood still to look and see what was going to happen.

Great, you gotta love an audience, Rebecca!

Cal took some things with long red tassels on them out of his pocket. He captured her right nipple in his mouth and pulled strongly. Rebecca yelped. He sucked so hard it hurt, but at the same time electric jolts shot to her core. When he let go, her nipple was nicely swollen and long. He rubbed it dry with his rough fingers, making her squeak. *Too much!* He didn't pay heed to her protests at all. Instead he moved his arm moved around her to hold her still. It might as well have been a steel band. *Why are you so damned strong!* Then he put a nipple clamp on, and Rebecca cried out.

"No, please, Master," she begged, "It hurts."

"Breathe through it, Becca," he said, as he ran his fingers over her cheek. "Breathe. You can take it."

His intent eyes were on her face as he slowly tightened the clamp. It bit down on her nipple and she tried to back away, but his arm wouldn't budge.

"That's just about right," he murmured, his eyes reading hers.

"No, Sir, it's too tight, please," she begged.

His strong, calm gaze held her steady. "No, it's exactly right. Breathe. That a girl."

As she did was she was told, the sting shot down to her pussy. She moaned, earning herself a sexy smile from Cal.

He put his mouth over her other nipple, and a minute later, she was wearing another clamp. Rebecca closed her eyes as she breathed through the pain. Both nipples were burning, and a blazing fire flared to life in her core. Her mind blanked, her knees buckled and she let out a long whine.

Cal put his fingers under one of the dangling tassels on the nipple clamps and lifted it. The tassel fell down again, but the hidden thin chains within, with little weights on them, didn't. He moved his fingers a bit higher until the weights slipped off his fingers and dropped.

Shocks shot through her body as the weights tugged on

her tortured nipple. Her clit was aching with need. She was so close to orgasm. If only he'd touch her there…

"Please, Master." Her words came out slurred.

"No, sweetie, not yet," he murmured. He lifted the other tassel until only the small weights rested on his finger.

"Are you ready?" He didn't wait for an answer and just let the weights fall from his finger. They bounced up and down. She jolted, making the weights bounce even more. The overload of sensations made her head spin, and if he hadn't held her with his strong hands, she would have fallen to the floor.

He drew her in his arms, stroking her back. "Easy, darling. Breathe." His power brought her back to planet Earth. When she was stable enough, he let go of her and guided her to another scene to watch.

* * * *

About half an hour, and a number of scenes, later, she was in dire need. Each scene they'd watched, he had played with the tassels and weights, driving her higher and higher. Just when she'd thought she couldn't get any hotter without orgasming, he had started to play with her pussy, as well. He had gotten her on the edge of coming again and again, and each time she'd needed just one more touch, he'd abandoned her pussy and breasts. She had protested so loudly, that Cal had threatened to gag her.

"I like your sexy sounds, baby," he had said. "but we cannot disturb other people's scenes. Understood?"

"Yes, Sir. I'm sorry," she'd mumbled.

He had hummed. "I think it's time for us to play, don't you?"

Rebecca opened her mouth to reply, but he put an arm around her waist and walked her toward a scene area.

When they got there, she looked at the bondage table that was standing in the middle. Inviting and daunting at the same time. She'd never been on one and could only imagine what it would be like. Now she'd find out. Excitement rushed through her.

Cal turned her around and removed the lace wrist cuffs.

"Up you go, on your back, please," he ordered.

Rebecca crawled onto the table, grimacing as the movement made the weights dangle from her throbbing nipples. When she was on her back, he put wide cuffs on her thighs, just above the knees. The way he curved his hands around her hips and resolutely pulled her bottom to the edge of the table made her gasp. She raised her head, seeking his eyes with hers, but he continued without looking at her. He grabbed ropes from his toy bag and worked quickly and with sure hands as he attached them to both the table and the thigh cuffs. Her leg muscles stiffened when she realized what he was about to do. Before she could react, he had pushed her legs up, bent her knees and pulled on the ropes until her thighs were widely spread. The posture opened her pussy for him. Rebecca's heart was racing. Being exposed like that was awkward. And sexy. Her hazy brain tried to work out whether she liked it or not.

There was no time to linger on the matter, as Cal kept working. He fastened a strap over her belly, another one under her breasts, and one above them. She inhaled sharply when she tried the straps and found she couldn't move. A shock ran through her, then panic welled up from her core. It was about to numb her when Cal put his hand on her stomach and said, "Look at me, Rebecca."

She obeyed and lifted her gaze to meet his. His dark eyes told her he understood, but that he would not relent. He'd rendered her completely helpless, had taken total control. He was looming over her, strong, confident, dominant. Instead of instilling fear, his power over her softened the tightness in her stomach. The panic dissipated and her muscles relaxed as she surrendered to his will.

He bent forward and took possession of her mouth, ruthlessly plunged in and out with his tongue. She was completely restrained by the ropes, the straps and his mouth, and she almost came spontaneously.

After a long kiss, he pulled back, his eyes heavy-lidded as he took her in. Pupils dilated, lips swollen and red from his hard, demanding kiss. *Gorgeous.*

His cock and balls were so tight they ached. Before he could start the scene he had intended to do, he needed release. Badly.

He walked to the end of the table, opened his leathers and sheathed himself in a condom. At times like this, he hated the club rules, although he understood them. But right now he would have given anything to be able to take her bareback.

He swirled the head of his cock through her juices. Damn, he loved her pussy. The swollen, inner labia welcoming him to ram himself home.

"You better be ready for me, Becca," he said, his voice thick with lust, "because I'm going to bury myself to the hilt and hammer into you until you scream."

Her "Please!'" turned into a cry when he thrust himself to the root inside her and held still.

"You're so damn wet and tight," he growled, "You're a dream to fuck, baby."

Her pussy clenched around his cock and she moaned loudly.

Cal pulled back and slammed into her again, keeping his full length inside her without moving.

"Oooohh...please! More!" she begged, her head rolling from side to side.

"Let's free your nipples, sexy," he said. His erection pushed even deeper as he bent over her to undo a clamp. He looked at the flattened nipple, loving it. Knowing overwhelming pain would hit her when the blood flowed back into it, he hammered into her.

Her loud whine filled the area, making his cock jerk inside her. A sheen of sweat covered his body as he pushed back his need to orgasm.

He undid the other clamp and licked over her nipple as pain hit her again. As groan fled his lips as she tried to writhe, but the straps held her immobile. Pain and lust showed on her face and in her dazed eyes. It was a mix he couldn't resist, and he slammed into her with fast, deep thrusts. Her pussy convulsed around his cock.

"That's right, love, come for me, milk me with your cunt." His words came out slurred. The fire in his core burned as intensely as hers.

Damn, this is utter torture. He knew the crude words and his brutal merciless hammering would put her over the edge. It almost took him with her, though.

Cal gritted his teeth, the effort to push back his own orgasm almost inhuman. His balls felt like they were going to explode inside and out. He couldn't last much longer, no matter how much he enjoyed what he was doing.

"Come for me again, Becca," he grunted. He angled his cock differently to hit her sweet spot.

Her body fought the straps as another violent orgasm shook her.

"Oohhhh… Cal, yesss… Oohhh." As her screams bounced off the wall, he finally let go of his control. He started to thrust into her hard and fast. His balls felt incredibly full, the pressure so high he had reached the point of inevitability. He roared his pleasure as the heat at the base of his spine exploded and pushed his semen up through his shaft in glorifying jerks. Sheer ecstasy rose from his core and raced over his nerves like tongues of fire, searing his flesh. He shuddered with exhilaration as her silky hot cunt sucked the last spurts out of his cock. One final push, then he surrendered to the deep sense of completion that filled his being.

Even through his after-orgasm bliss one thought kept pounding through his head.

Mine! My woman!

Chapter Nine

The next night, Rebecca finished rather late at the reception desk, and it wasn't until eleven that she met up with Cal at the bar in the dungeon. He greeted her with a steaming hot kiss, and by the time he let her sit down on a stool, her cheeks were hot and her pussy was wet.

After she'd finished her drink, Cal took her to a settee in a slightly secluded area. He sat and told her to sit with her back against the armrest, her legs over his. He rubbed her bare feet—no shoes for his subbie tonight—and a sigh of joy came from her lips. It had been a long night and her feet were aching.

"Thank you, Sir!" she whispered.

He smiled at her. "No problem, sweetie."

Rebecca relaxed fully now and almost drifted off.

"Stay awake, girl," Cal said with a laugh in his voice. "I got plans for tonight!"

She forced her eyes open to look at him. She knew he'd had a scene planned yesterday, but after their intense orgasms on the massage table, both had been spent. Cal had told her he'd decided to just go with the flow, enjoy the remainder of the evening and do the scene tonight instead. The eagerness in his eyes put butterflies in her stomach. Clearly, it was something he really wanted to do. And here she was, wanting to just sit there and doze while getting her feet rubbed by him. *A Master serving his sub.* She giggled at the thought.

He raised an eyebrow.

"Something funny, love?"

"I'm just glad you're so nice to me," she said in her

sweetest voice.

"Don't get used to it, subbie," he said dryly. "I give and I take."

When he dug his thumbs into a sore spot, she let out a sigh. "It's just so good to be off my feet for a bit."

"That happens to be exactly what I have in mind for you tonight," Cal said with a mysterious smile.

Rebecca narrowed her eyes. She was quite sure his idea of 'off her feet' was not the same as hers.

"Don't worry, sugar," he said. "You'll come. Screaming."

She pouted her lips. "Now, I *am* worried."

"Such an eager sub. Ain't I lucky!" Cal replied.

* * * *

Rebecca was kneeling in the middle of the scene area, her hands on her back and her gaze lowered. Cal was walking around, preparing things, and she waited patiently, occasionally peeking through her lashes. Before he came back to her, he clicked a floor switch with his foot and purple light bathed her naked body.

He sat behind her, caressing her belly, trailing up over her arms, down over her upper chest, caressing the swell of her breasts. Featherlight touches fluttered over her skin, while he pressed soft kisses on her shoulder, all the way up the side of her neck to her ear. Goose bumps bloomed across her skin and shivers of pleasure ran down her spine. She tipped her head to the side to allow him better access to the sensitive curve of her neck. Rebecca's closed her eyes as she enjoyed his touches, his presence enveloping her. Even when his hands and lips abandoned her body for a brief moment, she felt touched and held by him, as his aura of power and control surrounded her completely.

Soft fabric brushed over the skin of her upper body, making her nipples harden, as he tied a long white cotton strap around her that completely covered her breasts. The ends pooled on the floor behind her, the frayed edges tickling her back and ass.

Cal tossed coils of rope onto the mat, and the thud made her insides quiver. He sat behind her, pressed his head into the crook of her neck, deeply inhaling her scent, and he groaned. Gently, he tangled his hand in her hair and he pulled her head back to further expose her vulnerable throat and neck. He nipped her, and as she whimpered softly, he lapped over the sore spot with wet tongue. Her head rested against his shoulder and he slowly drew the length of a rope over the side of her nape, the harsh strands grazing her skin. A mewl broke from her lips.

Cal started working, all the while caressing and teasing her with his hands and rope, alternating slow and swift movements with both.

The feel of the ropes, and the reassurance in his touch made her head spin.

He put her arms on her back and tied her forearms together. Another rope slid over her body, as he wrapped it around her torso above her breasts several times, tying knots at the back and her sides. He gently pulled another rope over her skin, teasing, caressing and tantalizing. Moving erotically slow as he tied it under her breasts, pulling the skin taut and making them swell. She loved having her breasts tied up. Soft, husky sounds came from her lips when he moved the wrappings up against them with short, jerky movements. As she felt how tightly her breasts were bound, squeezed between ropes, her head dropped back and a long whine broke from her lips.

"Cal," she whispered, as she started to come undone. She was dazed and her head seemed to wobble on her shoulders.

He sat in front of her, held her head back by her hair and leaned in, his face inches from hers. A look of possessiveness fired in his eyes as he kept her pinned with his gaze, while he curved his other hand curved around her throat, claiming her. Rebecca yielded completely, bent to his will and control. She was dizzy, breathless, barely able to focus her eyes as his gaze held her.

"Master…" she mumbled.

"Breathe, Becca," he said softly, and ran his fingertips over her cheek, with featherlight touches. She automatically opened her mouth as the soft caress stroked over her bottom lip. Cal leaned in and kissed her. When he withdrew, he smiled into her eyes and started working the ropes again with sure, swift fingers.

"I'm going to get you off your feet now love." His voice a mere whisper. He put a rope through the suspension point he had made on her back, pulled it through the suspension ring above her and lifted her to her knees. A moan escaped her as the ropes around her torso tightened, feeling like a strong embrace.

After he had fastened the suspension rope, he started tying another one just below her waist, low around her hips and high up on each thigh. Never just one wrapping, but four times, so her blood flow wouldn't get cut off.

He pulled the rope from which she was hanging a bit higher, lifting her off her knees. Soft mewls came from her lips as the ropes above and below her breasts tightened and put pressure on them, making them swell.

Held by just the one rope, her body started turning slightly. Cal drew her closer and fondled her breasts. Her husky sounds enveloped them, the moment enthralling. A soft brush over her cheek, then he pulled her up even higher, until her feet barely touched the mat. He took another long piece of white cotton fabric and carefully tucked it under the ropes around her hips. He circled her and grabbed the long cotton strip, tugging it between her legs and through the windings around her hips at the back. It now loosely covered her pussy and most of her behind, like a makeshift loincloth, then flowed to the ground.

He wound a rope around her thighs, just above the knees, and pulled another suspension rope through it to lift her legs up. A tiny bit at first, her toes were still grazing the mat. As her weight was mostly on the suspension point behind her back, her body slumped forward. Rebecca surrendered to the feel of the ropes, embracing her, holding her, restraining her. Freeing her.

Cal tilted back her head. "Are you all right, Becca?" he asked softly, his gaze probing hers.

"Yes, Master," she whispered.

Cal smiled at her. "I want to take you a bit further, my love. If you get cramp anywhere, I want you to tell me straight away, understand?"

"Yes, Master. I will," she said, drinking in the care she saw in his eyes. And...love?

Please, Master Cal, love me. I love you so goddamn much!

She got a soft, sweet kiss before he continued to get her in a different position. A moment later he'd lifted her legs higher, putting her in horizontal, floating face-up above the ground. He tugged at the ropes around her torso, a reminder of his complete control and dominance.

Knowing that she couldn't move, that she had totally surrendered to his will, set her free. Allowed her to let go of everything and anything. It eradicated the need for worries and concerns, thoughts even. She could simply be. Float. Completely liberated. Ecstasy rose from her core and incoherent sounds came from her lips.

Her now hazy brain barely registered that Cal draped the long ends of cotton loosely over her body as if she was a work of art.

"You look stunning, my love," he said softly.

A throaty moan escaped her when he stepped closer and fondled her breasts, then grabbed the cotton he'd wrapped around them, and tore it apart. Her breasts spilled free and he cupped them in his hard hands.

"Oohh, Master, please..." she started begging. Her hazy brain didn't know what she was begging for, just that she didn't want it to stop. The harsh ropes, his hard hands and the freedom were mind-boggling and breathtaking. She was completely rope drunk.

She felt her body move as he slowly lowered her legs again

and removed the rope he'd wrapped above her knees. As she was floating in subspace, she was vaguely aware of his fingers and more ropes on her thighs, and a moment later she was lifted into the air again, her legs spread. Almost as if she was on a rope swing with her legs apart. All the while he was caressing her with his hands, the touch both reassuring and arousing. Then he draped the cotton fabric over her again and used the end of the strap that had been around her breasts to create a support for her head.

As he stepped between her legs, he slid his hand underneath the cotton that still covered her pussy. He started sliding his fingers through her labia, circling her wetness, and up around her clit. Rebecca tried to move, but found she couldn't. She could only hang and let the ropes carry her, float in subspace and take whatever he was doing to her.

Her eyes rose to meet his. The ruthless black eyes took her breath away. His face looked chiseled, his lips pressed into a thin line. He was towering over her, daunting and scary. And tearing at her heartstrings.

I love you!

The air shimmied between them as his smoldering eyes pierced hers. He knew and felt in his very core that if he took everything, he'd have to give her everything. He saw her love for him in her eyes, sensed it with every cell of his body. He couldn't help but to be drawn to her emotions like a moth to light. Even if he'd burn himself by getting too close, he couldn't stop it. Didn't want to, either. He needed it. Yearned for more. He wanted to get so close that her love would sear through his body and burn away the callouses from his heart and soul.

Kamikaze mission, Cal. She'll take your fucking heart.

The love and trust that beamed from her hazel eyes softened his hard gaze.

She's already got your heart, knucklehead!

"Tonight, I'm going to take everything," Cal growled.

"Keep your eyes on me."

A happy sigh escaped her and her muscles softened even more, yielding completely to his command.

He unzipped his leathers, quickly sheathed himself in a condom and circled his cock through her wetness. Rebecca moaned, clearly in as much need as he was. He didn't want her pussy, though, he wanted to take possession of her most private, intimate place. He slid his cock down toward her ass. A soft whimper came from her. While holding her with his gaze, he pressed against the tight muscle. She relaxed and pushed against him. Cal groaned at her willing surrender. She wanted this as much as he did, needed to feel owned by him. He pushed the head of his cock inside her and grabbed a small tube of lube from his pocket. Slowly he pushed in a bit more, stopped, dripped more lube on his cock, and slid in a bit farther. He carefully worked his way into her tight back hole, his intent gaze on her. Her whimpers turned into a constant soft wail at the thick intrusion that stretched her.

"Master... No... Cal, too much!"

Cal saw a delicious mixture of fear and lust in her eyes that made his cock jerk. He was aching to take her, but he controlled his own need and continued even more slowly as he caressed her cheek. "I'm careful, honey," he whispered. As he gently pulled back, he put more lube on his shaft before he inched in again.

Her satiny, tight ass woke every nerve in his lower body. Screaming for him to ram himself inside her. He suppressed the urge. *Not yet. Not just yet.*

His now slick shaft moved in more easily and the friction made her cock throb. Desire to pleasure her made him groan. He grabbed the lube and a visible shock shot through her as a cold blob landed on her clit. He started teasing it, rubbing, pressing, pinching and sliding.

"Ooohh, my God, Cal, please!"

Cal pulled back and thrust his cock into her ass. Her husky cry filled the air as he rammed his full length into her. Possessiveness coursed through his veins as he impaled her, and made her his. Took her as her Master, her man.

"More, please, Master." The words came out slurred. Her eyes had totally glazed over. "Please make me yours."

Cal growled and grabbed her hips, yanking her onto his cock.

"I want everything from you," he grunted. "Fucking everything you got to give."

He cupped one hand under her ass to hold her, so he could work her swollen clit with the fingers from his other hand while he slammed into her. Before long the sensitive nub was engorged.

The love in her eyes zinged over his nerves, straight to his core, poured back out of him to her and forged their hearts into one. A bond so strong it was almost tangible. The moment was breathtaking. Enthralling.

"Come with me, my love," he groaned. "Now!"

He pinched her clit and she came violently.

"Ooh, yessss! I love you, Cal!" Her screams bounced off the walls, her body spasming and shocking in the ropes.

His own mind blanked as the soaring fire in his core exploded and he bellowed his release. Wave after wave of brutal pleasure flooded his body as cum pushed up through his shaft in exhilarating jerks. He kept thrusting until he slowly spiraled down on the last ripples of joy.

As soon as his legs could carry him again, he pulled out of her and got rid of the condom. He thoroughly cleaned her off with wipes and got her out of the ropes. He worked quickly, simply tossing each rope aside. When the last rope fell to the floor, he scooped her up in his arms, grabbed a subbie blanket and walked to a love chair. He'd clean up later. Right now he wanted to hold his woman in his arms. The minute he sat, she snuggled against him, and he knew she needed to be held as much as he needed to hold. As soon as he had managed to get her in the blanket, he put his arms around her and pulled her as close as he could without hurting her.

He nuzzled her cheek. *You're mine. My woman. I goddamn*

love you, Becca!

Yet he couldn't say it out loud. Too much turmoil inside. She'd given everything to him, had trusted him completely. She'd screamed that she loved him, and it had made his own heart sing with joy. But he couldn't give that same pleasure to her just yet.

Emily, a submissive, appeared.

"Master Kyle sent me with water and chocolate, Master Cal," Emily said timidly.

"Thank you, Emily," Cal said. "If you could open the bottles and put them on the table."

After the submissive had gone, Cal made Rebecca drink a few sips and started feeding her bits of chocolate. While she was nibbling, he drank some water himself and also took a piece of the sweet, dark candy. He could do with some nourishment as well. He had been quite deep in topspace. That place where adrenaline coursed through his veins. Acutely aware of her every breath, every twitch of her muscles, every inch of her skin. The sounds of her pain and pleasure had taken him higher and higher. He too could crash-land after such a rush.

As he bit off another piece of chocolate, he kept a close eye on her. His experience told him that she was landing smoothly. Suddenly, her vibe changed and she stiffened. He didn't have to ask why. He wasn't a fool. The woman had told him she loved him, he knew she'd meant it, and he hadn't said a thing. He hadn't acknowledged her feelings, nor had he told her he loved her.

He cursed under his breath when she started to cry.

Nice work, Cal!

The woman was still high on endorphins, which would affect her judgment. As her Master, he had to deal with her, his sub, when she needed him. And she did, but he hadn't a clue how to. Not with this. Rebecca wasn't stupid. He was certain she had felt his love for her in his touch, had seen it in his eyes. Hell, he had known himself it had poured out of him. In spite of that, he was lost now. Simply holding her was all he could do.

When she finally looked up at him, he read the question in her eyes — "Don't you love me?"

"Please, don't force me to answer, Becca," he said softly.

She lowered her eyes, and Cal held her against his chest, but he knew something had changed.

Chapter Ten

"What the hell happened, Cal?" Kyle demanded.

Rebecca had called in sick for the weekend. Kyle had known she wasn't ill, but the woman had refused to answer his questions. Clearly, something had gone down between Rebecca and Cal that had upset her enough to stay away from the club.

Kyle wasn't chuffed to be stuck without a good receptionist and he was seriously pissed off with Cal for upsetting and hurting Rebecca.

"Mind your own business," Cal growled.

"Rebecca is my business," Kyle said, his voice calm but with a lethal edge to it. "She's a club trainee." He paused for effect. "One I entrusted to you."

"You saying you don't trust me with your trainee anymore?" Cal's eyes had narrowed, and he almost spat out 'your trainee'.

Kyle tried to read him, but found it impossible to penetrate the strong armor. But it was crystal clear the man wasn't happy. And good armor or no, he sensed it grated on Cal to say Rebecca wasn't his. Kyle sympathized with his friend, but unless he'd slap his cuffs on Rebecca's wrists Cal couldn't put his foot down. Nor would he let him.

"I trust you as a friend and I know you are a fine Master, Cal. But Rebecca's called in sick. For the entire weekend. I can tell the difference between a sick sub and an upset one. I need to know what's going on."

Kyle's unspoken words hung in the air. *My club, my trainee, my responsibility.*

A flash of shock ran across Cal's face, then he hid the

emotion.

What the fuck is going on? It was painstakingly obvious that the prospect of not being with Rebecca upset his friend. The man looked as if he'd gotten a blow to the gut.

"She's got feelings for me," he gritted.

Kyle waited patiently, sensing there was more.

"Told me she loves me. During a scene," Cal said.

Kyle could tell Cal was trying be casual about it, but he heard the pain underneath. He cursed under his breath. Had it been a simple case of a sub idolizing her Master, he would have found her a different trainer. But it was obvious Cal had feelings for the woman just the same, which meant the issue was in the gray area where his club responsibility overlapped with people's private business.

"Sort it out, Kyle. Sooner rather than later." Not a request. "I'd hate to lose Rebecca, or you, for that matter."

* * * *

Rebecca rang the bell and Olivia, her best friend, opened the door. Rebecca was glad her friend didn't say anything, even though she looked horrible. She didn't need a mirror to know that her face was lined by exhaustion and her eyes were dull.

"Come in," Olivia said. "I'll make us a pot of mint tea."

Rebecca took off her coat and followed her friend into the kitchen. She put cups on a tray, along with the cookie tin Olivia handed her.

"Chocolate chip," she said.

Rebecca nodded, appreciating her thoughtful friend. After all, there was nothing like chocolate to comfort a woman's broken heart.

After they'd settled into comfy chairs with hot tea and cookies, Olivia said, "Talk to me, Becca."

Rebecca sighed. She didn't know where to begin. Her friend didn't know she was working at a BDSM club, let alone that she was playing there too.

"A while ago I started working for a club. A posh club," she started.

Olivia raised an eyebrow. "What kind of club?"

"A sex club."

Olivia sucked in a breath. "A sex club? You mean...you are...?"

Rebecca's laughter filled the room.

"Oh, Olivia, don't look so shocked! No, I am not having sex for money," she giggled. "I work at the office. And the reception desk on club nights."

Rebecca decided it was best to not tell Olivia it was a BDSM club. Her friend wasn't into kinky sex, and didn't know the first thing about BDSM.

"So you work at a sex club, a posh sex club, and you didn't tell me?" Olivia pouted. "I want to hear all the sexy stories you've got to tell! But right now I want to hear what's going on, Becca."

"I can't tell you all that much. I had to sign a confidentiality agreement," Rebecca said. "As for me, I met a man."

"But, of course," Olivia said dryly, a slight smile around her lips to tell Rebecca that part was painstakingly obvious.

"I...errr... I met him a while back. And I fell for him," Rebecca's said. Her heart ached and a sob welled up in her throat. "I love him, Olivia. I love him so much."

Tears ran down her face and she swallowed, trying to get control over her voice. "I told him I love him," she whispered, "and I know he loves me. I can feel it. But he didn't tell me he does. He just said I shouldn't force him."

She started crying now, and Olivia got up and held her friend in her arms. When Rebecca settled down again, they sat in silence for a while.

"The shit always hits the fan when a man enters the scene," Olivia mumbled.

Cal had entered the scene all right. Olivia wouldn't understand that pun, but Rebecca couldn't suppress a giggle. Olivia gave her a quizzical look.

"Nothing," Rebecca hastened to say. "An inside joke."

"Must be one hell of a joke!"

"Well, yes…I…you know…" Rebecca stammered.

"It's all right, girlfriend," Olivia said with a faint smile. "You don't have to tell me."

"It's a BDSM club. And he's my…a Master." Rebecca blurted.

Horror appeared in Olivia's eyes. "You mean…you like to get hurt? By some asshole? And you love him?"

"It's not like that, Livvy," Rebecca said softly. "I don't know how to explain."

Olivia made a face. "I'm not sure I want to know. The thought of some asshole hurting my friend makes my blood boil." Fire shot from her green eyes.

Rebecca sighed. "It really isn't like that."

For a few minutes, neither seemed to know what to say. They'd clearly bumped into an obstacle that was difficult to overcome. Explaining what BDSM was like to her vanilla friend wouldn't be easy, especially right now, when Olivia was angry and upset about it. Rebecca didn't know what to do. Her heart seemed to be torn to shreds because of her feelings for Cal, and not knowing if they were reciprocated. The fear of losing her best friend on top of that was too much. She started crying again.

"I don't want to lose you, too," she sobbed.

Olivia's eyes warmed and she grabbed her friend's hand and squeezed it. "You're not going to, Rebecca. So we have different tastes between the sheets. I'm not going to let that come between us," she said, then chuckled before she continued. "I suppose our sex talks will change, though."

Rebecca giggled. They had always talked about their sex lives, or lack thereof, in great detail. "You're the one who's missing out," she said, laughter in her voice.

Olivia smiled.

Rebecca got serious again. "I love him so much, Olivia," she whispered. "What the hell am I going to do?"

"Well, what would you do if a client came to you with this story?" Olivia asked. "The woman telling the guy she loves him, and the man not saying the words to her?

Rebecca's mouth dropped open. *How could I have been so stupid? Why is it so painstakingly obvious when it is about someone else, and so...so...damn confusing when it concerned me?*

"I would have told her to not press the matter. You cannot force someone to tell you he loves you. Nor should you expect someone to say those words when you say them yourself," she said. "Damn, how could I have been so blind? If you really love someone, you don't pressure them, you accept them the way they are."

Olivia nodded in agreement and added, "And, of course, you don't stay in a relationship that is one-sided. But you said you are sure he loves you, too. He basically just asked for time."

"Oh, my God." Rebecca sighed. Panic rose in her eyes. "What if I've ruined it? Pushed him away? Damn!"

She started to cry again and Olivia got up to pull Rebecca into her arms.

"If he really does love you, he will understand. He will forgive," she murmured in her hair. "You will have to talk to him, though. But you know that, Miss Counselor."

"I really hate counseling," Rebecca said dryly. "Thank you for listening, Olivia. I don't know what I would do without you!"

"Glad to have been of service, BFF," Olivia said solemnly.

* * * *

Rebecca was nervous as hell. A fortnight had gone by since she'd last seen Cal, and it had been a long two weeks. After her conversation with Olivia the week before, she had decided she wanted her Master back. Her heart and body ached to be with him. Whatever it would take, she wanted him. If he needed time, so be it. She'd wait. In the meantime, she wanted him to be her Master again.

Rebecca had come up with a plan, and she had needed

Kyle's help to set it up. Kyle had freed her of her receptionist duties, set the stage for her, and he'd made sure Cal would be at the club.

Tonight she would do a striptease for Cal. Her striptease would be for him solely, but she'd do it in public, as he had told her some weeks ago she would.

She had read up on how to go about it, as she was no striptease expert. From what she'd learned, she had to choose an outfit and lingerie that made her feel good.

'Forget about what the audience might like, a good striptease is about exuding confidence and sensuality.'

She had gone for a lace thong, garter belt and seam stockings. They absolutely made her feel sexy and confident.

A striptease meant layers of clothes, and she'd bought a short black wraparound skirt that she was wearing underneath a tight red cocktail dress. A beautiful black cape with a trail finished it off.

She'd put up her hair in a chignon, held with one large pin, and she'd spent a lot of time on her makeup. Dark long lashes, pouty red lips. When she looked herself over in the full-size mirror, she was really happy. She looked stunning. Excitement bubbled up in her core.

Time to get my Master back!

* * * *

Cal was walking around the dungeon, pretending to be interested in scenes. He wasn't in the best of moods. He had hoped to see Rebecca again, but she wasn't there. As soon as he'd seen another submissive behind the reception desk, his hope had gone out the window, taking his good mood with it. He had decided then and there he would go over to her house. This bullshit of avoiding him had to end. They needed to talk.

He couldn't leave right away, since Kyle had made it very clear he needed to see him. The bastard was nowhere to be found, though, so Cal was sauntering through the dungeon.

He'd give Kyle an hour. Then he'd be off.

Somewhere in the back of the dungeon lights got switched on and music started to play. A lot of people sat down around the scene area, Doms on chairs, subs in their laps or on cushions on the floor. Cal strolled over to see what was going on.

A door opened and Rebecca came out.

What the fuck?

Anger started to rise from his gut. *She's been here all along! Has Kyle found her another trainer?* If he saw her with another Master, he'd punch his lights out. Best he leave right now. Yet he found he couldn't. The sight of her had him nailed to the floor. He couldn't even drag his eyes off her, let alone move his feet. She looked gorgeous. Fucking stunning.

My woman!

A black velvet cape trailed behind her on the floor as she strode into the scene area. A sexy red cocktail dress hugged her every curve as her body moved sensually, undulating, hips swaying seductively. As the lush, deep pink light bathed her, she lifted her gaze and met Cal's eyes. A sexy smile pulled at her bright red lips and she fluttered her eyelashes at him, raised a gloved arm and blew him a kiss.

Her sultry gaze sent a shiver down his spine. No way was he going to leave. He was enthralled.

The sparkle in her gaze conveyed she was more than happy that he was there. *So am I, baby!* His heart was thumping in his chest as he took her in. Her nipples had hardened, her breathing was fast, her lips slightly apart. *Gorgeous!* She began to move again, and his gaze glued to her body as she sensually danced across the area, undid the cape and let it pool to the ground behind her. She stood still, one foot in front of the other, and circled her hips in figure-eights. She dropped her head, exposing the delicate curve of her throat, and trailed the backs of her fingers up over the sides of her neck, then down again over the swell of her breasts. Cal swallowed when she looked at him from under her eyelashes as she erotically moved her hands down over her waist and swaying hips.

Cal's cock sprang to life. He had an overwhelming urge to drag Rebecca from the area by her hair and fuck her brains out. Instead, he sat down at the edge. *Isn't it peculiar that there is one empty chair still? In spite of the considerable crowd that mostly has to stand to watch the show? Kyle is a meddling bastard for sure!*

Rebecca swayed and twirled, running her hands over body, giving him sultry looks.

Cal imagined it was his hands, and when their eyes locked again, sparks flew across the area. He caught her soft moan and his cock jerked. The spell was broken when she turned around and strode to a Dom across from him. The way her ass jiggled under the tight dress made his mouth water. She bent over, showing the Dom her cleavage, while showing Cal her wiggling ass.

Jealousy stabbed through him. *Damn, the fucking Dom is looking at her tits!* He growled when Rebecca twirled around, moved her sexy ass in circles over the Dom's lap, then moved on to another Dom. She danced before that Dom, but her eyes kept locking with Cal's. He understood her message — she'd strip publicly, but she'd do it for his eyes only. Nevertheless, he growled when she pulled the Dom to his feet and turned around in front of him while putting his hands on her shoulders. She cast a sexy look over her shoulder, offering the Dom her back, asking him without words to unzip her dress. Her body moved sensually and she kept her eyes on Cal, then winked at him as the Dom teased the zipper all the way down to her butt. She held up the dress with her hands, danced away and blew a kiss to the Dom who had helped her.

Cal almost jumped up to deck the man. He might have done so if it wasn't for the fact that Rebecca came undulating toward him, then turned her back to him. She wiggled her butt as she looked at him over her shoulder and smiled. She twirled around with swaying hips and pretended to drop the dress, her mouth a big, sexy 'O'. She caught it with one hand, and the dress seemed to linger on the curve of her breasts, as if the fabric was kept in place by her jutting nipples only.

She gracefully raised her free arm as she danced around, circling her ass over his lap. Taunting him. She straightened, dropped her head back and pulled out the hairpin. Her long, brown hair tumbled down right in front of Cal's face and the sweet scent of roses filled his nostrils.

She'd sprayed her hair with perfume.

"Goddamn temptress," he said for her ears only.

Her husky giggle set his core alight. She straightened as gracefully as a ballet dancer and, as she spun around to face him, she finally let go of her dress, her arms up in the air.

He sucked in a breath as the garment pooled around her feet, revealing her full breasts. Red heart-shaped sequin nipple covers glistened as the light caught them.

Nipple covers. Fucking sexy! She sure as hell put the tease in striptease. His erection was having serious problems in his leathers.

Rebecca lowered her gaze as she struck a sexy pose, and stood still so he could feast his eyes. His smoldering eyes seared her skin as his gaze slowly ran from her breasts, down over her stomach, the very short wraparound skirt, her sexy legs and feet, and up again. Lingering at her breasts. Devouring her. Their eyes met, and the fire in his gaze sent a jolt through her body, straight to her pussy. A husky moan broke from her lips.

"Soon, subbie, very soon." His low, deep voice made her insides quiver.

Forcing herself to continue, she twirled, making the short wraparound skirt billow around her, giving him, and her audience, sneak peeks of her round ass. When Cal reached out to touch her, she quickly danced away, casting him saucy looks. She made arousing, sensuous moves in front of other Doms, keeping her eyes on Cal whenever she could.

I'm dancing for you and only you!

When she'd danced back to him, Rebecca put her right foot between his legs, the point of her high-heeled shoe almost touching his balls. He looked at her and lifted an eyebrow.

"Don't push me too far, sub."

She caught the barely audible words, pouted her lips in reply and blew him a kiss. A devilish smile pulled at his lips and she almost lost her momentum.

"Wolf Man," she mumbled.

Amusement flickered in his eyes and she blushed.

Her hand trembled slightly when she slipped it under the garter of her bent leg and slowly pulled out a condom in a red wrapper. She held out her palm with the condom in it. The promise in his gaze made her pussy throb and her legs quiver. He took the condom from her without releasing her eyes.

"Dance for me, baby," he said softly. Rebecca swallowed hard. Her body suddenly seemed heavy under his dark gaze. Somehow, she managed to snap out of it, and curled her fingers around the end of the long string that held up her wraparound skirt. With the words "If you please, Sir," she handed it to Cal. As he pulled on it, she started spinning away from him, and as if he was unwrapping her, the skirt fell to the ground.

All she was wearing now were the red arm gloves, stockings and garter belt, a red thong, the sequin nipple covers and ridiculously high-heeled shoes.

Murmurs of approval rose from the audience, but all that mattered to her was Cal's grunt. Slowly she approached him and lifted his chin with her finger. She leaned forward as if she was going to kiss him, then lightly pushed his head back.

His eyes told her she was seriously pushing her luck and in for a good spanking. Sparks of desire zinged across her nerves. She *wanted* to feel his hard hand on her ass. A low laugh rumbled through his chest. Her cheeks burned. *He knows?*

Damn mind-reading Master! As quickly as her high-heeled feet could carry her, she floated toward the other side of the scene area.

Time to end her little show. The many eyes that were feasting on her body were becoming too much. Her pussy was on fire and she was so very wet. She ached to feel Cal on her, groping and fondling with his hard hands, devouring her with his lips, and plundering her pussy with his large thick cock. A heady need rose from her core.

This last bit would take all her guts. She had made sure the area was bathed in a deep pink light as that would set off her body beautifully. It would soften her skin and emphasize her curves in the best possible way. Knowing that gave her more confidence, but in spite of it her body trembled. She drew in a deep breath.

You can do it!

As she kept her eyes on Cal, she kneeled gracefully, then lowered her gaze to the bulge in his groin, suggestively licking her lips. His low growl pleased her no end.

She put her hands on the floor, lifted her eyes to meet his. Then something inside her shifted. She was no longer a nervous woman trying to please her man, but a sexy panther goddess who knew what she wanted. She started to crawl toward him, slow, graceful and sensuous, like a tigress on the prowl.

The room fell quiet as she moved, deliberately pushing her hips out and making sure her breasts swayed.

When she got to him, Rebecca sat up, her bottom on her heels, thighs slightly apart. She pulled the arm gloves off with her teeth and let them drop to the floor. As she looked him in the eye, she cupped her hands under her breasts and lifted them.

"I'm yours, Master," she said shakily, suddenly insecure and afraid he'd reject her.

Her heart was hammering in her chest as she sat there, offering herself to him. Waiting and praying he would accept her.

For long minutes he didn't say a word, just held her pinned with the power in his eyes. The dungeon had gone completely quiet, as if everyone was holding their breath.

Slowly he got up from his chair and towered over her. "Stand up, sub." A harsh command, no warmth in his voice.

Rebecca scrambled to her feet, her heart thumping in her chest. She glanced up, trying to read his black eyes, only to find she couldn't. They were level. Ruthless.

Her heart sank into her stomach and she tried to hide a shiver of fear. *Oh, my God, please, no! Please, don't send me away!*

"The striptease deal was naked," he said in a level voice. He carefully peeled off the nipple covers and tossed them aside. He grabbed her thong in his hands and simply tore it apart. Rebecca gasped as the ruined piece of lace floated to the floor.

Cal straightened, fisted his hand in her hair and pulled back her head. There was nothing gentle about his movements, nor his words when he growled, "Your training is over."

He let go of her hair and she almost lost her balance. Tears blurred her vision. It was over. He had dumped her. Publicly.

"Hold out your hands."

Rebecca automatically complied, her bottom lip quivering as she choked on her sobs. She felt sick to her stomach. She just wanted to go home now, curl up into a ball and cry.

The touch of soft leather around her wrist almost made her jump. She blinked the tears from her eyes and looked down. While she was wallowing in misery, he had put a black leather wrist cuff on her. As she watched him, dumbfounded, he put the other one on. The bold silver lettering on them read *Master Cal's Rebecca*.

Her breath caught and she tried to swallow the lump in her throat. He'd had cuffs made especially for her. Her heart jumped for joy.

"Now, you're mine."

A sigh of relief rippled through the audience.

"Thank you, Master." Her voice was but a mere whisper, as she was overwhelmed by emotion. Happiness filled her core when she looked up at him. The dominant look in his smoldering eyes took her breath away. He curled a hand around her throat.

"Don't ever try to force me to do or say something, Rebecca." The power in his deep, low voice made her knees buckle.

"I'm s-so s-sorry, M-master," she stammered.

"You will be punished accordingly, lil' sub." His low-voiced threat sent a shiver down her spine. Cal gave her a wicked smile before he continued, "But, first, we'll finish what you started. Are you ready for the second part of the striptease deal?"

Rebecca remembered his words. *I will bend you over and fuck you hard until you come, screaming.'*

Her pussy clenched and excitement welled up inside her.

"On your knees, sub, and crawl to the middle. I want you in the spotlight," he said softly.

She started crawling, fully aware that her ass and pussy were exposed to him as he walked behind her. It was embarrassing as hell, but it turned up the heat in her core. Her skin tingled as if touched by him, and her swaying breasts suddenly seemed full and heavy.

By the time she got to the middle of the scene area she was soaking wet.

Before she could get in a kneeling position, he growled, "Stay on your hands and knees."

He took his place behind her, unzipped and sheathed himself in a condom.

"Brace yourself, subbie," he said, his voice thick with lust. Without further warning, he buried himself to the root inside her. His bellow drowned out her scream. Her swollen tissues struggled to accommodate the thick cock that stretched her and filled her completely. Cal bent over her, wrapped her hair around his wrist and pulled her head back so she had to look at their audience.

"Let's give them something to watch," Cal murmured. Her pussy clamped down on him and he hammered into her.

The head of his cock hit her hard, again and again, and the pain zinged straight to her insanely throbbing clit.

The tension and nerves about a public striptease, and the accumulating arousal while doing it, mingled with the sweet pain that shot from her cervix and coiled into a hot, white ball of fire. It coiled tighter and tighter, until the pressure got too high and it exploded violently, sending searing flames through her body.

"Yesss, oohhh, Cal!"

He growled when she screamed his name as she came, riding the tidal waves that shook her body.

"Mine, you are mine," he groaned.

He angled his cock differently and thrust into her sweet spot. Her wail filled the area. Over and over he slammed into her with deep, hard thrusts, stimulating that oh-so-sensitive spot deep inside her pussy. Instant heat flooded her core and her clit pulsed back to life, even as her vagina was still spasming from her first orgasm.

"Nooo…oooohh…no!"

"'Yes, Master, more' would be better, sub," Cal said. "Beg me for more."

He pulled her head back a bit farther to let her know he was in full control. He thrust his cock balls-deep into her cunt, hitting her cervix painfully. A shrill cry came from her lips and turned into a protesting moan as he held still, his shaft fully sheathed inside her, impaling her.

A sob welled up in her throat. Her pussy full, dominated and controlled by his large, thick cock, his hand forcing her head back by her hair. Too much. She couldn't move, could only take all he gave and give all he took. All control and choice taken from her. God, she wanted this. She needed this so, so much.

"More! Please take more, Master!" Her plea wasn't much more than a whisper. Tears dropped from her eyes. "Take all of me, please!"

Cal's growl made her pussy clench and his cock jerked in reply. As she felt the tiny movement against her cervix, something inside her snapped. Brutal pleasure raged through her as she came. Her vagina pulsed around the cock that gave her so much joy, her clit throbbed wildly and her nipples hardened to add to the magical buzz. A cry of inexplicable joy escaped from her lips as jolts of electricity seared through her center, again and again, until the currents seemed to shoot out of her every pore. Her entire body tingled and spasmed.

Her arm muscles were about to give in, and she was more than happy to sag on the ground. But before she could, her Master curved his hands around her hips in an unyielding grip. She was yanked onto his cock, and he started pounding into her with fast thrusts. The way he took her for his own pleasure woke up a weird desire inside her. The desire to simply be fucked by her man, hard and ruthless. Just like he was doing, fucking her caveman-style. The slick slide of his cock, combined with the sounds he made, made her head spin and her entire pussy throb. She couldn't stop a long wail of pleasure from escaping her lips. His loud roar echoed in her ears when he emptied himself inside her cunt, and as his cock jerked against her cervix, she came again.

Warmth enveloped her, soft and fuzzy on one side, hard and solid on the other. A blanket and Cal's chest. Her heart swelled with joy. She had her Master back. Better yet, he really was her Master now, not her trainer anymore. Rebecca opened her eyes, blinked to focus and looked at the cuffs around her wrists. *Master Cal's Rebecca.* She sighed happily and looked up at him. His black eyes sparked with possessiveness.

"Are you sure, baby?" he asked softly.

Rebecca managed a nod.

Cal put his fingers under her chin and lifted her face a bit more. "I hope you haven't bitten off more than you can chew," he mumbled. "I'm not an easy man."

She grinned. "I've got quite the appetite."

"So I noticed," he said dryly, and chuckled when her face turned a lovely pink. He ran the backs of his fingers over her cheek and nuzzled the top of her head, inhaling her rose perfume. "You're so goddamn sexy and cute."

Rebecca giggled. "Headline news — Wolf Man disarmed by Rebecca."

"Keep at it like this, and the headlines will read, 'Rebecca impaled by Wolf Man!'"

In spite of her burning cheeks, she giggled, as she said, "Uh-uh! You just…fired your gun. You can't."

"Don't count on it, sweetie." Cal moved his hips forward and she felt his erection. Rebecca's jaw dropped in disbelief.

"No way," she said under her breath.

His low laugh sent shivers down her spine. "Just how a Master likes to see his sub. Tongue-tied, shocked and impressed by her Master's firepower." Suddenly his eyes were hot and hungry. "And since you're claiming to be a big eater, I may feed you my cock."

She gasped, and even though the crude words shocked her, a spark of lust lit in her core, making her feel shy and aroused at the same time. Quickly she averted her gaze, not wanting him to see her feelings. She didn't want him to see just how much it turned her on. As if some inner voice was screaming, *'you bad, dirty girl'*. Judgment. Rejection. She shied away from that. And she certainly didn't want to share it with anyone else.

Cal sounded his disapproval. "No hiding, Becca." The steel in his soft voice shook her. Would she ever get used to this powerful man?

Don't play with the Wolf Man, Rebecca! He'll eat you alive!

She complied and looked up at him. The approval in his eyes melted her spine. His gaze warmed and he ran his fingers through her hair. His touch was breathtaking and erotic, the expression on his face so intense that her cheeks got warm.

"God, I love you!" he murmured, and took her mouth,

slow at first, softly nibbling her bottom lip, then he swept in.

Her head spun. *He loves me! He said it!* She felt it in his kiss. Her eyes filled with tears. Happy tears. Cal let go of her mouth.

"For fuck's sake, woman, I don't want to drown when I kiss you," he said, his voice hoarse with emotion. He gently wiped away her tears. Rebecca wrapped her arms around his neck and plastered herself against him.

"I love you so much, Cal," she whispered.

"I love you, too, Becca," he said softly in her hair, and held her close in his strong arms.

After long minutes he said, "You best love your Master, as well, lil' subbie."

She giggled and pushed herself up. "Or else?"

Cal chuckled. "You'll be in deep shit, cheeky thing!"

Rebecca pulled at the black chest hair that peeked through the opening of his shirt. Mischief bubbled up inside her, and she knew it showed in her eyes when she looked at him, a smile tugging at her lips.

"I'll take my chances. Sir." She couldn't keep the giggle from escaping her lips.

"Tonight, your wish is my command, my love." The hunger in his dark eyes set her core on fire. "Just remember it was your own wish when you can't sit for a week."

A week? She blinked, for a split-second thinking — hoping — he was kidding. But the gleam in his gaze trashed that hope. A shiver ran down her spine.

Oh, damn! I'm in deep shit!

"No, Sir, Master, please!" she begged. She could enjoy a mild spanking, but she sensed that tonight he'd demand more, and she knew his hard hand was very…hard.

Without paying heed, he lifted her off his lap, got up and tossed her over his shoulder. She yelled and pleaded all the way to the private theme room.

Cal slammed the door of the theme room shut behind him. He'd gone for the red and gold room. He put Rebecca down, turned her around and pulled her back against his hard chest. She looked around. Mostly red and gold with a few touches of black. A spanking bench with dark oak legs and red leather padding stood over to one side, a plush red chair without armrests to the other. A selection of whips, paddles and floggers hung neatly arranged on one wall. The room was dominated by a huge Medieval four-poster bed. Thick velveteen red and gold drapes hung off the four corners. Having seen the multitude of solid steel rings on the walls and rafters, Rebecca was quite sure the four-poster would sport them as well, carefully hidden by the drapes.

As she took it all in, he whispered in her ear, "The room totally befits a love couple."

She snorted. "Looks more like your wolf's den."

"Wolf dens are for delivering babies. I'm more interested in mating." His low, husky voice made her core pulse. "Rough mating."

Cal started fondling her breasts, kneading and squeezing them the way she liked so much.

"You know how wolves mate, Becca? It's quite sexy," he whispered, and started pressing little kisses under her ear. He licked around her ear and goosebumps rose on her skin. When he swept his tongue inside her ear, she moaned. "That's right, my sexy she-wolf, foreplay is part of a wolf's mating ritual. An Alpha wolf doesn't fuck his bitch until she's in serious need. Before he takes her, they bond and touch each other more and more and more."

Rebecca's heart rate sped up as he walked the talk and moved his hands over her body as he spoke. Caressing, squeezing, pinching. Arousing. Her head fell back against his chest and little sounds of pleasure came from her slightly parted lips.

"They make whining noises." Cal pulled her nipples, and she whined. "Yes, just like that, my little bitch. The Alpha sometimes puts his legs around her neck to flirt and claim his mate." Her spine melted when he curved his hand around her throat, and she moaned.

"See, works like a charm," he said, breathing heavy in her ear. "The bitch and the Alpha mouth each other, touch noses and bump their bodies together." He nuzzled her cheek and rubbed his erection against her bottom.

"Cal...please," Rebecca pleaded. "I need you...in me."

"Mating rituals don't go that fast, sweetheart," he mumbled against the sensitive curve of her neck. "A wolf woos his bitch, flirts...touches...smells...nibbles."

He buried his face in the crook of her neck.

"I love your rose perfume," he whispered, breathing heavily.

Then he ran his tongue in hot, wet traces over her neck, to her shoulder, and he nipped her there. She sucked in a breath as the tiny pain zinged across her nerves to her pussy, making her clit throb. Cal circled her and she had to put her head in her neck to look him in the eyes. Her whole being yearned for him. His control, his love and his touch. The pull was so strong it was almost painful. Without breaking eye contact, he got down in front of her.

"Then the Alpha wolf will smell her genital region to check if she's ready to be taken." He leaned in and smelled her pussy, inhaling deeply. "I can smell your arousal, lil' subbie. I think you are ready, but wolves lick their tongues in and out of their bitches to be sure. Spread your legs so your Wolf Man can taste your cunt."

Rebecca moaned as she complied. She was starting to feel light-headed. His words and touches were so erotic, so hot, that all her inhibitions got burned from her mind. All that remained was the fire in her lower belly, the throbbing of her pussy and clit.

Tremors shot through her when he lapped over her swollen nub, and she bucked her hips to get more. He just kept lapping, enough to start a blazing inferno, not enough to quench the flames.

"More, my goodness, Cal, more!" She instinctively tangled her hands in his hair in an attempt to make him lick harder, to suck her clit, and to give her the relief her body so needed.

A whine escaped her when he didn't give her that release. Instead he groaned and flicked his tongue in and out of her vagina.

"You taste so damned good!" he whispered against her pussy.

When he finally pulled back, he replaced his tongue with a finger, then two. Her legs started to tremble as he pumped his fingers in and out.

"Definitely ready to be fucked," he mumbled, sounding hoarse. "You know wolves stay connected for half an hour after he's come inside her? Maybe I should fuck you for half an hour, and make you come again and again and again, so you have an idea what it's like to be taken by a Wolf Man."

The vision blurred her mind and her clit jolted.

"Unfortunately, I want you so much, there's no way I can fuck your hot, wet pussy that long without emptying my balls inside you."

He pulled his fingers out of her and stood. He slid his wet fingers over her lips.

"Taste yourself, sweetling. Lick your nectar off my fingers."

She eagerly did what she was told and looked him in the eye as she lapped and licked, then she sucked his fingers into her mouth like she would his shaft.

He groaned and pushed her to her knees, lowered his zipper and took out his cock. The head was covered with precum.

"I'm going to feed you my cock and take that hot mouth covered with your pussy juices. Pleasure me, sub." He fisted his erection and pushed it through her willingly opening lips.

Rebecca closed her mouth around him and swirled her tongue around the swollen head of his dick. She sucked on it, making it swell even more. His low groan urged her on, and as she cupped his balls in her hand, gently kneading, she took more of him in.

God, he filled her up, whether he took her pussy or her mouth. She took it slow, and dragged her teeth over the silky soft skin that covered the solid steel beneath when she moved her head up. More suction on the tip. She loved a good cock with a mushroom head, and thoroughly enjoyed making it swell. It turned her on and her pussy got wetter and wetter.

A deep, husky growl rumbled through his chest. "Damn, you love giving head, don't you?" he asked in a gravelly voice. She giggled in her throat, and eagerly licked the sensitive frenulum at the underside of his cock. Tremors shook him. She purred, loving that she could arouse him, and that right now she controlled him with her mouth. Her gaze met his as she sucked him in again.

Comprehension shone in his eyes and he fisted his hand in her hair.

"You're mouth-fucking your Alpha male, woman." His unspoken 'Don't mistake who's in control of who' hung in the air. His powerful gaze was overwhelming and she wanted to swallow, but she couldn't with his large shaft in her mouth.

A corner of his mouth turned up. "That's right, girl. A good Alpha female obeys her Alpha male, so be a good bitch and take the whole of your Wolf Man's cock in your mouth. Every inch of me."

His jarring words and ruthless look in his black eyes made her pussy water and her clit ache. Her muffled mewl mingled with his low laugh. The bastard knew exactly how she felt. She thought he'd already taken everything she had to give. How wrong she'd been. Right now he was taking even more, and she willingly, eagerly, let him. Needed him to take her, use her, devour her. She knew he'd always find new ways to take more, that he would push her limits over and over again. God knew she loved it, loved him. Her Master, her man.

A slight movement of his hips pushed his shaft deeper into her mouth. Slowly, she started to suck him in, inch by inch. She flattened the back of her tongue to suppress the gag reflex, and managed to take his full length in her mouth. His cock jerked when the head touched the back of her throat. She moved up and down over his shaft, sucking hard as she moved down until he was again sheathed in her mouth, swirling her tongue over the tip and his frenulum when she'd moved up.

Cal tangled his hand in her hair and rolled his hips in synch, thrusting until he hit the back of her throat, taking complete possession of her mouth.

"That's it, baby. Pleasure me with your hot, hungry mouth." His leg muscles hardened and he threw his head back. His deep, husky groan filled the room. Her body responded to his arousal with an electric jolt through her core. When she next moved up over his shaft, he pulled himself out of her mouth and yanked her to her feet.

The sudden action had her off-kilter. Had she done something wrong?

"Master?" she whispered.

"You're entirely too good with that sexy mouth," he grunted, and took possession of her lips. He pushed in with his tongue, found hers, tangled with it, demanding a reply. He took her mouth so hungrily and fiercely that her legs turned to jelly and she had to cling to him.

When he finally let go, he pulled back her head. "You were trying to make me come, and trying to control me with your mouth. I think my sub needs to be punished for that."

"B-but, S-sir...you said..." she stammered.

"I said to pleasure me, yes," he said. "I didn't say 'make me come', though, did I?"

How the hell was she supposed to know what 'pleasure me' meant? Any man would want to come. But he wasn't any man. *Damn him.*

Amusement flickered in his eyes. "You should've asked."

"This is like walking a goddamn minefield," she muttered, and glared at him.

"It's called 'mind games', my love," he whispered against her mouth, and nibbled her bottom lip. "I did warn you that you might have bitten off more than you could chew."

"Maybe I should have bitten," she said.

"Sassy lil' thing, aren't you?" he replied, and his eyes glistened dangerously when he added, "Not to worry, your punishment will sort that out."

Rebecca gasped when he slid his hand to her ass, kneading it. A promise of what punishment she was to get.

"No, Master, please, no!"

He grinned at her, allowing her to see the merciless look in his eyes. Tremors of fear and need shook her.

"Aahh, my little sub is scared of her Wolf Man now," he said softly, as he ran the backs of his fingers over her cheeks. "But I think my wolf bitch is still in heat, isn't she?"

Without further ado he reached between her legs, and he ruthlessly pushed two fingers inside her. A soft whine passed her lips. "Yes, very much in heat. But before you get your seeing-to, you will have to receive your punishment. You want to stop, Becca?"

Rebecca's entire body was trembling with need. His harsh words kept poking up the fire that now was white-hot, scorching her. It needed quenching. She knew he was going to spank her hard, would probably make her cry, but she wanted it nonetheless. Just being taken wouldn't be enough to douse the fire inside her. She needed more.

"No, I don't want to stop," she said breathy.

Without breaking eye contact, he put his dick back in his leathers and zipped up, grimacing as he confined his unbelievably hard cock. A second later, she was dangling facedown over his lap, restrained by his leg over her ankles, and his left hand on her upper back. *How the hell does he always move so fast?* A shiver of fear and lust ran through her when he pushed her legs as far apart as he could without losing his grip on her. Rebecca's heart rate sped up as she expected the first slap. Instead, he gently caressed her ass.

"You know the flesh of your ass shakes when I slap it?"

he murmured. "And seeing that, just that, turns me on. The sound of my hand hitting your flesh makes my balls tighten and hearing your screams makes my cock swell and ache. Seeing how you love it, love taking the pain for me, damn near makes me come."

Hearing Cal tell her what effect a spanking had on him sent a jolt through her clit and her pussy clenched.

Smack!

Her ass was slapped again and again. He wasn't hitting her very hard yet. She knew this was just a prelude of what was to come. Right now he was only warming her skin. The real spanking would start when her skin had turned a nice pink. Then he'd slap her harder. And he did.

Smack!

Rebecca yelped.

Smack! Another hard swat. And another one. Her vision blurred. The swats made her belly get soft, softer, expanding, opening up, freeing her. Fluffy clouds carried her higher and higher.

She wailed when he suddenly thrust two fingers in her soaking-wet pussy and started a steady rhythm.

"You want more?" he asked, sounding very hoarse.

"Yes, please, Master."

Smack!

He had slapped the sensitive underside of her ass, then swatted both ass cheeks hard. She jerked on his lap and cried out.

Cal rammed his fingers in her pussy and sounded his approval. "You're very wet, darling. Are you ready to receive your punishment now?"

"Yes, Master," she sobbed.

"Good lil' sub," he murmured.

Time ceased to exist as he slapped her ass and played with her pussy, bringing her close to orgasm, only to slap her ass again and again until her entire lower body glowed, throbbing and aching. Both were on another plane of existence, totally sucked into the scene and the fire that was raging in their bodies.

Just when she thought she couldn't take anymore, he asked, "Ready for the last one, Rebecca?"

Her hazy brain could barely process the question.

"Yes, Master." Her words came out slurred.

He hummed, but instead of giving her the last swat, he started playing with her pussy again, thrusting in and out with his fingers, circling her clit, until she was wailing, begging, aching for him to let her come.

Then he slapped her ass. And she came. Hard. While screaming his name.

* * * *

Rebecca floated through the room with her eyes closed and landed on her back on a soft surface. She was still in subspace and enjoying the afterglow of her orgasms.

She sensed Cal around her, his aura encompassing her. She smiled lazily and mumbled his name. He caressed her cheeks with soft fingers.

"My love," he whispered.

When she finally managed to open her eyes, his were directly above her. Love and fire shone in them. She sucked in a breath as his gaze burned through her. Her nipples blossomed to life.

She started to reach up to stroke the face of the man she loved so much, only to find she couldn't move her arms. Sheer instinct made her try again, to no avail. Then the realization sank in that he had cuffed her to the four-poster. The corners of his mouth curved up.

"I like to see you helpless. Helpless and horny is even better," he whispered.

He vanished from her sight and she found herself looking at the reflection of her naked body in a king-size mirror on the ceiling. A shock ran through her and she gasped.

Cal chuckled.

"We're not done yet, baby." The lustful sound in his voice

woke her body.

God, would she ever get enough of him? One look, a sound, a touch, and she was ready for him again.

Before her still dazed mind allowed her to react, he had bound her legs with drapes from the four-poster and pulled them up in the air, angled slightly toward the wall. She watched him as he double-checked that the drapes weren't cutting off her blood flow. Feasting her eyes on his wide shoulders, the rippling muscles. *God, he's gorgeous.*

Her ass was lifted as he put a wedged cushion under it, and her pussy tilted up.

"Ready for my use," he mumbled. "And use, I will."

He leaned over her, his hands next to her head, and bent to kiss her sweet lips. When he let go of her mouth and spoke, his voice was raspy. "I want to take you bareback, Rebecca. We're both clean, are you okay with that?"

Lust and greed flowed through her. *Damn right she wanted that! All of him.*

"Yes! I want it all!" Her voice sounded smoky.

"Greedy woman!" he panted. "I'll shoot every single drop deep in that tight little pussy of yours. I've been hard for you for so long now, it's going to be a lot."

He leaned in and took his time to taste her mouth, plunging in deep and igniting a blazing fire in her core. She arched her chest, wanting friction on her nipples. He released her lips, put his mouth over her left nipple, and simply sucked it into his mouth, hard. She whined and tried to wriggle her hips to counter the sweet pain. Jolts raced over her nerves to her clit.

"Cal, oh, God, Cal, please! Please!" She almost screamed her need at him.

Her eyes were glued to him, and when he moved up to look at her nipple she followed his gaze. Her breath caught when she saw the long, swollen peak. The sight was so arousing a heatwave flooded her like a tsunami.

He glanced at her and her cheeks burned. She didn't want him to see how much the visual turned her on. The smile that pulled at his lips told her he did know. Then he broke the eye contact and put his lips around her nipple again. He pulled strongly while swirling his tongue over the crest.

Rebecca writhed as pain shot out from the tortured peak and mingled with the fire in her lower body, making her pussy so very, very wet. Just as she thought she couldn't take much more, he let go.

"Damn, you're beautiful, woman. So hot and totally fuckable," he said with a hoarse voice. "Look in the mirror, babe. Look at your sexy body while I please myself with it."

As her gaze rose to the mirror, he captured her right nipple in his mouth. A shot of lust seared through her when she saw her own reflection. Her legs up in the air, arms cuffed, his dark head over her breast, sucking her nipple hard while he toyed with the other one with his fingers. She almost came.

"Ooh damn…Cal, please," she begged, words coming out slurred. "I need you so much it hurts."

Cal's heavy-lidded gaze caught hers. "I know, baby. I'm hurting, too."

He swung his body from the bed, yanked off all his clothes, got back onto the four poster and he rose above her. His chest hair grazed her tortured nipples while his cock dragged over her swollen, wet tissues. They both groaned.

"I should really take you from behind, like a wolf takes his bitch." His voice was thick with lust. "But I want to look at you when I shoot my seed deep in your belly. I want to see your breasts shake when I pound into you, and hear every mewl and cry that comes from your sweet lips when my cock fills your cunt."

His words made her whimper, and her pussy clenched, aching for him to fill her completely.

"You're going to keep your eyes on the mirror, every single second, you understand, sub? You're going to watch how I plunder you, and how I make you writhe and moan underneath me."

Rebecca didn't trust her voice, so she nodded and sucked

in a shaky breath. If he kept talking like this, she was going to orgasm spontaneously.

Cal fisted his cock and rubbed the head over the sides of her clit, making her moan and beg.

"Before I'm through, I want to hear you scream your love for your Master." He slid his cock to her entrance and swirled through her juices. "Are you ready to be fucked by your Wolf Man, Rebecca?"

"Yesss, please!"

Cal rammed his cock in her pussy so deep, she screamed and threw back her head.

"Mirror," he growled.

She looked in the mirror, and embarrassment washed through her as she watched how he took her, hard. But within two of his deep thrusts, it turned into a dark, forbidden pleasure, so hot, and incredibly arousing. Every wanton urge woke as she watched his solid frame over her body. The way his ass muscles tightened each time he hammered his cock into her, how her breasts shook when he did. He just took her like an animal would take his bitch. A whine broke from her lips and her pussy clamped down on his shaft.

She was beyond desire. The need to plummet over the euphoric precipice of release was undeniable, unavoidable.

"That's it, baby, that's it," he panted. "Watch how I plunder your body. My body, you're mine. Tell me you're mine."

"Yes! Yesss, I'm yours... Take me... More. More!"

As he rammed balls-deep into her, she came violently.

"Yesss! Ooohhh! I love you!"

Her entire body convulsed as the heat in her core exploded and pushed up tongues of fire that raced over her nerves, searing her flesh. Sheer ecstasy pulsed through her in waves, shattering her mind.

"That's it, baby, enjoy my cock," he groaned through gritted teeth.

He kept pounding into her, right through her orgasm.

"Next time tell me you love your Master." His voice rough with lust and need. "Eyes. Mirror."

Still hazy from orgasm, Rebecca's lifted her gaze to the mirror again. Seeing, and feeling, how he took her without mercy, ruthless, just plundering and ravishing her, started another fire, its heat vying with the one that had just been quenched.

She saw herself with glazed-over eyes and sheer lust on her face as he fucked her animal-style. Her wildly shaking breasts made her pussy clamp down on the hard cock inside her.

Then he slapped her breast and a long whine welled up in her throat. She arched her chest in a silent plea for more. And he gave it to her, again and again.

Sounds of excruciating pleasure echoed through the room. She vaguely realized the shrill cries were her own. They mingled with his low growls and the burning heat in her pussy turned into a roaring fire. She was so close, almost to the point of no return. Her clit throbbed insanely. Then he grabbed her hips, yanked her onto his cock and pounded deep into her cunt, just taking. His rough action sent her over the edge.

"Ooohhh... I love you, Master! Oooh, yessss!"

Brutal, hot pleasure seared through her. Waves of sheer ecstasy flooded her like a tsunami. Then his wolf-like roar rumbled through the roam as he came inside her. Her clit pulsed in response to her man's need. His last hard thrusts made her whimper. Her pussy clenched around his hard cock, milking him as he rode the aftershocks out of her. Slowly she started spiraling down, totally spent and sated.

Cal collapsed on top of her.

"Every...fucking...drop," he panted in her ear. "I love you so much, Rebecca."

Chapter Eleven

Three months had gone by since Cal had told her he loved her. Rebecca was happy, and it was obvious he was too. Her heart had jumped for joy when he'd started talking about moving in together. Cal had told her he wanted her around him every day. To wake up each morning beside the woman he loved. And, of course, to have her lush body available to him whenever the Dom inside him felt like it.

Rebecca had pouted when he'd said that, at which he'd just grinned.

"You want your Master just as bad as I want my sub, Becca!" he had said.

She had glared at him, because, as per usual, he was right. It was good to be with a man who knew her so well, but sometimes it was too close for comfort.

Yet, when he had directly asked her to move in, Rebecca had been hesitant and had asked for a bit more time. Thank goodness Cal had not pushed the matter. He had nodded, his face unreadable, and told her he only wanted her to move in if she was ready for it and truly willing.

But, nevertheless, she felt his growing impatience concerning the issue. She also knew Cal wouldn't wait forever. He wasn't the kind of man to want a half-hearted relationship. He wanted it all.

That wasn't really a problem for her, Rebecca wanted that too. The difference was, she needed more than just living together. She knew in her heart that Cal was the man she wanted to grow old with. Moving in with him would be wonderful. But she didn't want to be just his girlfriend. She wanted to be his wife. And he hadn't talked about marriage, let alone proposed. Rebecca knew he had been disappointed in the past, but so had she. If he hadn't enough faith in her — in them — to be willing to make a complete commitment, she wasn't sure she was going to remain happy in the long run. Yet, she knew she couldn't end things with Cal, either. Their bond and love ran way too deep. She was stuck.

Another month went by, and Cal had been really grumpy a couple of times when she'd had to go home. His discontent had started to become apparent during their scenes as well. It seemed as if he was hurting. She didn't really understand, and normally she would try to talk to him about it. But she was too confused herself to raise the issue. Again.

Rebecca realized she had to do something or she would lose him. *If he isn't going to propose marriage, I will!*

Just the thought send a shiver down her spine. That was so bold. And not how she'd wanted to start a marriage either. She'd always dreamed about being proposed to, preferably in a very romantic way. Could she live with having to do it herself? Or would she blame him for the rest of their life for not proposing to her, and making her do it? Provided they had a 'rest of their life'. He could, after all, still decline.

Rebecca simply wasn't sure. But if she didn't act, things would only get worse between them.

She sighed. *Oh, well.* Even though she was in two minds, she knew that deep down she'd already made the decision. She was going to do the guy-thing and propose to her man. Her Master.

Before she could change her mind, she grabbed her bag and coat and went out to the lingerie shop to prepare.

* * * *

Saturday night had arrived. Rebecca was working behind the reception desk. She was nervous as hell. Tonight was the night. It took her longer than usual to process all the guests. She made a few mistakes here and there, and was blushing profusely when the Doms gave her stern looks. Of course, things went wrong with Master Luke, as well. The man was incredibly intimidating, and now that she was off-kilter, he got to her even more. He had threatened to get her Master so she could be properly punished.

Right at that moment, Master Kyle entered the reception area. He raised an eyebrow and walked over to the desk. He smoothed out the problem, and, after one last annoyed look, Master Luke went into the dungeon.

Master Kyle's strong gaze was on her, taking her in, assessing and probing. Making her more uncomfortable than she already was. Without taking his eyes off her he took out his cell phone and told one of the dungeon Masters to send another sub to work behind the reception desk.

Kyle took her aside and cupped her face.

"What's going on, Rebecca?" he asked in his smooth, deep voice.

"I'm fine, Master Kyle." she said, her voice trembling.

"No. You're not. Don't make it worse by lying to me, Rebecca."

She swallowed hard, tears pooled in her eyes.

"I'm sorry, Master Kyle," she whispered. "I'm just nervous."

"No shit," Kyle said dryly. "Why?"

"I'm... I have to do something tonight," she whispered. "With Master Cal."

"And you're this nervous about that?" Kyle asked.

Rebecca shifted her weight from one foot to the other, hoping Kyle wouldn't have noticed something between her and Cal was off. The man had a ridiculously sensitive antenna for such things, even when they were subtle. He was also very protective of submissives, and if he suspected Cal had done something to upset her, he would not hesitate to get involved. *Not what I need right now.*

"Have you talked to him, Becca?" he asked softly.

Rebecca averted her eyes.

"Not yet, Sir. I will." she said timidly. "Tonight."

"Good. Do it before you do the scene that makes you this

edgy," Master Kyle said firmly.

Rebecca almost burst out in hysterical laughter. The thought of telling Cal she was nervous about proposing to him before she actually did woke up her sense of humor. Kyle wouldn't understand if she'd start to giggle like a silly teenage girl, nor did she intend to tell him about her plans. And he was still waiting for a reply. It was good to know he was there for her when she needed it, and that he cared about her well-being. But right now, she had to get him out of her hair.

"I will, Master Kyle," she said. When she curved her lips up in a slight smile, he smiled back.

Kyle brushed a kiss over her cheek.

"Go now, subbie," he said. "Your work here is done for tonight."

Rebecca saw that the other girl had arrived and had already taken over. She gave Kyle a grateful smile, thanked him and sped off to the changing room.

Finishing early would give her another half hour to change into the outfit she had chosen for tonight. *Brilliant.* She could do with that time. After all, this was going to be the biggest moment of her life. Proposing and waiting, whether he'd accept or not. She sure as hell wanted to look her best. Not only for him, but also for herself. It would help boost her self-esteem and give her the guts to do this.

Her heart hammered as she did her hair, her makeup and put on her outfit.

* * * *

The dungeon door closed behind her and Rebecca swallowed hard.

Am I really going to do this? Oh, my God!

She glanced around the room, looking for Cal. She saw him in a sitting area, talking to another Master.

She started walking, very much aware of her unusual outfit. No one in their right mind wore a long, white lace chiffon gown in a BDSM club. It was a beautiful gown, but since it covered her entire body, it wasn't particularly 'sub-wear'. It screamed 'prude'. On top of that, it was white. She stood out like a sore thumb. Heads were turning and conversations around her came to a halt.

Oh, my God! Oh, my God! I can't do this! I can so not do this!

She almost ran away, but then Cal turned around and looked at her. His eyes widened when he took her in. Even in the dim lit room she saw mild shock and surprise in them. Then what seemed to be apprehension.

Shit! He knows? Or does he?

She couldn't read him. His face didn't give her any clues — it had that chiseled look, no expression whatsoever. His Wolf Man face. Dark, devilish, mysterious. Powerful. The only things that kept her from turning and running away were his eyes. His now almost black eyes, with a glint of…something. She couldn't figure out what. She just knew that he wouldn't let her go. Even from the distance, his aura of power enveloped her completely. His strong eyes forced her to start moving again.

As she walked, sashaying, the white chiffon nightgown swirled around her ankles. She could barely hold her own under Cal's gaze, but at the same time it kept her stable and strong enough to keep walking. Gracefully putting one foot in front of the other.

She stopped before him. Her bottom lip trembled as she reached for the front of the gown and ripped its press studs open with one swift movement. The gown slid off her shoulders and pooled around her feet.

The way Cal sucked in a breath as he took her in turned her nipples into hard peaks. She knew she looked great. But to see it reflected in his eyes made her feel sexy as sin. Hot as hell.

Her heart was hammering in her chest as his gaze roamed over her body, searing her. Melting her insides.

Her sexy white babydoll emphasized her full breasts and was loose underneath. The split in the middle revealed a thong with a white satin bow on her mound. It was a garter thong, its garters attached to white garter-belts that adorned her thighs. She knew he'd seen it when his lips curved up, and she gave him a cheeky smile.

"Wow!" was all he said.

Rebecca wet her lips and reached out, her hand shaking a bit, ready to propose to him.

"Cal, I…" she started, her voice soft.

He seemed to move quicker than light when he got up, put a finger across her lips and pulled her against him with his other arm. "No, my love. This is not how we will do things." His voice was barely audible over the music. He gently caressed her cheek with his fingers and his lips curled into a smile. "You do not have permission to deprive your Master of his task, little subbie."

Without breaking eye contact, he dropped to one knee in front of her and reached out his hand.

"Make me a happy man. Marry me, Rebecca," he said, sounding rough. "And, for fuck's sake, move in with me."

Rebecca blinked tears from her eyes and smiled. "Yes. Yes!" Her voice came out a whisper.

Cal stood, drew her into his arms, and on a throaty groan, took her lips for a kiss that blew her mind.

Cheers sounded around them and Kyle ordered bottles of champagne to be opened.

Her head was spinning when Cal finally released her.

"Gorgeous!" he whispered. "You move in tonight!"

"But…"

"No more 'buts', sub!" His deep voice reverberated through her. "I want you with me. And tonight we're going to celebrate our engagement until the cows come home."

Rebecca giggled.

He looked at her with love and sheer happiness in his eyes, making them sparkle like black diamonds. "Witchy woman, I love you!"

* * * *

Cal and Rebecca sat on the lounge set on the patio. He looked at her as she read through a sample contract for their collaring ceremony. He knew it was quite drastic, but it was merely to give her an idea, something to work from. Much of what was on the sample wasn't what he wanted, but as they'd already agreed to alter it until both were happy with it, he didn't really see a problem. He should have known that his subbie would react differently to it. Clearly, she felt as if the sample contract was the finished thing, and took it accordingly.

He smothered a chuckle when she grumbled, the frown between her brows deepening as she read more. When she was done, she looked up defiantly at him.

"I am not going to sign this!"

Cal had her on her knees at his feet before she had a chance to plug in her brain. He smothered a laugh when he saw the shock on her face. Most people underestimated how agile a man his size could be, and she was no exception. She'd learn. Her reaction to the impact, and being on her knees, pleased him. Instantly submissive, her recalcitrant attitude gone, all puppy eyes.

"Let's try that again, shall we?" Cal said dryly.

"Yes, Sir. I'm sorry," she said softly. "I don't like the contract, Sir."

"Look at me, Rebecca." When she did, he continued. "It's only a sample, sweetie. You know what a sample means, don't you?"

Amusement flowed through him, and he smiled at her.

"I...I got carried away, Sir," she said timidly.

Her widened eyes and pink cheeks showed that she realized she had overreacted.

Cal leaned forward and gently stroked her cheek with the backs of his fingers. "Honey, we will work on our own version, together, until we are both happy with it," he said. "Let's hear what you don't like."

"I don't like to be referred to as a slave," she exasperated. "Nor do I like the thing about giving up my worldly possessions. I will not go along with that."

Cal mouth curled into a smile. "But, of course, you wouldn't. You're not a slave. Good thing is, I don't want a slave, nor your worldly possessions. What else?"

Rebecca didn't reply. Cal put his fingers under her chin, tilted her face up and held her with his gaze.

"Let me guess. The statement that your Master is allowed to take on other submissives and lovers."

Her eyes sparked. "Y-yes, Sir. I... F-for me... I d-don't..." she stammered.

"Becca, all I want is to marry you both the vanilla and non-vanilla way. I want you to be my wife in every possible way. I love you, woman," he said. "If there was yet another option to make you my wife, I'd probably want to do that, too. I have no intention of taking another wife, another lover or another submissive. Only one woman will receive my love and lust, and only one will wear my collar and wedding band."

Tears rolled down her cheeks and she wrapped herself around him, sobbing in the crook of his neck.

"Dammit, woman, stop trying to drown us every time I tell you I love you," he grumbled into her hair. "Do you have any idea how much tissues cost? You'll bankrupt me." Her sweet giggle tickled the skin of his neck.

Rebecca sat up and looked at him. "You know, there is another way."

Cal lifted an eyebrow. "And you want that. Tell me."

"Handfasting," she replied. "And yes, I'd want that. Very much."

"Handfasting?" Cal chuckled. "My wrist cuffs and collar aren't enough for my greedy subbie? Now you want to be tied up on our wedding, as well?"

She grinned at him. "Yes, but tied to you."

"You want to have me tied up? On our wedding? Bad, bad subbie," he growled, as lust lit his eyes. "I will have to punish you for even suggesting it."

"But, Sir!" Rebecca started.

He treated her to his Master-look, and put enough warning in it to shut her up on the spot.

"Lose the shorts and drape yourself over my lap." His command shook her visibly. "And you'd best convince me that you're happy to receive your Master's punishment, lest I accidentally choose large instead of medium."

Her eyes widened. He held her with his gaze and could almost hear the cogs churn as she got that he was talking about a butt plug. He smothered a laugh, fully aware the woman wasn't keen on large ones. Or medium ones, for that matter. He, on the other hand, loved to see her struggle with the discomfort of wearing an anal plug.

While she quickly wiggled out of her shorts and thong, he grabbed the toy bag he had put on the patio earlier. Out of her sight. He liked the element of surprise.

A few minutes later she was at his feet again, and slowly sat her bottom on her heels so she wouldn't shift the plug too much.

"So, about this handfasting," Cal started.

"Yes, Sir?"

"You want me in a kilt, as well?"

Rebecca's mouth dropped open, and she closed it again, confusion in her eyes.

Cal enjoyed the moment. He had deliberately said that to her out of the blue, knowing that mentioning a kilt suggested that he was familiar with handfasting—a pagan wedding ritual during which the hands of the bride and groom would be tied together.

"My love, I have Scottish ancestry, so I know what it is. And I am entitled to wear a kilt. A real one at that," he said with a slight smile.

"Scottish? But…you've got black hair and dark eyes?"

Cal grinned. "Scottish ancestry nonetheless, babe. Maybe I am the black sheep of the family."

"Oh, I don't doubt that for a second," Rebecca said, her eyes sparkling with laughter.

He leaned forward, cupped her head, and mumbled

against her lips, "And you love me for it." Then he kissed her, soft and teasing, knowing she preferred a hard and demanding kiss over a lovey-dovey one any time. She moaned a protest in his mouth when he didn't give it to her. A smile pulled at his lips.

"Such a greedy sub," he mumbled against her mouth. A delightful pink colored her cheeks. He licked over her bottom lip, then nibbled it.

"Cal, please!" Her husky whine sent a tremor through him and made his already hard cock strain against the confinement of his jeans.

"Yes, Becca?" he breathed as he kept licking and nibbling her bottom lip.

"Please just kiss me," she begged.

"I am kissing you," he said, and softly took her mouth again for a sweet, tender kiss. He slid his free hand under her top and cupped her right breast. Her nipple jutted in his palm, an invitation to play with it, but he simply held her breast in his hand.

He chuckled softly when she started to squirm. Moving would shift the butt plug, wake up nerves and heighten her need. He gently squeezed her breast to add to it, and a moan broke from her lips.

Cal started licking and nibbling her lips again, and she made little protesting sounds.

"What do you want, subbie?" he whispered.

"I want more, Cal."

"Wrong answer, subbie. You shouldn't demand," he said, as he kept pressing soft kisses on her lips, the corners of her mouth and her throat.

"Fucking sadist," she moaned under her breath.

His low, husky laugh melted her insides. "Give me the right answer, lil' subbie."

"Please take more!"

He growled as his lips landed on hers and he plunged in, kissing her deeply and thoroughly with a hunger that shook him.

When he finally lifted his head, she keened a protest.

"Greedy woman," he mumbled, "Way too greedy, we got to work on that."

He curved his hands around her waist and lifted her onto his lap.

"Time to serve your Master," he said, his eyes half-lidded.

He yanked off her top, unhooked her bra and groaned when her breasts swayed in front of his face. He leaned forward and closed his mouth around a nipple. He circled it, and her areola puckered tight. He circled the crest of her bud, and her moan turned into a husky cry when he sucked it hard. He let go of it with a pop, admiring the red, swollen bud.

"I damn love your tits," he groaned, then captured her other nipple in his mouth. Her soft mewls of excitement turned into moans. Sounds that stoked the fire in his core. When he had taken his fill of her nipples, her eyes were dazed, her breathing ragged. A lovely overheated sub.

He moved her off his lap so he could unzip and pulled his jeans down a bit, freeing his erection.

"Put your legs over the backrest."

Rebecca complied and he hummed his approval.

"Now let's fill up that tight pussy." His voice was hoarse with lust. "Put your hands on my shoulders." He cupped her ass and lifted her pussy over his cock, then lowered her a bit. As the head of his cock slid into her, they both gasped. Cal held her there and their eyes locked.

"Ready, baby?" he asked.

She blinked. "Ready for what?"

He started lowering her and his cock pushed in farther, struggling for space with the anal plug. Rebecca's eyes widened.

"No, no! Stop! Too much, Cal!"

A long whine broke from her lips as he moved her down a bit more. He kept his eyes on her, both to see if she could handle the double intrusion and for his own pleasure. The emotions that were warring in her eyes made his cock hard to the point of pain. Concern, lust, disbelief and need showed on her expressive face as he filled her cunt inch by inch.

"Still too much, sexy?" Her pussy clamped down on him. His cock jerked in reply. "I think you like it. A lot."

Finally, her ass touched his thighs and he was in all the way, balls-deep. He groaned. She felt so good. Like a silky soft, wet fist around his cock. Tight and hot. He gritted his teeth to suppress the urge to take his pleasure. Instead he focused on her. She was struggling with the invasion and trying to move up. But with her legs over the back of the garden sofa, she had no leverage.

Her dazed eyes held shock, and she gasped, "Too much! Too much!"

He gave her his devilish smile. "You did call me a sadist."

Rebecca hissed. "You are! You're a fucking sadist!"

"No, darling, this is a fucking sadist." Cal thrust his hips up, hitting her hard with his cock, and a shrill cry came from her. "Now, I'm fucking, and, yes, I like your pain, as it gives you so much joy. So you could call me a sadist."

He lifted her up a tiny bit and kept thrusting into her, his rock-hard cock pressing against the butt plug, just taking, and there was nothing she could do to stop it.

"Too much, oh, my God, too… Ooohh, please!"

Hearing her plead and seeing her breasts bounce each time he thrust into her made his cock swell further. The way her cunt clamped down on him, tighter and needier, made his balls draw up. He wasn't going to last much longer.

"Yesss, ooohhh, yesss! Please don't stop!"

"I'm not going to, baby, feels too fucking good," he groaned. "I'm going to fill your pussy with my seed." He lifted her up and simply dropped her down on his full length. She shrieked as she came violently, her cunt clenching and tugging. It pulled him over the edge, his core exploded, and his balls pushed up his cum. The brutal pleasure of orgasm raged through his body and he roared as her convulsing pussy sucked him dry.

* * * *

It took Rebecca and Cal several more sessions—and a lot of thinking—to plan all the ceremonies. Since they had three, they decided to not go for very lengthy vows. Rebecca had giggled. "You aren't a man of many words anyway," she'd joked.

"My hands usually speak for me, doll," he'd retorted, to which she'd given him a "hmff".

But she didn't see the need to repeat what had already been said, neither did he, so they agreed to keep their promises for each ceremony short and sweet, while making sure they expressed everything that mattered to them.

Rebecca wanted a fantasy wedding dress, and without giving away any details, she gave him a few small samples of the fabric so he could get a matching outfit. Cal had decided to wear a kilt during all three ceremonies. She would wear her wedding dress for the first two, but not for the collaring ceremony.

"I'll choose the moment to start the collaring, and I want to be the one to strip you from your wedding dress," he said.

Rebecca was confused. She knew that traditionally a submissive was supposed to be scantily clad or completely naked during a collaring ceremony.

"I thought I'd change clothes for that?"

"Not going to happen. You're my bride and I will be the one to get you out of your gown. As your husband, that's my right and my task. And I insist."

One look at him made it clear he would not give in on that one. It was indeed tradition that the groom got his bride out of her dress, and the fact that he insisted on that made her feel utterly feminine, and wanted.

"So, if I can't change clothes, what am I to wear?" she asked, knowing she couldn't wear much underneath her wedding gown. Plus, she'd have to wear it all day long, so latex was out of the question and leather was too thick.

"Very little, I say," Cal said dryly. "But I do not want you naked. As for the rest, it's entirely your problem."

Rebecca looked at him, surprised by his answer. She was happy he'd allow her something to wear, because she had expected him to want her naked.

Cal put his fingers under her chin and lifted her face. "I don't want everyone to feast their eyes before I've even had the chance to feast myself on you."

"Cal!" she said shocked. "We're discussing our wedding! Do you have to be so crude?"

"Do you have to ask silly questions?" He grinned. "Just thinking of how I will take you when you're mine has me hard as rock. You best make sure you're very well rested."

"In that case, we'd better not have sex before the wedding," she said teasingly, and giggled.

"Don't taunt me, sweetheart, you'll come to regret it." His eyes held a promise she really wanted him to keep. Or maybe not. She swallowed.

"Cal…" she started.

"Denying your Master orgasms is so, so wrong, subbie," he whispered in his low, dark voice.

How could a soft voice sound so threatening? Arousing?

"Let's discuss orgasm denial. Lose the trousers." A command.

She quickly complied. One look made clear her thong had to go, as well.

He slid his fingers through her folds and hummed when he found her adequately wet. He played with her pussy until she had to hang on to him for support. Her legs were shaking and she was throbbing inside and out.

"Such a sweet little sub. So wet, so needy," he mumbled. He took a vibrator and two leather straps from his toy bag. He pushed the vibrator inside her, and when he switched it on, it sent jolts of pleasure out from her lower body. It buzzed in waves, alternating between fast and slow vibrations. It turned up the heat in her core, but didn't give her enough stimulation to be able to come. He put a leather strap around her waist, pulled the other strap between her legs, and attached it to the one around her waist to keep the vibrator snug inside her pussy.

"Master," she said on a moan.

"Yes, lil' subbie?" he asked with a devilish smile.

"I...please...I," she said, stumbling over her words. The thing inside her melted her brain. She couldn't think straight.

"You don't like orgasm denial, Rebecca?"

"No. Yes. No. I don't... Sir!" She looked at him, not sure what to say.

"Mmm... I don't like it much, either," he mumbled as he caressed her cheek. "When on the receiving end, that is."

He motioned for her to get on her knees and unzipped his leathers. His erection sprang free, and when she eagerly opened her lips, he fisted himself and fed her his cock.

Chapter Twelve

Rebecca emerged on Kyle's arm, and the sigh of admiration that went through the crowd mingled with Cal's exclamation of "Holy fuck!"

Rebecca sucked in a breath when she saw him, and she leaned heavily on Kyle as her knees almost buckled. He looked dashing, dark and dangerous, and to-die-for sexy. Her ruggedly handsome Wolf Man. Her spine melted when their eyes met. He held her gaze for a few seconds, then his gaze moved over her body. Her heart thumped in her chest as she waited for a sign that he liked what he was seeing. She knew she had never looked better in her life. Before leaving the dressing room, she had checked herself thoroughly in the mirror to make sure of that. And what she had seen reflected back had pleased her tremendously.

Her breasts were pushed up by the dress's fronted corset in purple silk with a swathe of embroidered decoration, ruched chiffon, embroidered dragonflies in aqua, and crystals. The sleeves were tight around her upper arms, then flowed into a wealth of chiffon. The dress had a full ball gown skirt with a medium train. The purple satin had a beautiful sheen when she moved. She looked like a lovely fairy.

Now she was standing here with her husband-to-be on the other side of the aisle. The light breeze played with her hair and the wealth of ribbons on her dress and sleeves as she waited for Cal's reaction. She couldn't miss it – the expression on his face told her all she wanted to know. Her breath caught when their eyes locked. The open admiration and love made her heart swell. The desire she saw turned her nipples into hard peaks underneath the corset.

"Please help me spin around," Rebecca whispered to Kyle. He gave her a puzzled look, then gallantly took her hand and made her twirl. She stopped with her back to Cal and cast him a sultry glance over her shoulder.

A smile curved at the corner of Cal's mouth when she showed him how her corset was laced up. The beautiful aqua and purple ribbons were laced through a ridiculous number of grommets.

His smile and the sparkle of amusement in his eyes told her that he understood it would take forever to get the dress undone. Needless to say, Rebecca had made sure there was no zipper. She giggled softly at the thought of him fumbling with the ribbons, impatient to get her out of the dress.

He held her pinned with gaze, and slapped his right hand on the left. Rebecca swallowed as she got the message of how he would reward her for her cheek later on. His low, husky laugh floated through the air, making her blush profusely. The laughter and giggles that rose from their guests, as they got the message just the same, made her cheeks burn more, but she couldn't help but smile.

She dragged her eyes from Cal, spun around to face him again and put her hand loosely back on Kyle's arm. As she slowly approached Cal, she feasted her eyes on him. He was wearing a loose-fitting black Ghillie shirt with a distinct lace-up part that ran from the middle of his chest to his throat and was tied with a silver-colored lace. His dark chest hair peeked through the opening and Rebecca's fingers tingled with the need to touch him there. His kilt was such a dark anthracite she could barely distinguish the typical tartan weave. Underneath the kilt a bit of bare skin showed, revealing just a hint of his tan, muscular legs, then they disappeared into long anthracite socks and black biker boots that fastened with straps and pewter buckles. Rebecca smiled as she saw silver-colored wolf heads on the sides of the shafts. Clearly, her man was chuffed with the title she'd given him. As she got closer, she saw that the large pewter buckle on the wide black leather belt around his waist featured two wolves, a male and a female.

She got overwhelmed by emotions as she realized he'd chosen that buckle especially for their wedding, and her eyes brimmed with tears. She blinked them away as well as she could. This was a happy day. Their big day. She didn't want to cry. At least not just yet.

They got to Cal, and Kyle guided her hand to Cal's. Kyle stepped aside, but she didn't really notice, as she was totally absorbed in Cal. Breathless. Awed.

"I love you!"

Had he said that, or had she? Or both? She wasn't sure.

Cal took her hands and put her palms on his chest. "Keep them there, or I'll bear-hug you," he whispered for her ears only.

After she'd complied, he carefully slid his hand under her hair to cup her head, leaned forward and kissed her. Rebecca expected him to only steal a short, tender kiss, but when she opened her lips for him, he swept in and kissed her until her toes curled.

Cheers and yells from their guests only vaguely registered.

"Get a room!"

"Damn, they're skipping straight to the wedding night!"

"Oh, my God, he's roughing up the bride!"

"Let him enjoy his last kiss as a free man!"

Cal released her mouth, leaving her panting and aching for more.

"You ruined my lipstick," she said, not really caring about it at all.

"He'll ruin a lot more before morning comes, love," someone yelled, and laughter filled the air.

Cal looked at their guests. "If you can all shut up now, I would love to take my bride," he said with a gleam in his eyes, then finished his sentence, "to be my wife."

Everyone quieted, and Cal opened his black leather sporran. He took out a delicate silver wire-work collar with purple and turquoise Swarovski crystals. Rebecca sucked in a breath. It was a stunning piece of art, some two inches high, and the colors of the crystals matched her wedding dress.

"My love, this is your collar for dressed vanilla occasions," he said softly. "Lift up your hair for me, please."

His eyes fired with possessiveness when he put the delicate collar around her slender neck.

"Beautiful," he mumbled. "Hold out your hands, my Rebecca."

As she did, he took two matching bracelets out of his sporran. When he put them around her wrists, she felt his dominance trickle through her skin and fill her entire being. She lifted her gaze to meet his, and he groaned.

"Mine! Now and forever!" he said softly, and brushed a kiss across her lips.

Someone coughed politely behind them, and Cal dragged his gaze away from Rebecca and turned around to stand next to his bride.

The officiant was ready to start their wedding ceremony. Rebecca was nervous as hell and let out a sigh when Cal grabbed her trembling hand, and squeezed it.

The officiant cleared his throat and welcomed everybody.

"We are gathered here today to celebrate the very special love between Rebecca and Caleb, by joining them in marriage."

Rebecca giggled under her breath as she heard the officiant use Cal's full name, which hardly anyone ever did. He gave her a sidelong glare that contradicted the smile that pulled at his lips.

The ceremony floated past her like a dream. She tried to focus, but only managed to catch a few phrases.

"Marriage is about sharing your lives together, to stand together to face life and the world, hand-in-hand."

Both smiled, as they were holding hands already. Cal squeezed hers, and they exchanged a loving glance.

"May you wake up every morning, look each other in the eye and fall in love all over again."

"Not a problem," Cal mumbled under his breath.

Rebecca smiled and gave his hand a soft squeeze.

The officiant finished his speech and it was time for their vows. Kyle stepped forward, holding a cushion with the two wedding bands on it.

Rebecca turned to face Cal and he took her hand. The emotions she read in his eyes made her heart skip a beat.

"I, Caleb, take you Rebecca to be my wife, my partner in life and my one true love. I will cherish our union and love you more each day than I did the day before. I will trust you and respect you, laugh with you and cry with you, love you faithfully through good times and bad, regardless of the obstacles we may face together. I give you my hand, my heart and my love, from this day forward for as long as we both shall live."

A few tears ran down her cheeks, and when she started her vow — the same one, but with the names reversed — her voice trembled slightly.

Even as she spoke the last words of her vow, he ran the backs of his fingers over her cheek, gently brushed away her tears and licked them off his finger.

Without taking his eyes off her, he picked up the ring from the cushion and slowly slid it onto her finger with the words, "This ring is a symbol of my love. I marry you with this ring, with all that I have and all that I am."

Rebecca's gaze dropped to the wedding band on her finger and she swallowed hard, trying to force back more tears.

"Stop crying, woman, and marry me," he said softly. "I want to kiss my bride."

"Impatient Wolf Man," she whispered as she took his wedding band from the cushion. "Now give me your finger."

Cal chuckled at her words, and when she realized what she had blurted out, her cheeks burned.

Rebecca looked into his eyes as she slid the wedding band on his finger.

"This ring is a symbol of my love. I marry you with this ring, with all that I have and all that I am." Her voice was tingling with love and happiness.

Cal growled and pulled her in his arms.

"Not yet, cowboy!" Kyle's said with a laugh in his voice. "Wait for it, and do it right."

Rebecca giggled softly when Cal glared at Kyle, then looked at the officiant, his eyebrow raised, urging the man to get on with it. She knew what it was like to be on the receiving end of Cal's Master-mode. The poor man stammered the last words as he pronounced them man and wife.

"You may now kiss your bride."

"Finally," Cal said, and he took complete possession of her mouth.

* * * *

After the official wedding ceremony, waitresses and waiters appeared with champagne. As soon as everyone had a glass, Kyle made a toast to the newlywed couple. Everyone cheered and congratulated them.

Kyle continued when everyone quieted again. "This wonderful day is far from over. Cal is a greedy man, and he has decided to take his Rebecca three different ways today." He paused when people cheered. "To be his wife, of course."

He asked everyone to attend the next ceremony, a handfasting, in half an hour at the lanai on the other side of the gardens.

After the handfasting there would a reception, and time to congratulate the couple, followed by an outdoor roast meal. In between, the photographer would take the married couple through the gardens for their wedding pictures. The third and final ceremony would take place in the evening. There was no set time for it. Cal himself would decide when he wanted to put his collar on his woman.

Before people could swarm round them, Cal guided Rebecca toward a quiet place in the gardens. He wanted a private moment with his bride before the next ceremony started. When they got to a secluded spot, he drew her into his arms and just held her. Rebecca wrapped her arms around his neck and burrowed against him.

"How do you feel, my love?" he asked.

"Happy, excited. Overwhelmed," she said softly.

He kissed the top of her head.

"My wife," he whispered into her hair. "Damn, I'm happy."

"My husband," she sighed and smiled at him. "You know, the first time I saw you, you scared the hell out of me with that look. Yes, that one."

"Are you trying to tell me it doesn't work anymore?" Cal frowned. "Damn, we've only been married fifteen minutes. It wasn't supposed to wear off that fast!"

Rebecca giggled. "Oh, you'll always be able to knock the wind out of me," she said.

"Wait a minute," Cal's frown deepened. "Are you trying to reassure your Master that he still has his mojo?"

Her sweet laughter filled the air.

"Maybe I'd best consummate our marriage right here," he murmured against her lips. "A good seeing-to might shut you up."

A spark of lust appeared in her eyes and she nibbled his bottom lip. "You'll ruin my dress. I can't have that happen."

"Then stop begging with your eyes for me to fill you up." His voice sounded hoarse. "Or you will end up looking like a very well-used bride before we even have our wedding pictures taken."

A soft mewl broke from her lips. "Please, kiss me, Cal."

Cal took the lips she so willingly offered and kissed her gently, nibbling and exploring. Without releasing her, he cupped her bottom and yanked her against his erection. When she moaned, he swept in and kissed her intensely and deeply, groaning when her soft body melted against his.

After a long, passionate kiss, he lifted his head. "God, I love you, Rebecca," he said as he looked into her eyes. "And fuck if I can wait until tonight before I make you mine."

"That best be a promise," she said in a husky voice, "because I don't think I can wait that long, either."

He flashed her smile, and drew her into his arms. She put her head on his chest and he simply held his woman, reveling in her presence and the love he had for her in his heart.

A bell chimed thrice, telling them it was time for their handfasting. Hand-in-hand, they walked over to the lanai.

* * * *

A beautiful white and pink round wedding tent was set up near the lanai. The High Priestess was already waiting for them near the altar. The tent was a good thirty feet in diameter, which allowed all their family and closest friends to be in the circle the High Priestess would cast.

As the bride and groom took their places, the High Priestess walked around clockwise to do so. She called on the Guardians of the four Quarters, asking them to witness the ceremony and to stand in protection over the circle. She ended with, "In the names of the Goddess and the Great Horned God the circle is cast. So mote it be."

After welcoming the bride and groom on their day of love and addressing the guests to welcome them too, the High Priestess started a simple but effective grounding meditation. When she had finished, she motioned Cal and Rebecca to join her before the altar. They cast each other an intense look as the High Priestess started the ritual.

"I call upon you, Lady and Lord, to join us here and to witness the holy union of Caleb and Rebecca."

A few moments of silence went by before she continued, a moment during which even nature seemed to quiet. The air felt pleasantly full and warm around them, as if the spirits and angels had indeed descended to envelop everyone with love. Family and friends, who stood in a circle around them, grabbed each other's hands. A huge circle of love with the beaming bride and groom in its center.

"With love in your hearts you are declaring your intentions here today with the Goddess and God, and family and friends as witnesses," the High Priestess started. "This handfasting will greatly deepen your union. Remember your intentions and words often so they may guide and support you throughout your life together."

The High Priestess took the handfasting cord from the altar. The cord had been made from the same ribbons used on Rebecca's wedding dress and a thin strip of tartan from Cal's kilt. She turned to Rebecca, reverently holding it in her hands.

"Rebecca, do you join us here today of your own free will, to acknowledge before the Lord and Lady the bond that is shared between you and Caleb?"

"Yes, I do." Her voice sounded strong and clear.

The High Priestess repeated her question to Cal, and his "I do" was equally loud and clear.

With a smile the High Priestess said, "I ask you to face each other and look into each other's eyes."

The entire world seemed to become one big blur to Cal. All that remained were the love that shimmied in the air between him and his woman, and the High Priestess' voice.

Cal and Rebecca held each other's left lower arms in such a way that their wrists were touching, his steady pulse on her faster one. Heart to heart.

"Rebecca and Caleb, will you share in each other's laughter and look for the brightness and the positive in one another?"

"We will," they answered together.

"And so the binding is made," the High Priestess said as she looped the cord loosely around their hands.

"Rebecca and Caleb, will you be present in challenging times and support each other, so that you may grow strong in this union?"

"Yes."

"And so the binding is made." The High Priestess looped the cord around their wrists again.

"Rebecca, will you trouble Caleb?" the High Priestess asked.

"I may," she answered, mischief dancing in her eyes.

Cal smothered a laugh.

"Is that your intent?"

Love shone from Rebecca's eyes when she said, "No."

The High Priestess addressed Cal. "Caleb, will you trouble Rebecca?"

"Hell, yes!"

Laughter and giggles rose from their family and friends.

The High Priestess's expression was of shock. Obviously, she hadn't expected such a reply. Cal gave her a friendly smile to reassure her, and the woman continued.

"Will you intentionally cause her grief?"

"Never!"

"And so the binding is made." Another loop around their wrists.

"Rebecca and Caleb, will you always love, honor and respect one another?"

"Yes, we will," they answered in unison.

"And so the binding is made," the High Priestess said, and loosely wound the cord around their wrists again.

"Rebecca and Caleb, do you wish this union to last till death do you part?"

Rebecca opened her mouth to say "Yes" as they had agreed, but Cal put his finger across her lips to silence her.

"No, I wish this union to last for as long as it serves our Highest Good," he said without even a hint of hesitation.

Rebecca's eyes widened. Cal held his eyes on her, knowing full well he'd surprised her. He knew what he had said was big. It could mean a month, a decade, or forever. They had argued about blood vows, and both had been hesitant about that. Cal knew that blood vows would go beyond death and would not necessarily be desired. What the human heart wanted was not always congruent with the needs and wishes of the soul. But he'd thought of a beautiful alternative. His vow didn't mean forever by default, and left room for the Cosmos and their souls to decide what their Highest Good would be.

The impact of his vow was clear on Rebecca's face, and his heart hammered in his chest as he waited for her reply.

Even their guests had gone quiet and a solemn silence encompassed the wedding party.

"I, too, wish this union to last as long as it serves our Highest Good," she said softly. "I love you so much!" she whispered as a few tears dripped from her eyes.

"I love you too, my woman." Cal softly ran his fingers over her cheek and wiped away the tears.

Even the High Priestess was blinking furiously and had to swallow before she could speak the words, "And so the binding is made."

She wound the cord around their wrists and tied the knot.

"Your union and bond is symbolized by the tying of this cord. Your union is formed by your love, friendship and your commitment to the vows you have made today, and will be strengthened by the way you live your lives together. You entrust yourself and each other with the making or breaking of this union. As I now remove the cord, the knot will remain tied, symbolizing your lives becoming one."

The High Priestess gently removed the cord from their joined wrists and put it on a velveteen cushion on the altar.

Cal took Rebecca in his arms and gave her a long, deep kiss and put all his love in it. As a result tears ran from her eyes again. He chuckled and released her mouth. With a demonstrative sigh, he pulled a tissue out of his sleeve. He knew her well, and had expected she'd end up bawling her eyes out on their wedding day, so he had prepared for it. She gave him a smile.

"I like having a few tricks up my sleeve," he grinned.

Rebecca wrapped her arms around his neck and pulled

his head down. With her lips against his, she whispered, "Kiss me, please!"

"Don't ever stop being needy and greedy, woman," he whispered back before he took her lips. She willingly opened up for him and he swept in, releasing his hunger for her. Her fiery reply made him groan. He yanked her hips against his groin and rubbed his hardness against her.

When he finally let go of her, her lips were swollen and her eyes dazed.

"Fucking beautiful," he said softly. "I fell for you after I kissed you on that dance floor."

She looked at him in shock. "But I bit your lip?"

"Tell me about it," he said dryly. "That was one for the book."

A giggle came from her.

"You better not remind me too often, little subbie." He gave her a devastating smile. "Your pretty little ass won't like it."

"Cal, Rebecca." The High Priestess drew their attention with a smile. "It is time to jump over the broom."

"Let's do this," Cal said.

Rebecca's mother and Cal's father held up the wedding broom, which was decorated with pink and purple ribbons and an abundance of white roses. They held it some eight inches above the ground for them to jump over.

Cal looked at Rebecca as he took her hand. With her other, she was holding up the skirt of her dress, showing a fair bit of leg. Recognizing her bratty expression, he guestimated she was about to pull it up higher, likely to show the garter on her thigh.

Cal raised an eyebrow.

"Any higher and you'll jump over the broom with a very red ass!" he said without raising his voice, but making sure he put enough warning in it to let her know he dead serious.

A moment passed as he waited for her to make up her mind. The sparkle in her eyes revealed that she was still tempted to sass him, then something about her changed and she lowered the skirt a bit. He drew a deep breath of relief. He'd indeed have walloped her ass, hard. He hadn't been joking when he'd said he wanted to be the first to feast his eyes on his wife. But he would not have enjoyed the spanking. Not one bit.

"I'm sorry, Cal," she whispered.

"You will be." A corner of his mouth lifted. "Now let's see if you can jump." He slapped her ass so hard that she felt the impact through the layers of her dress. Even as she squeaked he grabbed her hand and jumped over the broom with her.

Everyone cheered.

"Can't you two ever do things normally?" Kyle asked, a big grin on his face.

"Nope," they said in unison, and laughed.

The High Priestess smiled as well when she walked up to them.

"Blessed may your holy union be," she spoke, after which she thanked the Goddess and God and bade them farewell. She hugged and congratulated both the bride and groom, and went on to close the circle, thanking and bidding the Guardians of the four Quarters farewell. When she was done, she gave Kyle a nod, indicating he could take over as Master of Ceremonies

With a booming voice, Kyle made everyone cheer for the newlyweds, after which he took the chance to congratulate Rebecca and Cal before the guests flooded around them to do the same.

Waitresses in colorful pagan dresses appeared with jugs of mead, traditional pagan honey wine. After a toast and many, many congratulations and shaking hands, Cal and Rebecca went to the lanai to cut the wedding cake. They fed each other tidbits of the first piece they'd cut, laughing and kissing and whispering "I love you."

Tables with finger-food, wine and juice were rolled out and soon everyone was mingling, laughing and chatting.

Rebecca was happily talking to a group of other

submissives when a tingling sensation in her neck sent a shiver all the way down her spine. It was as if Cal was touching her. She sucked in a breath and her nipples hardened against the corset of her dress. She turned around and looked into the smoldering black eyes of her husband standing on the other side of the lanai. He kept her pinned with his eyes as he slowly weaved his way through the crowd to her. As if by magic, everyone moved out of the way, clearing his path. Her breathing sped up as he got closer and closer, and her legs quivered. He looked every bit as ruthless as when she'd first seen him. Dark, mysterious, powerful. Dominant. He stopped barely an inch from her, and the fiery hunger in his gaze set her core alight.

"Time to find the photographer." His unspoken words hung heavy in the air. "I want my wife!"

Everything inside her yielded to his power. Suddenly her breasts were full and she felt herself dampen. A soft moan broke from her lips.

"Now!" Cal's husky growl made her even needier.

"Yes, Sir," she said, her voice shaky.

They spent the next hour with the photographer in the gardens. Rebecca had been looking forward to the photoshoot. Much to her surprise Cal seemed to enjoy it as much as she did. Then again, no matter what she and Cal did together, it was always good. She giggled when the photographer wanted to take pictures of her on a swing with Cal pushing her. The way he laughed made her heart swell. There were pictures of them kissing and holding each other, on a bench, and all kinds of other poses. Love and desire shimmied in the air between them, and the photographer hummed, obviously pleased.

Then the man wanted to take a few pictures of Rebecca on her knees, looking at Cal as he tipped up her head with his hand. Sparks flew as Cal devoured her with his gaze. Rebecca was surprised the soil beneath her didn't melt.

"Goddamn," the photographer mumbled under his breath. "Hold that thought!"

As if they needed encouragement. Whenever his Wolf Man gaze seared through her, she had no choice but to surrender. Everything inside her yielded as he held her pinned with nothing but the possessiveness in his eyes.

Cal let the photographer take a number of pictures of them in that position, then he almost shooed him away with a short "Enough." He didn't even look at him, but the man quickly made himself scarce.

When he was gone, Cal pulled Rebecca to her feet and swung her up in his arms.

"I want to consummate my marriage," he said with a gravelly voice as he carried her indoors. "I hope you are prepared. I plan to take you hard."

She just sighed longingly and wrapped her arms around his corded neck, keeping her eyes on his face. Love and an intense need washed through her. She felt totally feminine and desirable, all woman, being carried by her handsome, sexy husband.

Cal carried her upstairs and entered the purple theme room. When the door slammed shut behind him, he took possession of her mouth without even bothering to put her down.

After a long, electrifying kiss, he pulled back and gently put her on the ground.

"Cal, I need you. In me. Deep. Now. Please!" Her smoky voice made his cock pulse.

"Today your wish is my command, baby."

He pushed her farther into the room, and when he stopped her, she turned around. Her eyes widened when she saw the stocks. She looked at him, startled.

"Tempting, but not today, baby," he said with a slight smile. "Choose where you want to be taken."

Stocks, a bondage table, chains, and a spanking bench took up most of the room.

"Not exactly the Holiday Inn, is it?" she said dryly, then walked to the bondage table.

"Good enough," Cal said, and she squeaked as he pushed her facedown over it. He slid his hands under her skirts and he groaned when he felt lacy boyshorts that left the undercurve of her ass exposed. He started pulling up the skirt of her dress, carefully folding it over her back. He snorted a laugh when he saw the pink text on the white boyshorts. "Please Fuck Me!"

"Trust you," he said with a laugh in his voice, and she giggled. "'Please fuck me'… I will do just that."

He yanked the boyshorts down, lifted his kilt to bare his cock, and fisted himself.

"Brace yourself, love, you're in for a rough ride." Without further ado, he thrust balls-deep into her slick pussy. Her scream made his cock jerk. He kept himself sheathed inside her and pushed even deeper. Rebecca yelped as he impaled her.

"That's it, baby, feel your husband's cock," he growled. "Every inch of me."

Her pussy walls pulsed in response to his rough words.

"I love how you react to dirty talk, baby." His voice was thick with lust. When she clamped down on him, he curved his hands around her hips and slammed into her, hard and deep. Rebecca's cries aroused him even more, as did the way she clawed at the table to hold on, digging her fingernails into the leather.

"Cal…no…too much…oh, my God, no!" she whined.

"You want me to stop, Rebecca?" he panted, slowing down a bit.

"No…it's…oh, damn, please! Don't stop!" Her plea drove him wild.

With a growl, he tore her panties off so he could shove her legs farther apart, allowing him to get even deeper. His mind blanked and his vision blurred as he just took her like he had promised. Hard. By the time he shot his seed into her womb, she had come twice. He sagged over her, kissing her neck.

"Mine. You're mine," he said in a rough voice.

When his breathing had returned to normal, his cock had hardened inside her and he took her again.

"Oh, my God, Cal," she moaned as he hammered into her pussy. He hit her cervix, and she whimpered.

"I'm sorry, baby," he groaned, "But I want you so much. You feel so fucking good…your cunt so hot…and tight."

Her cunt clamped down on him. He sensed she needed this as much as he did. She wanted him to take her completely.

"Please, take more!"

With a growl, Cal pulled her off the table and put her on the floor with her ass up in the air. He yanked her back onto his cock and pushed her torso down.

"Fucking insatiable, demanding fury," he groaned as he pounded into her. "Is my cock not enough to satisfy you?"

"Yes. Please, take me…hard. Ooh, Cal." She screamed his name.

Cal growled, gave her what she asked for and slammed his hard cock into her. He held her down with a hand on her back to make her feel restrained and used. He needed that like he knew she craved for her man to take everything from her.

Then he slapped her ass and angled his cock differently to hit her sweet spot. He kept thrusting into her, his climax approaching fast. Holding her down, impaling her with his thick cock, sensing she was about to come, almost took his head off. Then she came, her body shaking and spasming. Her shrill cries of ecstasy made him groan.

Her cunt tugged and sucked at his cock, and the pressure in his balls became unbearable. Another deep thrust and the fire in his core exploded. Glorious heat shot up and out from his groin, pushing his cum up through his shaft. He screamed her name as he kept thrusting until he had completely emptied himself inside her.

After a few minutes, Cal's brain started functioning again. He got up, cleaned himself off and scooped up his wife. He sat down on a chair with Rebecca in his lap. Her eyes were still dazed as she wrapped her arms around his waist and snuggled against him.

"Becca?"

"Mmmm."

"You all right, my love?" he asked softly, realizing he'd taken her really hard—had needed to take her hard—as if to mark her as his own. He knew she could take a lot, but he had almost lost control of himself.

"Not sure if I can walk. You may have to carry me for the rest of the day," she mumbled against his chest. "On my wedding day!"

Silence. Guilt washed through him. He'd been too rough. On their big day.

"I'm sore," she said.

A soft growl rumbled through his chest. *How the hell can I make this right?* His muscles tensed.

"I'll walk bow-legged for a week."

She sounded disgruntled, but he heard something else underneath. A suppressed giggle? He put his fingers under her chin and tilted her head up. Her eyes gleamed with laughter and relief washed through him.

"You little bitch! Making me think...making me feel guilty and bad," he grumbled.

"Oh, but you are bad!" she said, sounding husky. "And you're mine now. My bad Wolf Man husband."

The possessive tone of voice and look in her eyes made him blink. Then the realization sank in. He had never taken her, or any woman, that hard, almost mindless and animalistic. On the brink of losing complete control. But as he had penetrated her, her softness had completely enveloped him on a far deeper level than just his cock in her pussy. She owned him as much as he owned her. Right then and there he knew that he would never be able to love another woman again. Would never be able to take another woman again. Ever. He swallowed.

"You've ruined me, woman." His voice sounded gravelly. "And I'm goddamn happy for it."

It had been a beautiful day, filled with joy, love and laughter. When the sun had set, a band had started playing and people had danced.

Around ten p.m., Kyle had announced that the day had come to an end. By eleven, all the vanilla friends and family had left after saying their goodbyes.

The remaining group went indoors and changed into clothes that would fit the collaring ceremony that would be held at a time of Cal's choosing. Everyone was wearing BDSM outfits, but according to the dress code, all subs' bodies were fully covered, at least from the neckline to mid-thigh. Cal hadn't wanted anyone bar his wife half naked for the collaring ceremony.

Right now, everyone was dancing, chatting and having a good time.

Rebecca was nervous. She had no idea when Cal was going to start the ceremony. She was still wearing her wedding dress, so he could her out of it.

Her best friend, Olivia, had stayed for the evening, even though she was vanilla. Rebecca appreciated that Olivia had insisted on being there, especially since she knew her friend was so awkward about all the BDSM stuff. The woman had done her best to try and fit in the crowd, but somehow, she still looked out of place in the dungeon with its torture devices.

When Rebecca had asked Olivia to assist her, she had expected her friend to decline. It meant a lot to her that she'd accepted. Being the bride's assistant also meant helping her get into the outfit for the collaring ceremony. Rebecca had found the ideal outfit for that, one that wouldn't be in the way during the day, and that could easily be put on underneath her dress. She'd laughed when Olivia had blushed when she'd seen it.

"That barely covers a thing!" she had gasped.

"That is sort of the idea." Rebecca had giggled.

It was a two-piece outfit. The top part was a gold-colored bra that she had been wearing underneath her wedding dress. It was soft, so the corset of her dress wouldn't push any underwires into her breasts.

She hadn't been wearing the bottom part during the day. It was easy enough to slip into that, with Olivia's help. In the bridal dressing room, Olivia had carefully lifted Rebecca's skirts so she could step into the flimsy garment. It was a slave skirt, which was nothing more than a few golden straps around her hips with a dark red strip of fabric in the front and back. The strips were floor length, but barely wide enough to cover her mound and behind. The outfit had come with gold-colored hot pants that she was not going to wear. It was perfect the way it was. Like Cal had ordered, she wouldn't be naked, but it would be incredibly sexy and seductive.

Olivia had carefully lowered her skirts over it and smoothed out any crease or fold with her hands.

Her hair needed to be pinned up on her head, so Cal could easily put the collar around her neck. Olivia had done a beautiful job, leaving a few sexy curls dangling over her ears, while the rest was loosely put up.

Now, in the dungeon, knowing what was to come, Rebecca was nervous. She kept eying Cal, wondering how long he was going to make her wait. Cal caught her glancing at him and gave her a dashing smile before continuing his conversation with Rafe.

Rebecca glared at his back. *Damn him!* She grabbed her skirts and walked to the bar to order a stiff drink. She needed it. Badly.

Before she could take a sip, a strong hand curved around her nape. She sucked in a breath.

"No alcohol for my moody wife." Cal's deep, dark voice sent shivers down her spine. Suddenly her heart was pounding and her insides melted. Just that, his voice and his hand on her neck put her in full sub-mode. He turned her around and she looked up at him.

"Master?" Her voice was a mere whisper.

"That's right, little sub," Cal said, his eyes flashing possessively. "I'm going to make you mine."

With his hand on her nape, he pushed her to the center of the dungeon. Everyone had quieted and formed a circle around the couple.

Cal slowly walked around Rebecca, tickling her slender neck. He pressed his lips on the sensitive curve, and she shivered.

He faced her again.

"Are you ready to become my submissive, Rebecca?" he asked softly.

She hesitated. "Yes, but...no..."

Cal's eyes turned darker, ominous, and seemed to cut right through her.

"I am, but...my dress, Sir," she hastened to say.

He stepped forward, towering over her, which forced her to put her head in her neck to look up at him.

"You think your Master had forgotten, sub?" His voice sounded rough.

"N-no. I'm sorry, Cal. Master." Her voice shook.

Why does he have to make this so awkward? This isn't how the ceremony is supposed to go!

"Good. I think you deserve a good spanking for even hesitating."

Rebecca heard the tinge of hurt in his voice and suddenly it dawned on her that he had thought she was going to refuse him.

"I'm so sorry, Master. Please make me yours."

His eyes softened and he caressed her cheek with his knuckles.

"Let's strip this beautiful fairy and reveal the sub underneath," Cal said. "Get rid of your shoes."

Rebecca quickly kicked the high heels off her feet and Olivia rushed over to pick them up. A shiver ran up her spine when Cal held her with his eyes as he undid the ribbons of the sleeves, then slid them off her arms. He called for Rebecca's assistant, Olivia, again, and the woman turned up with a velveteen cushion. Carefully he removed the silver bracelets and collar from Rebecca's neck and wrists, the touch of his fingers so soft that goose bumps rose on her skin. Another stroke over her cheek, then Cal put the jewelry on the cushion Olivia was holding up. She walked away, as carefully as if she was carrying the queen's crown jewels. Cal took his handcuffs from his belt and put them around her wrists.

"Don't move, baby."

A minute later, Rebecca heard chains clanking above her head. *What the hell is he doing? This really isn't part of the plan!* Clearly her Master had decided to improvise. *Damn it.* Now she didn't have a clue what was going to happen. It got worse when he came back and fastened her handcuffs to the chains—not part of the plan, either—and raised her arms up in a vee. Then he tightened the chains until she was on tiptoes.

She was totally off-kilter, her heart was pounding and her chest was heaving. The position made her breasts bulge over the corset.

"Damn, you're beautiful," Cal said. He traced his finger over the full upper curve of her breasts.

Rebecca almost glared at him for changing their ceremony without talking it over, but she didn't dare. Not when he was looking at her like that. The controlled power and heat in his eyes seared through her. She dampened.

He gave her a knowing smile and she blushed. He bent his head and took her mouth. Hard. Deep and passionate. Utterly dominant. She moaned into his mouth. Sparks sizzled over her nerves and her insides quivered.

When he let go of her mouth, her legs wobbled and her head swam.

"This is how I love to see you. Confused, aroused and ready to receive my cock."

Cal circled her and undid the knot from the top set of ribbons that closed her corset. Slowly, as if he had nothing else to do that day, he slid them out of the grommets.

With everybody's eyes on her, Rebecca got suddenly shy. She had grown quite used to doing scenes in the club, but this was different. Today was different. And somehow, it didn't seem right to be chained like this while wearing her wedding dress. She was still the happy, blossoming bride, yet the chains woke up her submissive side at the speed of light. Both emotions collided in her head. Her body was trembling.

"Cal…" she whispered, needing his strength.

"I'm here, baby, I'm right here."

He wrapped his muscular arms around her and pulled her against his strong chest. This was where she belonged. Home.

"Just breathe, baby," he whispered in her ear, and nibbled on her lobe.

"It's so…" Rebecca started.

"Overwhelming?"

His soft, deep laugh melted her spine.

"I know, baby. I love it. Love to see you struggle, have your body tremble with anticipation while your brain is trying to work things out," he said softly. "Now, let go. Enjoy."

He continued with the ribbons, and when he got to the top, he pulled them out. He simply tossed the long ribbons on the floor and started undoing the second set.

Rebecca was wobbling on her tiptoes. *Why is he taking so long?* She really wished she had gone for fewer grommets. She had wanted to tease him with it. Had envisioned him wild with lust, fingers trembling as he tried to rip out the ribbons, not being able to control his need to get her out of her dress. Somehow, he had managed to reverse that, and was teasing her, driving her up the wall. Her own need to be stripped by him made her nipples pebble and her pussy throb.

His soft laugh told her he knew, and he continued, ever so slowly, to pull the ribbons out of the grommets.

"Please, free me, Master!" she begged. "Please!"

"Patience, sub!" he growled. "I'm enjoying myself!"

He slid his hands under the corset, cupped her breasts and started to knead them. A moan broke from her lips.

"Silence, sub!" More mewls came from her as he slipped his hands underneath the bra top and found her hard nipples. He toyed with them until they were swollen and aching. Electric currents raced over her nerves to her core. She knew that she was very, very wet. When he withdrew his hands, she protested softly.

"Such a needy, hot sub," he groaned.

Finally, he pulled the ribbons out of the last grommets. He held up her dress and tongued her spine from the neck to her waist, drawing erotic circles that made her head spin.

Then he stepped around her, still holding up the dress.

"Look at me, Becca!"

When their eyes locked, he simply let go of the dress, and with a *woosh* it fell to the ground.

A low, rumbling groan came from his mouth, and she vaguely heard appreciative mumbles from the crowd.

"Wow!" Fire lit up his eyes when he took her in. The golden bikini top with shining beads, the cups barely big enough to hold her full breasts. Two thin golden straps on her otherwise bare hips, holding a narrow flimsy, maroon strip of fabric in place over her mound. The excuse of a skirt almost reached the floor.

She blushed, suddenly a bit shy. His gaze rested on her breasts and she actually felt them swell under his gaze.

"This is not what I'd had in mind, sub," he said, sounding rough, "but I like it. A lot!"

Knowing that she pleased him filled her heart with joy. Cal walked around her, gently caressing her skin with featherlight touches. She could almost feel his gaze burn her ass, which was barely covered by another narrow strip of maroon fabric.

Please like what you see!

When he groaned, she almost let out a sigh of relief. He

cupped her ass underneath the fabric and kneaded.

"Cheeky sub." His whisper sent a shiver through her. His hard chest against her back, his dark voice, the touches. She could nothing but surrender when he reached around her, slipped his hands under the front strip and found her pussy. Her very wet pussy. Her heart was pounding in her ears as he moved his finger through her slit to her entrance.

Rebecca's legs quivered and a husky mewl escaped her when he went over her swollen clit.

Kyle broke the spell when he cleared his throat.

Cal almost growled. Kyle chuckled.

"However much I like this unexpected scene, I fear people will get overheated if you continue," Kyle said. His eyes sparkled with laughter.

Slowly, Rebecca's brain started to work again, and she saw Olivia looking at her and Cal with shock on her face. Her friend's bottom lip was trembling. She clearly didn't know what to think or do.

Kyle noticed Rebecca's concerned expression, turned his head to see what she was looking at, saw Olivia and immediately understood what was going on. As Master of Ceremonies, he had to make sure everything went smoothly, and an upset bridal assistant was not okay. He walked over to the woman.

"I do apologize, Olivia," Kyle said. "A collaring ceremony is usually a very solemn, serious event, but these two…" He gestured at Rebecca and Cal. "They never do anything the way it's supposed to be."

Kyle sensed the woman was very ill at ease, and when she looked at him, he read in her eyes that she needed an anchor. Someone who'd give her a sense of normalcy. He could do that. He smiled reassuringly and was pleased to notice her shoulder muscles relax. The woman knew he was a Master, owner of the club, but a friendly face was still a friendly face.

"Are you okay?" he asked gently.

She nodded. "I'm all right. I'm just…"

"Overwhelmed?" Kyle said with a grin.

When she glared at him, Kyle burst out laughing. It put a smile on her face. That pleased him. The girl deserved a bit of a break. During the day, he had kept his eye on everyone and he had seen how she'd handled herself among the BDSM crowd. Awkward as hell, but still doing her utmost to fit in, mingle a bit and be a good assistant for Rebecca. Quite admirable. And he'd been in the game long enough to be able to tell that even though she was overwhelmed by it all, she had gotten aroused by the scene just the same. The poor thing probably didn't understand what had hit her.

"Are you ready for the ceremony, pet?" Kyle asked.

Olivia looked at him with shock on her pretty face. Kyle hastened to apologize. *Force of habit when addressing a sub. Damn it.* And the woman sure as hell was one, even though she didn't seem to be aware of it herself. He could smell one a mile away. As could his cock.

He kept his gaze on her and she lowered her eyes, blushing profusely.

Back off, Kyle, back off!

"Yes, I'm ready," she said, a slight tremor in her voice.

"Good. Let's get on with it." Kyle moved to face Cal, only to find him passionately kissing his wife. He cleared his throat to get Cal's attention.

Rebecca's head was spinning from the toe-curling kiss when Cal let go of her lips, and glanced over his shoulder.

"About time, Kyle! For a minute, I thought you were going to rough up Becca's assistant!"

Rebecca was still hanging in chains, and when he turned back to her, his expression changed. It softened, yet there was a mysterious gleam in his dark gaze. She swallowed. *Oh dear, no more surprises, please!*

He stepped closer, invading her space, and again she had to crane her neck to look into his eyes.

"Are you ready, my love?" he asked softly.

"Yes, Cal," she replied.

"Rebecca, my beautiful wife, are you ready and willing to accept my collar and wear it with pride and honor?"

"Yes, I am." Her voice came out a whisper.

Cal nodded at Kyle, who lowered the chains for him. Cal freed her arms and Rebecca gracefully got on her knees in front of him, her eyes lowered.

"So beautiful!" Cal murmured. "Look at me, Rebecca."

She complied, even though she was confused. A sub was supposed to keep her eyes down during the collaring ceremony. He was breaking every protocol in the book, but it was clear he didn't give a toss.

Protocol or not, Cal wanted to see her eyes. Watching her pupils dilate made dominance fizz through his veins. Without breaking eye contact, he held his hand out to his right and took the collar from Kyle.

"Do you willingly accept this collar, my collar, as a symbol of my devotion to you and my ownership of you?"

"Yes, I do."

Cal opened the collar, gently put it around her neck and fastened the dangling lock with a small key, as he said, "I will guide you and protect you, my sub. You will be the only one to wear my collar. You will be the only one who will receive my love, albeit through my cock, my flogger, my whip or my hand. It may be joyful, it may be painful, but I will always love you, respect and cherish you."

A few tears ran from her eyes and she touched the lock on her collar.

"Thank you, Master," she said, her voice rough with emotion. "I'm honored to be your submissive, to wear your collar. Yours is the only one I will ever accept. I will do my utmost to serve you well, but I might need some help with that."

Amusement trickled through him.

"Not a problem, subbie!" he promised. The longing spark in her eyes tugged at his heart.

Rebecca reached out for her assistant, and Olivia, who was standing close by, put something in her hand.

"Please accept this token of my submission and wear it on your heart, Master." She placed her gift in his hand. Cal looked at it and saw a beautifully designed silver wolf pendant.

"That is gorgeous, my love," he said.

"Turn it around," she said, and when he frowned, she quickly added, "Please."

He looked at the back and read the engraving. *Rebecca's Wolf Man.* A laugh rumbled through his chest. Then he touched her cheek. "You couldn't resist, could you, my little sub?" he asked with a smile. "And you're right, you own me as much as I own you. Just that I get to smack your gorgeous behind."

Rebecca grinned.

"I accept your token of submission, and I will wear it on my heart," he said, sounding rough with emotion. "Now, get up and help me with it, sub. You're mine."

Swiftly she got up and helped him with the silver chain.

"You may now kiss your Master," Kyle said with a grin.

Cal pulled Rebecca against his hard body, tilted her head up and took her mouth on a groan.

Kyle sighed and shook his head. "She was supposed to kiss you, asshole!"

But Cal had other things to worry about, like plundering his sub's hot mouth, kneading her ass under the skirt, and enjoying the feel of her breasts against his chest. Rebecca yielded completely.

People cheered, and drinks were served.

Cal let go of her lips, accepted a glass of champagne, and grumbled. More champagne. He was fed up with it. He was longing for a glass of whiskey.

"If you've ordered a champagne breakfast for us, I'm going to make you wear a butt plug for a week. The largest one I can find!"

Rebecca giggled.

Cal gently put the thin glass against her mouth.

"Drink, my love." Their eyes met as she took a sip and licked her lips. Cal groaned.

"I love to see you drink and swallow." Lust flickered in his eyes. "Do remind me to put that on tonight's menu!"

Rebecca's cheeks turned red and desire lit her eyes. Cal laughed.

"My greedy sub!" He drew Rebecca close to his side as people came over to toast their new bond.

"You really are such an ass for not sticking with the program!" Kyle said, and he thumped Cal's solid arm muscles.

"Stop whining, pal! I made her an honest woman, I already consummated my bride, thoroughly," Cal said with a broad smile. Both he and Kyle grinned as Rebecca gasped and her cheeks turned a delightful crimson red.

"She's wearing my ring, my collar and my cuffs. I think I did quite well!"

More books from
Totally Bound Publishing

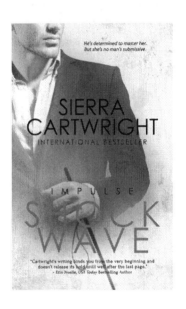

Book one in the Impulse series

*When Master Nathaniel Stratton catches Alani Dane,
a professional submissive, yawning during a scene with
one of his club's most prestigious members, he vows to
personally deal with her.*

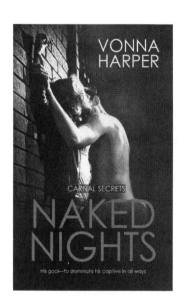

Book one in the Carnal Secrets series

Freedom is everything to jockey Marina until an emotionally scarred man kidnaps her. His goal -- to dominate his captive in all ways.

Book one in the Kitchen Confessions series

Being a single mother running a catering business isn't easy. Finding time for love is nearly impossible. Adding in a man with his own family issues could be a recipe for disaster.

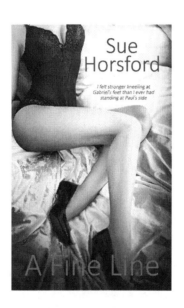

*No one would understand that my submission empowered
me, that I felt stronger kneeling at Gabriel's feet than I ever
had standing at Paul's side.*

About the Author

Dani Rose

Born and raised in the Netherlands, Dani Rose moved abroad as an adolescent for a few years where she fell in love with the English language. She spent some time in Australia and picked up a lot of new words, and a nice Australian accent. The love for English remained, the Australian accent didn't.

Dani's always had a love for writing. Her first work was published when she was barely six years old. Okay, it was published in the kiddie section of a newspaper, but that's not the point! At the time she couldn't even write herself so she dictated the short story to her mother who then sent it in. Little Dani was ecstatic when it got printed! A writer-to-be was born.

As a teen she wrote romantic love stories for her best friend and became known by all her classmates as a wannabe-author of short love novels. More projects were started, some never got finished. Then, around 2006 Dani became intrigued by the realms of BDSM. Now there was a subject she could—and wanted to—write about!

Unfortunately life got in the way and it wasn't until 2015 that Dani found her mojo again and could be seen writing for days, weeks, months on end, working on several stories at the same time.

Finally, in 2016 her first book was finished! The first of a series that loosely evolves around an exclusive BDSM club.

Today Dani lives in the Netherlands with her four-legged furry creatures that occasionally meow to let her know they need food and she has to take a break from writing.

Dani Rose loves to hear from readers. You can find contact information, website details and an author profile page at https://www.totallybound.com/

Home of Erotic Romance

Made in the USA
Middletown, DE
18 September 2021